Plague Wizards

by
JP Wagner

PLAGUE WIZARDS

First edition. November 27, 2023.

ISBN: 978-1-990862-29-8

Written by J P Wagner.
Edited by Beth Wagner

Dedication

To Lois, Tricia and Lila, your support has meant the world to me.

Introduction

I thought a lot about whether to publish this book. Alison's trauma really made me concerned, I did not want people to think that either me or my father took the subject of abuse lightly. There wasn't anything graphic in the book and as I reviewed the manuscript, I found that it was important to see Alison's journey. It is dealt with in a very real way.

As a survivour myself I was able to identify with Alison and I tried to ensure that her journey through the story felt genuine, to myself anyway. Everyone deals with trauma in different ways and so people may feel differently about this story.

It's also important to realise that people are more than their trauma and in this book I hope to show that

Content Warning

This book may disturb sensitive readers as it deals with

a survivor of trauma and how she copes with her life as

it is now.

Please take care when reading.

Chapter One

Alison McHarg peered through the metal fence; the tree was only remarkable in that it couldn't exist. It looked much like a poplar. But there were, on closer inspection, subtle differences in leaf-shape and texture of bark.

She clucked her tongue against her teeth. She would have to go find the farmer who owned the land and pay him the exorbitant fee to have the gate unlocked so she could have a closer look.

She shook her head at that thought. He'd had people tramping over his land for weeks. Eventually, he put up the fence just to keep people away. And he'd set a steep fee, not in the expectation of getting rich, but just to keep everyone from pestering him to open the gate.

She'd come all the way to this wild bit of Scottish shoreline. It'd be a waste of time to go back without actually looking at the thing, close range.

The farmer, one Glenn Alexander, had changed his story about the tree. First off, he said he'd suddenly found it, grown to sapling size, one morning. There had been a spate of people who knew that visitors from outer space had left this tree, of course.

Mr. Alexander later changed his story to a more believable one about how he'd "never noticed the tree before," something a little more likely.

Botanists had come in and argued over the tree, claiming it must be a mutant of this or that variety. Cuttings had been taken (with hefty payments to Mr. Alexander), but every single one had refused to grow.

The cuttings proved to be remarkably difficult to extract DNA from. When the DNA was successfully extracted, the researchers claimed that something was wrong with the sample. Researchers were perplexed, as this DNA could not exist.

Altogether, it had been a six-weeks' wonder. But then other things came along and shifted this impossible tree off to the back burner.

Alison, a biologist from Toronto who'd specialized in medicinal herbs, had allowed herself to observe the strange specimen. A book of hers (written under a pseudonym) describing an entire list of medicinal herbs, their preparation and uses, had made her enough money that, carefully spent, could support a brief visit to Scotland.

So here she was, looking at the impossible tree, and feeling annoyed. Not that she couldn't afford to pay Mr. Alexander;

she'd been careful with her money, and that was no real problem.

Thing was, she just didn't like to go talking to some strange man.

That was--- No, she cut that thought-path off. She'd gotten past it, through it, though obviously not over it, but she wouldn't let herself dwell on it.

It seemed to her she might find a better view down there off to her left, so she moved along the fence.

Then the sky went dark, her head buzzed, and in her ears was a long chant in some strange language.

Pain blazed in her chest, numbness ran down her arms. She recognized the symptoms of a heart attack. Then they were gone as if they'd never been. She stumbled to the ground, caught herself, and stood upright.

No sign of the fence, no sign of the tree. In fact, it seemed to be early morning, and she could barely make out the surrounding trees.

She shook her head. Something was wrong. There hadn't been more than a few trees here. She felt strange and tried to figure out what had happened. Not likely a heart attack, or she'd be dead. Where did her packsack go? There wasn't much in it, but there was some survival gear in it.

She had a dress on---! That stopped her. She'd gone out this morning in a pair of bluejeans, hiking boots, and a cotton shirt. Now she was wearing some kind of rough cloth dress, and no underwear that she could feel.

On her feet were a pair of soft leather boots, but not in any style she'd ever seen, fastened with a series of large hooks going into thumb-sized eyes.

"I think perhaps I should panic about now." Alison thought to herself.

But she didn't.

She turned around again, looking in all directions. A narrow path wound through the forest off to her right. For want of any better goal, she wandered off in that direction.

It was a well-used path, worn several inches below the ground's surface in some places. She could see traces of tracks, though none of them meant anything to her. "I deal with plants, not animals," she muttered. "And plants don't have feet."

She looked both ways along the path. "Next decision, which way to go? Or should I just stand here waiting to be rescued?"

She bent down and picked up a twig from the ground. She tossed it in the air. 'Whichever way the narrow end points, that's the direction I'll go.'

And, of course, the narrow end landed, pointing pretty much straight off into the woods.

"Bad test," she muttered. "Let's try that again. Facing along the trail, this time."

The stick went up and came back down, pointing toward her. "It didn't turn over. Might as well have pointed in that direction and headed out. Try again."

Two more tries had the stick falling down butt-first, then toppling to point straight off the trail in one direction and then another.

She was feeling as if she were getting just a little too fixated on having the stick point a way for her to go.

This time it fell butt-first, pointed off into the forest, but just a little off the right angle. She bent down to pick it up again, then said, "Damn! No, it's pointing off just a little that way. No more fooling around. It's time to get going."

Still holding the stick, for no other reason than that it hadn't occurred to her to toss it aside, she started tentatively up the trail.

She began noticing footprints in the dust. Hoofprints, to be more precise, three-toed hooves, each as long as her own foot, or longer. "No lions, tigers, or bears, so far. Though I don't know if I could tell a bear-print from a giraffe."

Having picked a direction to travel, she did not bother moving fast. One direction was likely as good as any other and moving was at least not standing still.

The light grew rapidly better, and Alison could make out the trees and plants around her. None of them were recognizable, though none of them were too extremely odd. The leaves were all of greenish hues, and most of the trees seemed to be near relatives to the tree that she'd gone to see---

Now, how should she refer to that? Back on earth? Well, maybe just "back there." She'd never had much patience with the people who described in great detail (and vaguely at some points) their abduction by "space aliens."

This didn't seem to be the case. For starters, she hadn't been taken aboard some ship and operated on, or anything like that. Just that one instant when she was there, now she was here. And dressed like this.

"Stop it! You're about to go into a panic. Don't think about that. Look at what's here, and play botanist. Give your mind something to do."

Then something even weirder happened. She seemed to know names for a lot of the plants, particularly the trees. The strangest part was that the names were not English nor French, nor any other language she'd heard of.

Some of them seemed to have deeper meanings, as though made up of two or three words. But she had no meanings for those words. Also, she got several colour terms attached to words which had no meaning other than that plant.

But why did "blue" cover some shades of green as well? No, don't be quite so Anglo-centric; field-trips to wild countries had taught her that colours could fall in very different categories depending on the language.

"Worse than operations! The Aliens have mucked around with my head!"

She stopped. This was getting just too scary.

She wasn't sure what she might have done next if she hadn't seen a movement up ahead. It looked like the shape of a man.

"People? Are they friendly or hostile? Whoever's playing games with me, they wouldn't just drop me down where the next people along would kill me, would they? And if I run, where should I run to?"

In the end, sheer survival instinct kept her where she was as the men, three of them, came closer down the trail.

They had brown hair, save for one who had black hair. Each had their hair tied back with a cloth or leather band tied round the forehead.

They wore trousers, calf-length, and bare feet, two wore sleeveless vests that laced up the front, the leader's chest was bare.

They were all carrying spears, carrying them as if they were very familiar with their use. Panic started up again, but now she beat it down, using some hard-learned techniques.

Three with spears. Not much hope to fight against them, if they turned out to be hostile. Running wasn't a much better option; they could run her down fairly soon, if one of them didn't just save the bother by throwing his spear into her fleeing back.

The leader stared at her, with no expression showing on his face. He spoke to her. "Malum ikteshil vrin gi?"

She was about to answer, "What's that? Klingon?" when she immediately realized that she understood him. What he'd said was, "Do you come in peace?"

The comprehension also hinted that this was more than just a polite phrase of greeting. It was a question of her intentions as well.

She answered in the same language, "I come in peace." Whatever, whoever, had put the language in her mind, hadn't forced her mouth to form the sounds correctly, so that even she knew she sounded foreign. She couldn't quite get the stress-pattern right, and the 'l' sound had a strange quality to it that nearly defeated her.

Puzzled for a moment, the leader then spoke a phrase similar to the one he'd spoken before, but without the 'gi' at the end, which made it a statement rather than a question this time, "Malum ikteshil vrin."

"Yes," she answered, "I come in peace."

One man in the back muttered a word that meant "Foreigner."

Actually, she realized, the word meant more than "foreigner," it seemed to carry overtones of "untrustworthy," as well.

She also hoped they would not leave her alone with that guy. There was something in his face that brought back memories she'd much rather not recall.

But the leader paid little attention. He was concentrating on her. Unlike the other man, he appeared to be looking at her as she was, weighing all the evidence of her appearance and her somewhat flawed ability in the language. Finally, he nodded, "She's the one the Woman told us of. Let's go."

The word he used for 'Woman' meant something more, something like 'studious woman,' but even that did not seem to fit.

"Walk along the path, just in front of us, please," he said.

It was a polite request, not a command, so there seemed to be nothing to be gained by arguing. Less, because she had no grounds for arguing, no place she could actually claim as a preferable destination.

It wasn't much further before she smelled wood smoke. Shortly after that, they were coming to cultivated fields. The people had cleared the fields of most trees and all underbrush, with rocks dug out and stacked beside the fields. In the fields, there were mostly stands of what seemed to be cereal crops. Though she knew the names, and something of their uses, mostly they were just names to her.

The village, or whatever one called the conglomeration of huts from which the fields radiated, consisted of low log buildings with peaked roofs thatched with straw. None of them appeared to have windows.

There was no wall around the village, but the appearance of the men's spears suggested to her that the men were willing and able to defend themselves. Suggesting further that there were enemies to be defended against. Though not so many to require the effort of building a wall.

The leader of the trio said, "The Woman's house."

"Which one is that?" The houses all seemed essentially the same to Alison.

He made a noise of exasperation. "The Woman's house! The one with the vine!"

Alison considered a moment defending herself as a stranger who didn't know these things, but that seemed likely to cause more problems.

The vine was none that she'd ever seen. In fact, the vocabulary in her head didn't even have a specific word for it.

Alison jumped as the voice behind her shouted, "Kooowa! Moralei! Here she is!"

The door opened, and a woman stepped out. Alison was wondering if there were differences between the language she'd been 'taught' and the local dialect. Maybe 'studious' meant 'wise'?

Whatever the proper translation was, the woman was short and trim, with longish brown hair. She eyed Alison up and down, and didn't seem to like what she saw.

"You're the cause of it, then?"

Which annoyed Alison. "No!" she shot back. "I didn't 'cause' anything. One minute I was back in my own country looking at a tree I'd never seen before, the next minute I was here. None of my doing. If you know how to put me back, I'd be pleased."

The woman thawed, minimally. "Not a wizardess, then?"

"No." Alison considered for a moment saying "Just a botanist," but decided that would open up all kinds of other topics she might not want to get into. Such as, if the plants were so different from what she knew back home, then her story might seem to be a lie.

"So, then. Well, come on in, we'll talk inside."

Moralei stepped back and to the right to let Alison come in. As Alison was stepping across the threshold, she felt a pat on her behind. As tightly wound as she was, the reaction was immediate. She spun round; her left hand whipping up towards where a face would be. The man himself had stepped back, so the next move was a snap-kick to the groin.

Later on, going over the matter in her mind, she suspected that the business of coming over to this world had put her timing off just slightly, because instead of a solid hit, her foot only grazed him, enough to send him staggering away.

Then the shirtless leader had his spear up and was ready to thrust. Alison knew that, barehanded against someone who knew how to use a spear, she was in trouble. She settled into a defensive stance.

"Daro!" the wise woman's voice was commanding. "Flan got what someone should have given him years ago. Lady, whatever your name is, relax. I'll have no bloodshed on my threshold!"

Alison heard in that more than a command not to kill. But of bad luck following the very act of shedding blood on the threshold of the house.

She pulled herself out of the rigorously drilled-in self-defence mode. An act that required more than shifting hands and feet to a neutral mode. But required pulling her mind out of the state where nothing counted but protection of self. It was difficult when faced with that still-poised spear blade.

Her mind was saying first, 'No one's going to get me easily again!' Followed by, 'Does this mean I'm not over it yet?'

Her mind flashed back briefly to that night, waking alone in her room, with that man standing over her bed---. *'Stop it! That's the past! It's never going to happen again!'*

She turned to look at Moralei, who was looking her over. The wise woman nodded. "Something still haunts you, then? No, no, don't bother about it.

"Daro, thank you and your men for bringing her safe here. You might try to convince Flan that those kinds of liberties could have him stretched out for the burial rites, but I doubt he'll listen."

"A seeing, Moralei?" asked Daro.

"I see very seldom, Daro. Sometimes I read the way a present course of events may end, but it's only 'may end.' If someone chooses to adjust his behaviour, the outcome is likely to be different. Thank you, you may go. I will remember your assistance."

As Daro and his men left, Moralei closed the door and turned to Alison. "May I ask a name of you?"

"I'm called Alison."

"Alison, eh? Well, Alison, magic brought you here, most likely magic cast by someone in the City." She muttered, almost to herself, "What're they up to now, in the City?"

Alison shrugged, hoping the gesture had the same meaning here. The question seemed to be rhetorical, anyway.

Moralei was thinking. "Well, they'll likely be coming to search for you sometime. I suppose we'd better keep you until we can send someone to the City, or until they find out where you are.

"This is a small village, though, and everyone has to help out or we don't live. What sorts of things can you do?"

Alison understood what she was being told. A guest was a guest, but if the guest stayed for long, they ought to help somehow. And it was well-known that 'City people' weren't much use on a farm. Connection with the magicians suggested Alison was a City person herself.

Instead of answering that question, Alison asked one of her own. "How far is it to the City?"

"About three weeks' trip, but nobody in town can be spared to take you there, not for six weeks more."

"But I can---. No, never mind." She'd been about to do the 'field-worker to native' thing of offering payment. Unfortunately, she had literally nothing but the clothes she wore. Furthermore, she had a feeling that the villagers had never seen money, and even if they had, they didn't really understand the concept.

Alison would have to earn her keep until someone from the City came to collect her. She couldn't believe they'd go to all the trouble of bringing her here just to abandon her. She felt her mind go into a grim line. When they came, she'd give him/her/it an earful!

"I see. Well, as for what I can do, I'd say I could lend a hand at what needs to be done. And I can learn fast," said Alison finally.

"Can you indeed? Well, that's a help, if true." said Moralei.

The implied doubt annoyed Alison. Unfortunately, with no actual knowledge of the things villagers did as daily work, she was in no position to start an argument.

"I believe I can," was all Alison said.

Moralei gave her a considering look. "So, then, we'll have to see."

Chapter Two

Royin Gredion's-child woke up to hear a voice. "He's waking up!"

Someone else said "Maker be thanked!"

Royin wondered at that; why should it be such a wonder that he was waking up? He tried to reply, but suddenly he was drifting off into dreams of vividly coloured plants and trees.

When he woke again, it was full daylight. One of the Household servants was leaning over him. After a moment, his hazy mind recognized Valyan, Chief servant of the Household. But Valyan's job was overseeing other servants; what was he doing at Royin's bedside, like an ordinary menial?

"Are you awake, Royin-sir?"

"Yes, I believe I'm awake. Is something wrong?"

"There is great trouble in the House, Royin-sir! Everyone is dead, save for those who still sleep. The House is in ruins! All the Masters are dead, save for some who still sleep. The king himself has been asking in regard to this!"

Royin's mind, still hazy, refused to comprehend all this. He held up a hand. "Wait. The House is in ruins, you say? What caused it? Earthquake?"

"No, Royin-sir, not the House, not the building, but all the Masters! No one knows what happened, but there is suspicion that a spell went awry and caused the deaths of many who are most capable of magic. All the most learned in the city are dead, so far as can be determined. The less learned---, ah, those not so learned as the Chief Masters, were put into a sleep from which they could not be wakened. You are the most learned to recover."

"Surely not the only one!"

"Well, Royin-sir, it is said that Olibaj-sir and Naram-sir have awoken, but their minds are---, are affected."

"The Grand Master?"

"Dead, Royin-sir. You are the only one left to give instructions." The servant said this as if it relieved him of an intolerable burden.

Royin attempted to sit up and fell back. He attempted again, and the servant sprang to help him. It occurred to Royin that Valyan was dreadfully afraid of having to give orders that were the prerogative of the Master. However, Royin, son of a nephew of the Grand Master, knew the Chief Servant mostly by reputation. In theory, any family member could give orders to Valyan, but Valyan's primary function was seeing to the smooth running of the Household.

Royin shook his head again. "All right, Valyan. I am awake, for now, and I'll do what needs to be done. First, have someone bring me a bowl of broth and a loaf of bread. I don't know how long I've been asleep, but I feel weak. Prepare lists and reports for me as to what has happened, and I'll deal with matters as soon as I'm able."

"Yes, Royin-sir." As Valyan hurried out, it occurred to Royin that Valyan could do a fair job of running the Household, where its daily functions were concerned. What he had lacked was someone at the top, in whose name he could give orders.

He did the best he could, but even the bowl of soup and broth didn't restore him altogether. One moment he was reading lists, the nest he was waking up in his bed again.

He recognized the servant bending over him this time, a young man named Daivalma. "You are awake, Royin-sir?" There was concern in the young man's voice and features.

"I'm awake." It took Royin a moment to recall the situation as he'd learned it previously. "Yes, I'm awake. How long was I asleep this time?"

"Only over the night, Royin-sir. But a Royal Messenger has come three times to inquire if anyone in the Household can shed light on the strange happenings. Is it an attack from Saljashin, and if so, how do we counter it?

"The Royal Messenger desires any information we can give."

"I see. At present, I know nothing. No, don't tell the messenger that; tell him we're working on the problem."

Just as the servant was about to leave, Royin called him back. "A moment. The Grand Master is dead?"

"Yes, Royin-sir."

"The circumstances?"

"He was in the midst of a working when he was struck down. No one knows what the working was, save that it required the sacrifice of a large djasa."

Royin's eyes went wide. The djasa was a large hornless animal, with three-toed hooves, used for milk, meat, and hide. A working involving a djasa was a powerful one. Cold shivered down his spine. "A large djasa? And he died during the working?"

"Yes, so it seems, Royin-sir."

"And the shield-spells did not contain the power?"

"Uh--- I don't know, Royin-sir."

*'Of **course**, he doesn't know! He's a servant, not a magician, and he wouldn't know a working from a wardrobe. No Wizardly Household would employ a servant with the least amount of magical capability.'*

Royin nodded. "I'll have to have a look at his workroom. Get me a cup of rizil-infusion."

"Yes, Royin-sir."

Rizil-infusion, stalks of the rizil-plant soaked in wine over a low fire, was a concoction used to keep magicians awake and alert during long workings and, more clandestinely, to keep students awake for extensive study-sessions.

Royin knew that it was not safe for him to be taking it in his condition, but he also knew that his alternatives were limited. If something had killed the Master of the Household, and all those others, not to mention disabling so many, it was necessary to find out just what it had been.

The rizil was, as usual, not very palatable going down. Also, as usual, it took only moments take effect. First, his eyes saw patterns they had never noticed before, the grain in the wood-panelling of the room, then the precise make-up of the diagonal lines in a piece of tapestry.

He pulled his mind from these. "Let's go to the Grand Master's workroom."

"Yes, Royin-sir."

The servant hovered as Royin moved slowly toward the door. As Royin kept his feet moving, one after the other, he realized he was in a bad way. Without the rizil, he'd likely have fallen flat on his face.

He made his way to the Grand Master's suite, restraining himself several times from shouting at Daivalma to stop fussing at him. He managed this mostly by remembering that he was the highest-ranked Master presently in command of his faculties, making his welfare of utmost importance to the servants.

There was a whiff of blood and corruption at the door of the room, but otherwise, the room was clean. "The bodies?"

"Your pardon, Royin-sir. The animal was burned, and the Grand Master buried. They were beginning to---uh---."

"Smell? Yes, of course. A djasa, eh?"

The last was spoken mostly to himself, but the servant answered it anyway. "Yes, Royin-sir. A large one."

"I see." Royin looked around the workroom. "One of those jars over there will have grain in it. Bring one grain over to the lamp."

"Yes, Royin-sir." The man went quickly to the jars and found grain in the second one.

Royin wondered why the jars were not labelled, but the answer came to him immediately; the Grand Master would pride himself on knowing where everything was in his workshop, and his conceit forbade him from resorting to labels.

Daivalma came back with a small handful of grain and Royin, with difficulty, held himself back from saying, "Only one grain, fool!"

Instead, he picked out one grain and said, "Put the rest back, please."

It probably wasn't a good idea to try doing a working in this state, rizil or not, but this was a very tiny one. He spoke a bidding-formula and tossed the grain into the flame of the lamp. It blazed for an instant and was gone.

Without any spectacular flashes or flares, a set of dotted green lines showed along all the edges of the room, on the floor and ceiling, as well as all the corners.

Rapidly, he counted the number of dots from the floor to the top of the moulding around the floor, then made the calculations. The rizil permitted him to finish the calculations long before the lines died out.

"Three months! It's been three months since shields were raised in this room!"

"Yes, Royin-sir."

"But I was told that this disaster happened---when?"

"Two weeks ago, Royin-sir."

"Then the Grand Master was doing a working involving the sacrifice of a djasa without first establishing shields? Ridiculous!"

"Uh---yes, Royin-sir."

Royin looked at the servant. "Sorry, not something you'd know about, of course."

"No, Royin-sir."

"Where are his notes?" Foolish question; they were over on the table.

Yes, they were on the table, in a jumble, too. It seemed likely that they had been scattered during the course of the disaster, and the servants, unable to make head not tail of them, had simply stacked them. Royin cast an eye over them. Grand Master Tangral was very well known for his distrustful nature, among other things.

It came, Royin thought, mostly from the continuous rivalry to be the next Grand Master. They made the choice based on who was the most powerful wizard. This meant that every aspiring wizard got into the habit of keeping his experiments carefully hidden from all other wizards, until he had them perfected, and could demonstrate them for others, and have the Keeper scribe them in the Books.

After one had become Grand Master, he could not be removed until death, or the conclusive proof of certain crimes, but the life habits of secrecy were difficult to break. Thus, the greater part of Tangral's notes were in a code of some kind.

He looked at Daivalma. "No notion at all of what he was working on?"

"No, Royin-sir."

"Hmm." His eyes fixed on the servant's face, and he had to pull his mind away from considering the pattern of wrinkles found there. "What does gossip among the servants say? And if you claim not to know, I'll have you dismissed as too stupid to serve in this Household."

He was immediately ashamed of his bullying tactics, as he saw the terror showing on Daivalma's face. "It's said he was working at the Ascension Gift, Royin-sir."

Royin nodded. According to custom, every year on the Anniversary of the King's Ascension to the Throne, the Head of the Pengwa Household, as Chief Wizard to the King, would present to the king a gift, produced by the Master's magic. What that gift might be depended very much on the mood of the King; some previous Kings preferred something useful, such as a better grain, an improved djasa, or the like. King Tandwil preferred something frivolous and flashy, something that said that his power was so great he could have his most powerful Wizards waste their time making something for him.

"Thank you, Daivalma. Would you please see to having lists of the wizards, of whatever skill, still capable of functioning, delivered to my quarters?"

"Yes, Royin-sir."

The man was looking mystified at the sudden change of topic. Royin realized that, rizil-infusion or no, he could not handle all the problems that would need to be dealt with. (Or perhaps the rizil-infusion made him realize the fact that he was going to have to pass on some responsibility, keeping for himself the question of just what the Grand Master had done to cause this.

❀

Royin looked around the table. There were only three of them, enough to share the load somewhat, but not as many as he would have liked. At this point, though, they didn't want any youngsters messing around with things. A sixteen-year-old might well have a good deal of magical ability, but he—or she— didn't have the life-experience to deal with political things.

Ormant Lipion's-child was next-eldest after Royin, and capable enough to dislike taking Royin's orders. He was large and bulky, with wild hair. His fingers were thick, but much more agile than they looked.

Faral Pidrona's-child was youngest, very slim and pale-looking, unsure of himself, and trying not to show it.

Royin looked down at the gleaming dark surface of the table, on which were three piles of paper. "I've divided things up into three sections, one for each of us. Most of my time is going to be taken up with finding out just what happened to Grand Master Tangral.

"Further to that, I need to know any hints, even gossip, about what he was going to do. Ormant?"

Ormant shook his shaggy head. "Nothing."

"Faral?"

"Well, uh--- I didn't feel it right to pry into the Grand Master's business." He drummed his fingers on the table, then jerked his hand into his lap.

Royin gave him a stern look, still feeling a fraud in the Grand Master's position. "All right, what have you heard? No matter how ridiculous it might sound, this is for King Tardwil's Accession Gift, remember?"

"I heard it said that he was looking up all the works on the 'outside worlds.' Some people said he was planning on taking the king on a tour of one of the worlds. Impossible, of course. Nobody could gather that much power, let alone work it."

Royin grinned. "Thank you. It's not likely, but it may lead to some other hint. Thanks."

He paused. "All right, then. Each of you take your stack and read it over. See what you can get started at immediately, then we'll have a meeting tomorrow again, to discuss any difficulties. Any questions?"

"Yes. What puts you in charge?"

Royin nodded. It was the question he expected Ormant would ask. "Seniority, the way we always pick a Grand Master."

"Grand Master?" Ormant's hands pressed on the table-top. "You're calling yourself Grand Master?"

"We have to have a Grand Master to speak to the King, and to the other Households. I'm the senior Master left, of any capability, which makes the job mine." He stopped before adding, 'Much as I don't want it.' Some little bit of sense told him he daren't admit any weakness or indecision to Ormant.

"You really think you can manage the Household?"

He gave Ormant a firm look. "I know that I'm senior in years and ability, and that I've been working at this mess already. We've got to get ourselves sorted out, then we can argue about who's best for the job.

"At present, we've got the king demanding to know what's happened. We've got a disaster that's hit all the Wizard-Households in the city, and that's a much bigger problem than whose butt warms which chair. Or do you really want to force an election in these circumstances, Ormant?"

Ormant shook his head, looking down at the papers stacked before him.

Royin put his own hands on the table. "If there's nothing else, I declare this meeting adjourned."

❊

Hadjalloni siFantanna, Watcher for the Kingdom of Saljashin, looked out the window at the battered grey stone plinth, then frowned down at the report in his hand. It had been sent and received through fire, a magical means. No, he didn't enjoy using magic, for all that it was necessary sometimes to see what the life-twisters in Rosthan were up to.

Disaster had, apparently, stricken the life-twisters. All of their most powerful Grand Masters were dead or incapacitated, or at least those Masters who lived in the King's city of Gagapeng.

That was a stroke of fortune. He tapped a finger on the table before him. How badly were they weakened? Might it be possible to use this opportunity?

He looked out the window at the battered statueless plinth, the piece of stone left there as a reminder to everyone. Once, long ago, a statue of the Blue-Blossom Wizard had stood there, a wizard born and bred in this very city of Lunchmachor. The man had carefully built up, over the years, knowledge of various herbal concoctions and an army of men and terrible animals.

With these, he had taken over the kingdom of Saljashin.

For many years, the Blue-Blossom Wizard had ruled, with increasing harshness, until the Man of the Harmonious Hand had come, one who was immune to the narcotics the Wizard used to prevent uprisings among his subjects.

Over a space of several years, the Man of the Harmonious Hand had organized a covert resistance to the Wizard, and had at last overthrown him. They had dragged down all the Wizard's statues, leaving this one in the centre of Lunchmachor as a reminder. On feast days, people would come to throw rocks at it.

They had to maintain constant vigilance to prevent such a person as the Blue-Blossom Wizard from rising again.

The difficulty was, the Kingdom of Rosthan stood next door to them, Rosthan, which not only permitted magic, but gloried in it. Rosthan, where wizards boasted of their abilities to cause plants to change into what they desired, to produce this or that new effect, even new medicines.

The rulers of Saljashin had always known that something must be done about Rosthan, but it was difficult to decide just how.

It was known that Saljashini were slipping over there to be trained, some even attempted to slip back after having trained. Any of them might be another Blue-Blossom Wizard.

So far as could be determined, none of these people had survived.

But that battered plinth still stood as a warning.

Hadjalloni rapped on the workroom door, then opened it without waiting for a response from inside. A chubby little balding man looked up as Hadjalloni entered, then looked back to his work. Figures and computations scribbled in charcoal on a large square plank of wood.

Hadjalloni, irritated at the man would so casually ignore him, said, "How is the work, Melungtal?"

Melungtal siTalrun looked up again. "A few little wrinkles to smooth out, Hadji, my boy. Wouldn't want to turn these things loose too soon. Could turn around and bite back at us."

"How long?"

"How high is up? How far is away? You have at least a bit of understanding of what we do, Hadji. It's a matter of slow and careful steps, sometimes finding an answer that puts us way ahead, sometimes finding a problem that keeps us at a stop for months. Saying when we'll have it ready to put into action, that's something that only a fool would attempt."

"Not the answer I need, Melungtal. I've just received word that there's been a catastrophe among the Life-twisters. Most of their wizards are dead or incapacitated. This would be the ideal time to strike, when they wouldn't be able to deal with it."

"Can't do it, Hadji. There's still one possibility in a hundred that the things we're working at will take a wild change, and that would mean them coming back at us, and us as defenseless against them as the Rosthanites."

"One in a hundred? I'd say that was fairly safe."

Melungtal gave one of those 'you-don't-know-what-you're-talking-about' looks. "Don't think of it as 'the hundredth one is the bad one.' Think of it more like having a handful of a hundred grains, one of them deadly poison. You start eating them, one by one. Is the first one the one? Or the second? Or the seventy-sixth?

"Still an extremely simplistic analogy, but more representative of the danger. I'll be sure to tell you when it's safe to use."

He turned back to his calculations. Hadjalloni knew that trying to continue the discussion was futile. Jaws firmly clenched, he left the workroom.

Royin had to do a good deal of digging, but the situation grew clearer. The notes didn't say exactly why, but Tangral had apparently been working at touching one of the 'outside' worlds.

Not all scholars agreed on the existence of the outside worlds, and Royin himself had just recently been able to accept the theory. The theory was that there were other worlds besides this one, worlds with strange people and animals, worlds with walking trees and enormous flying animals.

Even touching one of the other worlds took a lot of power, though. Observing would be terribly difficult, and for all that might be learned, the power could be better used in other ways. Moving things between worlds. No, that wasn't something to even think of.

Unless, of course, you were Tangral, with an intense belief in your own ability.

Among the papers was a chart of planetary conjunctions, a chart which had no relation to bodies in the sky above Gagapeng.

He had, it seemed, dragged something out of that other world, a living being, apparently. A calculation of the power that required, even with the planets—both here and there—in favourable conjunction, suggested that Tangral had done away with everything not directly necessary to the task. That had included the shields.

Of course, Grand Master Tangral did not need shields; nothing could go wrong.

Except that it had.

When one was doing a working involving the sacrifice of a large djasa, the strain would be severe. Apparently, it had been too much even for the Highly Superior Grand Master Tangral.

With no shields, when Tangral collapsed, that huge amount of magic had gone wild, striking hard at every magically competent person in a wide circle around the Household.

"Burn it to powder!" And all this for what? Bringing someone over from outside? Why bother? The only clue seemed to be in Tangral's notes, a question, 'What sort of plants might be over there?'

If that had been the question, why bring a person over? He might have to do some tracing, see if someone had indeed been brought over (and possibly destroyed in the blast of power?) No, the blast of power would only have killed him. Or her. Or them. Whatever the gender, there should be a corpse. Yes, he was going to have to do some searching.

❈

The King's Messenger, a small man in a beaded jacket, displayed obvious impatience. "Certain other Wizardly Households have declared that a reprehensible act has been committed, which centred around the Pangwa Household. It is suggested that this was a hostile action, aimed directly at them."

Royin kept an expressionless face. To admit any fault risked having the Pangwa Household broken up, and its people and possessions distributed among its rivals. At the end of it all, he might well be the last Master of Pangwa Household, but he would do all he could to prevent that.

"The Pangwa Household has been badly affected by this disaster, probably no less so than any other. No one ought to say that it was a deliberate act on our part."

'Only in that Tangral didn't intend the disaster. But we won't talk of that.'

"So you say."

Royin calmly raised his eyebrows. "Does not the fact that it is I, rather than some senior Master, standing here meeting with you suggest something?"

"Suppose the King requires an inspection of your Household to ascertain that it is as you say?"

"Has the king made such a request?"

"No, not yet."

Royin spread his hands. "I will not make decisions based on a hypothetical possibility. When the king makes such a request, I will make a response at that time."

The King's Messenger was clearly annoyed; he had tried a bluff on Royin that he would never have thought of trying on one of the senior Masters who were now dead or incapacitated. Royin himself was trying hard not to show any sign of the lack of assurance that haunted him.

The Messenger nodded. "I will take your word to the king."

❀

Royin stared deep into the dark glossy finish of the Council-table, then raised his eyes. He mustn't seem to be burdened with matters, for the sake of Faral's morale; as for Ormant, they didn't need any rebellion in the Household Council, truncated as it was.

"I've put the king off temporarily, but we can expect a demand for inspection in three days to a week. At that point, I may be able to put the matter off for another few days by appealing the decision, but we should be ready for the worst. We have to have our Household in condition to be seen by that time, including the hospice-wards."

He paused. "Faral, our financial status?"

Faral flinched, as though he'd been accused of something. "We might be said to be on a sound footing, financially. Over the decades, we have gathered a good deal of wealth, and held on to a considerable sum of it. We could possibly survive for another five years without any further income.

"A good deal of money has been invested in loans to merchants and caravan-traders, such that we will continue to have some small income.

"I have also worked out the costs of maintaining the incapacitated seniors; that will continue to be a burden to us in the future. I would suggest accelerated training from some of our junior people, so they might be able to augment the Household income."

"What of outstanding contracts? Are there any we can fulfil with our present resources? How many will have to be cancelled, and what is our liability for the cancellation?"

Faral's eyes went wide. Clearly, he had missed something. "Ah—I, ah...."

"Young fool!" Ormant flared. "You've---!"

"Ormant!" Royin's voice overrode Ormant's. "We're all having to do things we'd never had the least training for. We'll get nowhere if we shout at each other for failings. Faral, you'd best look into the matter. Find out which contracts can be delayed, without penalty, which ones cancelled without serious loss. Bring us a current report at the next meeting."

"Ormant, do we have anyone capable of teaching? And do we have anyone capable of being taught?"

Ormant drew a breath. "Not as many as we'd want. We have a couple of hundred youngsters who can put together simple spells, but I'd hate to see any of them turned loose on a major working.

"We don't have any teachers left. We have some of those who were assistants, but that meant mostly that they saw to it that all the equipment and supplies were set out for demonstrations, and put back in stores afterward. I'd hate to see any of them turned loose as teachers."

Royin nodded briefly. "I accept your concerns. However, if Pangwa Household is to continue, we are going to have to bring our youngsters along, and bring them faster than usual."

Pick the students you think best able to profit by it, and have them given advanced lessons, as far advanced as seems safe to you, consonant with the need to have more Masters."

"Masters! Try to make Masters of them, and we'll ruin the Household for sure!"

"That's why you'll be overseeing the matter personally. Are you able to do so?"

"I? Able?" Ormant stopped a moment. "I suppose I'll have to be, won't I?"

He looked up, frowning. "Why did Tangral take such a risk, anyway?"

"As I understand it, he was working at providing something spectacular for Ascension Day. In order to do so, he needed the power that should have gone into the shields. His body couldn't take the strain of that much magical power, so he died in the midst of the spell, with the results we're all so well aware of."

"What on earth was he doing?"

"I've only been able to find out some general things. The rest I'm still working out."

"Why should it take out all the more powerful Masters first?" Faral asked.

"Missed that part of training, eh?" Ormant eyed Faral with annoyance. "You know that the way to build our power up is to use it, press against the boundaries, so to speak. Something like exercising muscles. But the increase in power comes along with an increased susceptibility to wild magic. Take note of that fact."

Royin frowned. "All right, Ormant, no use running the thing into the ground. He's right, though, Faral. We survived because we weren't quite so susceptible to the wild magic let loose by Tangral's death.

"Nor is it as simple as Ormant suggests; there are a few Masters of less power than we who have survived, but whose minds are still badly affected. There are even some students who had a moment of unconsciousness and are well save for having lost some part of their memory.

"The whole subject is something that needs to be studied, but not at the moment, not until we have the Household back on sound footing again."

Ormant leaned forward. "All these people who are still unconscious. We know for a fact that they'll be of no use to us, even if they wake. Might it not be best for the whole House if we quietly do away with all of them? Our resources are not totally unlimited."

The difficulty with quashing the notion immediately, Royin realized, was that it was something that had occurred to him, too.

Still, he shook his head. "No. I will not say 'absolutely not'; there may come a time when keeping such people is no mercy to them. I will not murder people simply to avoid the expense of caring for them."

Ormant merely nodded; Royin had a suspicion he had just been testing to see how far Royin could be pushed.

After the meeting, he went back to his investigation of Tangral's working. Some things were not altogether clear, but some things could be determined. For instance, using the proper conjunction of planets for such a thing, he had sent a seedling tree over to this other world. That one had required power, but not so much that he had had no power left over for shields.

There were certain spells on this seedling, which would attract a person of a certain sort; these spells were all derived from other spells, so that their general nature was easy to determine. The specific sort of person they attracted, however, was quite another matter, but he left that aside for a time.

So the Old Master had taken a living person, willy-nilly, from their own world, as an Ascension Gift? It fit with his high-handed personality, but something was missing. How does one prove to an unwizardly king that this person before them was indeed from another world? It allowed too much scope for other Households to start rumours of fraud, proof or disproof of which depended on the word of Wizards, any of whom either had ties to Pangwa or rivalries with them.

However, magic did not appear to work reliably on the other world, so it had apparently taken some time to attract the proper person. Why had Tangral required a woman, specifically? Had it been merely the fact that a woman was likely to be smaller, hence less difficult to bring over?

The effect of the conjunction of planets would last two, perhaps three days, which meant that whoever Tangral was bringing, it would have to be done within that time-frame. The trap, for he could no longer think of it any other way, had been sprung at near the last possible moment, just as the conjunction was passing.

That was the likely reason for the overstrain that had killed Tangral.

He looked up. How necessary was all this, or were there things more immediately necessary to the survival of the Household? There was probably going to come a tie when he would have to set forth the results of his investigation, at least to the king. How deep, though, did he need to go?

Well, there was at least one thing remaining. There had been no strange people found in the Grand Master's workroom; the servants would have let him know. The spell, therefore, didn't seem to have worked.

On the other hand, there were two phases involved in the spell: bringing the person into this world, and bringing her to the Master's presence. If the first part had succeeded, but not the second, the person might be anywhere in the world. Likely dead, of course, but still Royin felt he should look.

Seeing if someone was presently in this world who belonged in another world was mostly a matter of knowing what to ask. He took the little knife from his waist and pricked his thumb. Dripping two drops of water onto a piece of paper, he tossed the paper into the fire.

A picture formed in the flames, a picture of a woman dressed in the fashion of

Gagapeng, though the fashion was of about five years back. She was seated in a rough wooden cabin, to all appearances, in good health. At a guess, she was in one of the farming villages in the hinterlands.

He wondered if Tangral had tried to mix some good luck charms into his spells, just in case. Not only had she come on farmers quickly, but farmers who didn't just kill her as an outsider and appropriate her clothing.

Something ought to be done for her; it really wasn't fair, jerking her out of her home and leaving her in a farming village in the middle of nowhere.

He cancelled the fire-seeing.

No, it wasn't fair that Tangral's overweening conceit and self-confidence should destroy Pangwa Household, let alone all the Wizardly Households in Gagapeng. There were important things that needed to be done right now, and many people besides one dark-haired woman depended on his decisions.

But the raven-haired outside woman strayed into his thoughts from time to time.

"Yes, we are willing to allow the king's men to come and see the status of our Household. We are not willing, though, to allow members of other Wizardly Households to inspect us, gleaning whatever they may of our secrets.

"If, however, the king is willing to issue a command that our representative be allowed to inspect their Households, with Royal Troops accompanying us, we will consider the matter."

The men wearing the robes of Masters in various Households stood still, clearly at a loss as to what to say. Royin was fairly sure that all of them, with the possible exception of the Representative of Pantetikwa Household, were dressed-up students, nowhere near capable of dealing with political matters at this level, and likely afraid to speak for fear of fouling things up.

The fellow from Pantetikwa, though, was less than willing to hold his silence. "Is it not a fact that, rather than fear of our discerning their so-called magical secrets, the Masters of Pangwa are more concerned about one secret, that rather than the mere focus of disaster, this was an attack on all our Households?"

It was a predictable line of attack. The Representative of Pantetikwa House has proof of this assertion, of course?"

"It is clear that the magic that caused the ruin was centred around Pangwa House."

"I see. And by whose evidence?"

"By the evidence of all Households represented here!"

"None of whom, of course, have any reason to make trouble for Pangwa House?"

'Got you!' Royin thought to himself.

The Representative of Pantetikwa Household glowered. Everyone present knew that the disaster had centred around Pangwa House. Everyone present also knew that their status as competitors to Pangwa House made their witness suspect in unbiased eyes, and where could any serious witness be found who was not either beholden to Pangwa, or to one of the rivals?

It was likely that the next visit by the king's soldiers would be accompanied by an order to allow the inspection, without conditions, on pain of Royal displeasure. The longer this was delayed, though, the better Royin would be able to shore up matters in the Household.

The Royal Messenger looked as if he'd swallowed something ill-tasting and indigestible. "I will take your words to the king. I do not think he will be pleased."

"Very well." Royin knew that mention of the king's displeasure was intended to push him into backing down, but he did not comply. If he buckled under such a nebulous threat, the carrion-eaters would descend to pick Pangwa's bones.

Chapter Three

Hadjalloni tapped on the workroom door and opened it.

Melungtal marked the place in his scroll with a small block of polished stone. "So, Hadji. my boy, you've got the authorization to force me to put all our necks in the noose and hope that the worst won't happen? No, it's not just that you're easy to read; I have friends passing me a bit of gossip from time to time."

Hadjalloni's face was grim. "Hah! Pray that the worse won't happen! We've been doing that for years. The 'worst' Melungtal is that some power-mad fool decides to be the Blue-Blossom Wizard come again. And now we have a chance to see it doesn't happen, and you keep dithering around, wanting to make the soup taste just a bit better."

"Oh?" Melungtal was not argumentative. "Is that what you think I've been doing? Just adding little bits and flourishes? It isn't as simple as all that, and I did try to explain it to you, Hadji."

"Yes, you gave me your explanation as to how there was still some danger in putting this project into operation. But I think, on the contrary, it is that simple.

"I'm going to have to remove you from the project. According to rules, every step of your progress has to be recorded, so that any competent wizard can take it on and complete it. So you really aren't needed here, are you?"

"I see. Going to lock me up in a deep, dark dungeon, are you, Hadji?"

"No. I don't think you're a criminal, just a bit misguided. You're to stay in your suite, under guard, until the project is put in place. If you don't cause any trouble, you can be quite comfortable."

"I see. You'll have an escort for me, will you, Hadji? Certainly you're not going to trust me to report to my rooms like an obedient student sent for chastisement?"

Hadjalloni didn't allow himself to be baited. He opened the door and signalled to the five soldiers who stood outside, all clad in breastplate, greaves, and helmet, each with a short spear in hand. "Escort the Scholar to his suite, and hold him there. Remember, he is not a criminal, not to be mistreated. Off you go."

"Yes, sir."

Melungtal said nothing and merely marched off quietly.

❀

"What can you tell us of the Colony Farms, Faral? Projections on profits, and so on?" Royin looked down the table at the nervously twitching Faral.

"Their status is good enough, sir. If we were to take all their profits, it could ease our own situation considerably. I really think, though, that at least some of the profits ought to be put back into the Colonies.

"We can certainly use the profits immediately, but if we can forgo them, we can stretch our budget just that much further into the future."

That Faral had actually expressed a recommendation caught Royin so much by surprise that his answer did not come immediately. "Fine. We'll go with your proposal."

Before Faral could spoil the moment for himself by expressing doubts, Royin turned to Ormant. "Have we any Masters, even potential Masters?"

"Hah!" Ormant's meaty hands slammed down on the table. "We have eleven youngsters, most of whom I wouldn't ordinarily trust to wash dishes in the kitchen, let alone do any sort of complicated working. I've been driving them a bit, though, having them read everything available, particularly stuff just a bit above their level.

"Next week I plan to have them start actual practice. The Purple Flower, I think."

Royin nodded. "The Purple Flower? Hardly a test of power, is it?"

"You think we really want tests of

Power just yet? This is a test of following procedures."

"I see. What about the baby wizards?"

Ormant grinned, a bit nastily. "Altered the reading and writing lessons to mostly reading and copying simple spells, rather than old histories and poems. Might just speed up their actual magic-training a little."

"See that they're ridden hard on actual comprehension. If a kid gets a wrong notion in his head early, it may be hard to train out later on."

"You just keep on fending off the King and all, leave me to run the teaching."

Royin nodded.

"Speaking of fending off the king, I'll have to let you handle that, Ormant. I'm leaving for a week, possibly ten days; there's another matter that needs taking care of."

"What?" Ormant was angry. Faral appeared his usual uncertain self, only more so.

"It's about the Ascension Gift. I really don't know what Tangral intended, but there's a young woman from Outside sitting out in a farm village. She's part of the Ascension Gift, somehow. Not that she was the gift, but Tangral was planning on using her somehow. I've got to go see if I can find out what."

Royin surveyed the table. "We all know how the king is; a good Ascension Gift could go a fair way towards putting Pangwa House back into his favour.

"Ormant, anything that really needs the Grand Master's approval, put it off until I'm available. Make emergency decisions as you have to."

❋

"It's only the Ascension Gift, and the prospects of the Household," Royin thought to himself.

'Love at first sight' was one of those things that happened in the old stories, usually with two people for whom it would cause the maximum social or political difficulty. In real life, one's family chose one's mate, and the two learned to get along well, sometimes even extremely well.

In his own case, Royin was an orphan, adopted into Pangwa Household, and so far there'd been no talk of him marrying anyone. He had a fair idea of his own abilities, and he knew that sometime, in the next few years, tentative offers ought to be coming to his seniors---.

Royin caught himself. He was the senior! No, it was something he was still having trouble accepting. It would be up to him to accept or reject, and possibly even up to him to choose a wife.

He shook his head. Not for a year or two, yet. They had to get Pangwa House out of this mess. Then he could consider possibilities of marriage.

There was something about this dark-haired woman, though....

He pulled his mind back to the task at hand.

Royin had worked out the position of the village, and its distance from Gagapeng. He might have ridden a duka, but pushing one of those long-legged riding beasts to the utmost would require a week and a half riding. Then, a week and a half back--- no, more, because the woman would hardly be used to riding duka, and they wouldn't be able to push the pace.

On the other hand, there was one project which Royin had been working on for several weeks before Tangral's disaster. This project was fully ready and only needed testing.

He smiled; yes, a four-day trip out and another four days back again would constitute extreme testing. He couldn't guarantee that it was altogether safe, but then there was danger everywhere.

Royin had started with the observation that hot air rose. Why could not that power be harnessed to lift and carry things, possibly even to carry things over long distances? It had not been quite so simple in practice. First of all, an enormous amount of hot air was needed to lift the smallest thing.

He had then developed spells to augment the lifting ability of the hot air. It had also been necessary to produce a bag large enough to be worthwhile. It had to be a very fine weave, in order to prevent the hot air from escaping, or at least prevent it from escaping at too great a rate. Certain forms of experimental flora produced a sap that could be either extruded into long, very strong thread, or into large sheets of soft fabric.

Unfortunately, they had been given up as too expensive to be worthwhile.

Like so many other things, though they were not economically viable at the moment, the Household had saved at least a few samples, just in case.

Royin himself had done the spells that had brought several fields along from seed to adult in a matter of weeks, rather than months. People were hired for the specific purpose of producing the thread and weaving it into the closely woven fabric Royin needed.

He took the small ebony box from its workshop shelf, the small polished cubical ebony box that would do all the work. It held the mechanism that would blow hot air up into the bag, augment the lifting power of the hot air, and provide the propulsion as well.

The power that worked the spells inside the box were stored within in a device commonly used for lower-level spells. The device had to be re-powered, from time to time, and was more wasteful of power than a spell charged with its own sacrifice.

On the other hand, the power-mechanism permitted a person to do a spell or spells for a long time, without the physical burden having to be borne for the same time.

Royin spoke the words that started the mechanism which, in turn, began filling the bag with air, then began storing the supplies he had requisitioned into the basket that would ride beneath the bag.

Even so, he had to wait a while longer for the bag to fully inflate, to the point where it was straining to leap for the sky. He got into the basket and spoke the word that released the spells that held it to the ground. With gathering speed, he rose into the night sky.

He had chosen the middle of the night for his expedition to begin, when most folk would be in bed, or at least indoors. This way, Pangwa Household would not be immediately besieged by people demanding to know what sinister contraption Pangwa House was letting loose now.

Some people—such as astrologers—might catch sight of it in the sky, but were unlikely to tell just where it had come from. Besides, in Royin's experience, astrologers were a notably unworldly lot, and their greatest concern would be to an anxiety that this might be some new heavenly body that must be considered in their calculations.

It grew colder as he rose, and it occurred to him he knew that mountain-tops were cold, so he ought to have dressed properly.

Royin drew a little power from the ebony box in order to warm himself a bit. He dared not take too much; that could cause the warm air for the bag or the propulsion effect to fall off. The one would have him falling to the ground sooner than he wanted, the other would make it difficult to fly either against or across the winds.

At present, judging by the moon and the stars, he was travelling pretty much westward. He intended to correct his course from time, especially in the latter days of his journey, as the exact effects of the wind became known.

The feeling of flight was elating, though flight in this manner was much more cumbrous than the swooping, swerving flight of birds. It occurred to him that this might be the salvation of Pangwa Household. Merchants would pay well to have their cargo lifted and taken from one city to another, ignoring the winds and bends of the caravan roads.

Royin would have to do something to maintain the Pangwa House monopoly on the device as long as possible. Possibly have people trained to use the devices, with each device keyed to a particular person. Even go so far as to arrange a set of spells to cause the device to burst destructively if tampered with.

Any set of safeguards that could be imposed magically could eventually be unravelled magically, of course. But if Pangwa House could continue to develop the notion, making constant improvements, by the time any of the other Houses had put out their version, Pangwa would be established in the market.

He smiled. 'Moving a little before yourself, aren't you?'

Dark night air continued to flow by as he went along.

Royin suddenly woke, with his head leaning on the rim of the woven-wood basket. The cool air was still flowing past, and he was still flying west, but behind him the dawn was lightening the horizon. He tried to estimate how long he'd been asleep, then shook his head. No, he wasn't altogether recovered from the results of Tangral's disaster yet.

There was one thing to be said about being Grand Master, Royin thought. He could order the servants to prepare supplies of this and that nature, and there was no one higher for the servants to check with whether he could actually requisition all this. He was thus well-stocked with food, most of it the sort that could last several days.

He picked up a loaf of bread and attempted to break it. Yes, his logical thinking was still impaired; when he had tapped the power of box to warm himself, it hadn't occurred to him to consider the effect of the continued cold on his food supplies.

He took the small knife from his waist, pricked his thumb, and flicked away a drop of blood into the wind. Burning was the preferable means of sacrifice, but this casting away was enough to power a minor working.

He repeated a formula, then touched the loaf of bread, a sausage, and, almost as an afterthought, the skin of wine.

He smiled at the thought that, if he had done this sort of working in the presence of a client, he would probably have wasted a touch of power on some kind of display, flashing lights, colourful auras, or the like. Lay persons often needed that sort of thing to convince them that magic had actually happened.

He'd reckoned the thing fairly closely; the bread was thawed, but not hot, and the sausage was still cold in the middle.

He was going to have to take note of everything he was learning on this trip. First, warm clothing, or at least robes or blankets to wrap the travellers in.

About the food, well, they could work up some sort of chest to keep things from freezing.

The wine was still cold. It had not been the best of wine, but the taste now was just somewhere sort of appalling. He didn't think the freezing and thawing could account for the deterioration. Perhaps the actual magic spell he'd used had had unexpected effects.

He grinned slightly. A little test to give some of the better students a chance to see if they could devise a spell to warm wine without destroying the taste. A little working, a trivial amount of magic used, practically no possibility of the production of wild magic.

The grin went away; for the foreseeable future, Masters of Pangwa House were going to go at every working with a strong concern for wild magic and shielding.

On into the west he flew, with the rising sun at his back.

"This village, Strick's Bolg, is way west of the City, in what they call the New Lands." Moralei smiled. "Not so much 'new' as 'wild.' People came here from further east, when the land back there was starting to fill up."

"I see." Whoever or whatever had taught Alison the language had neglected to fill in some gaps. She had no idea who or what 'Strick' had been, nor what a Bolg was. She didn't bother asking; it was something she could find out about later, and in the meantime there were more important things she needed to know.

"Where's the outhouse?"

"Follow the path around back."

The outhouse stank. There was no pleasant word for it. On the other hand, Alison had done fieldwork in some primitive conditions, so it was no shock to her, considering the rest of the society.

She wasn't sure if it was something that showed in her expression, or just Moralei's bias against 'the City,' but the wise woman's immediate comment when Alison returned was "This isn't the City, where they take care of all the smells from their outhouses by magic."

Alison considered, for a moment, explaining flush toilets and sewage-treatment plants, but decided that this was another thing she should just let go.

But Moralei's mood seemed to change almost immediately. She offered Alison a piece of flat bread and an earthenware cup. "Bread and chalberry wine. For you, my guest."

The last part sounded like some kind of formula, and Alison, though she couldn't find in her own command of the language any answering formula, said "Thank you," and took the bread first, then the wine.

The bread had been cooked in a flat cake, much like a pita, and tasted as though the chief ingredient were potatoes. The wine was red and sweet, with a hint of something like cranberry, but not quite.

"Sit, Alison." Moralei gestured toward one of several wooden stools next to a rough log table which, from the look of it, was used more for preparing herbal remedies than dining.

"You know anything about medicine?"

"Not a lot. I know something about the plants we use back home for medicine, but pretty well, everything's different here."

Moralei nodded. "I see. Well, maybe we can start in with that a little later. Suppose you just follow along with me and learn something about the village first.

"First, Samishak has some tangal in his vorish. I'd better go over and take care of that."

Apparently whoever had brought her here had put terms for various crops and weeds into her head, so that she could see in her mind the vorish, similar to the oat she knew back home save that the leaves each divided in three slender spears, and the grain itself, when ripe, was either red, black, or yellow.

The tangal was blue-green, with a thick stalk, and a head that eventually ripened into a bright white flower, and still later, scattered its seeds around for the next year.

Samishak was a tall, skeletal man, very tanned, with hair beginning to go grey. He grinned when he saw them. "A good day to you both," he said.

Alison reflected that her arrival must have been the talk of the town this morning.

"A good day to you as well, Samishak. This is my guest, Alison."

"Fine, fine. Will you deal with my tangal now?"

"Yes, yes, don't push, Samishak." Moralei looked at the field.

Alison thought it only barely possible to distinguish what was tangal and what was vorish at this stage, and sometimes, not even that distinction could be made. Was Moralei supposed to have some special knowledge that would allow her to decide which could be pulled up, which left behind?

But Moralei did nothing of the sort. Instead, she took out a small knife that hung at her waist, a bronze knife, Alison thought, and pricked the ball of her thumb.

She let a drop of blood fall on the earth, then spoke a quick phrase that wasn't in Alison's command of the language. In fact, it seemed like some other language altogether.

Moralei paused for a moment, then said, "There you are, my friend. They'll begin dying this evening, tomorrow morning at the latest."

"Good, good." Samishak's white teeth showed. "I'll have one of the youngsters bring you over a loaf of Andami's bread this afternoon. Next time I go hunting, I'll remember you."

"Good. The crop looks quiet."

Alison thought she might have misheard. 'Quiet' didn't seem like a term to apply to crops.

But the old farmer answered, "Quiet, yes."

Now, was that a mythical way of complimenting the crops, so that the spirits or whatever wouldn't feel insulted and cause problems? Or was it some sort of dialectical thing that the "teacher' hadn't prepared Alison for?

Moralei walked from here to there in the village, looking at the crops, and giving a commentary on things that seemed (to her) to be interesting.

"Flahas," she pointed to a small crop that appeared to have gotten an earlier start than Samishak's vorish. it looked a little like pea vines, though even now they were a blue colour. Alison's mind whispered 'Lakos' at her and gave her a vision of what looked much like a dark purple pea-pod. Inside it would be something that looked like a purple kidney bean.

What shocked her most of all was the potato. Everything about it said that it was what she knew as Solanum tuberosum. They knew it locally as allom, with only a slight difference of vowels in the form Alison knew. Moreover, what she 'knew' about the allom was that by all surface indications it was a potato, complete with the edible tuberous roots. Furthermore, it was ground and made into flour, from which someone had baked that pita-like bread.

So how had the potato gotten here, and how had it gotten here sufficiently long ago to be so common?

On the other hand, Alison was here. If she had been brought here, couldn't someone bring a potato? Actually, it wasn't that simple; they'd have to bring enough to actually grow, and produce enough of a crop to even begin to spread.

But they were undeniably here, and presented a puzzle, but it was a puzzle that she didn't have enough pieces of to even attempt a solution.

They visited a few houses, mostly houses where Moralei had been treating people for this or that, anything from coughs and colds to broken limbs.

She met practically everyone in the village, though it would take her some time to remember all the names. Everyone was wary of her. Some were unfriendly, which she read as the way they showed their wariness. After all, she was an outsider, and who knew what those City people might do?

She also got a feeling that Moralei's acceptance went a long way towards gaining the villagers' tentative approval. She also met Old Kangasa, the nearest thing to a Headman the village possessed. His position was due to a combination of his years and a general reputation for wisdom. His hair had turned white, and he carried a staff which had nothing to do with a symbol of his office.

He nodded to Alison. "I see the wise woman has already made you welcome."

"Yes, thank you."

"Good. May no trouble attend your stay among us." It was said with the sense of a formula, but Alison got the feeling that it was not 'just something the Elder was expected to say.'

Like too many other things, her 'language-teacher' seemed to have left out any notion of how to respond. She said, "I'll try not to cause trouble," and notice looks from both

Kangasa and Moralei that suggested she was hardly fit to be in polite company.

She almost burst out with, "I didn't ask to be sent here!" She realized just in time that this would be on a par with complaining, "It's not fair!" Instead, she held her peace.

But Kangasa had other things on his mind than instructing strangers in proper protocol. He turned to Moralei. "They say Norvallik and his family are unhappy about the sharing of the crops."

She nodded. "Usiyin had twins in early spring, when the stores were already low."

He almost smiled at that one. "They are that way, aren't they? Always first among the complainers, and sometimes if there's nothing to complain about, they'll find something."

"Maybe it's time someone told them to go find some village they'd be more comfortable at."

Kangasa's face was unreadable. "Don't like that sort of thing. It always causes division, no matter how gently it's handled. I'll go soothe them, tell them they're being no harder done by than anyone else in the village."

He was off on his way, and Moralei continued on her own way. Alison followed along.

An old man in a bed dominated one of the next houses they visited. He said nothing, did nothing, but everyone appeared to be aware of his presence, and it seemed to be a presence that made them nervous.

A woman, possibly a few years younger than Kangasa, looked up when Moralei came in. "Ah, Moralei. You still can't do anything for him, then?"

Moralei shook her head. "I told you before, Antalga, there's nothing I can do. It's his time, the time for him to go dwell among the stars, but Goradin is too strong. His body, his mind, have given way, but his spirit still holds fast to this world."

"In his day, he was a good man, a respected man, but now he lies like this! I'd rather see him passed and gone to the stars, Moralei. This doesn't honour his memory."

Moralei shook her head. "I do what I can to ease his passing, but I can't hurry it."

Antalga sighed. "No, I suppose not. Will you eat with us?"

"We ought not. We'd be a bother."

"No, no, you won't be a bother! I wouldn't have it said that my house dishonoured the wise woman."

So they ate bread there, along with some sort of meat, which resembled turkey. It didn't seem polite to ask what the meat was, and it was offered with one of those dialectical words, rafti, that her 'language-teacher' hadn't prepared her for.

They wandered from place to place in the village, no set of regular 'rounds,' and some houses Moralei didn't visit. Alison could only guess that it was because no one was sick in those houses.

Some people were introduced by nicknames, such as "Knees," because of his knobby knees or "Hunter," or "Little Fellow" (who was tall and broad.)

One cheery man, Sethanki by name, was working in a field. After they'd passed him, Moralei said, "You'll probably hear him called 'Holder', but not to his face. They call him that because any time anyone wants to borrow his spear, or shovel, or hoe, or whatever, he almost always claims that he's just about to use it. Not enough that it's worth the disruption to ask him to find a village better suited to himself, but just enough to be aggravating."

There was a large house in the approximate centre of the village, which Moralei pointed out as "the bathhouse."

'Bath House' in the local language put into Alison's mind a large marble building, where men and women came to sit in the steam. This wooden building was clearly not that, but Alison had difficulty figuring out the questions to ask to clarify it, so she just asked, "How does it work?"

Which, of course, got her a strange look from Moralei. "How does it work? Everybody takes part, seeing that wood is cut and supplied, seeing that water is brought. How else? How does it work in the City?"

"I'm not from the City, I'm from somewhere else altogether. The city supplies water, for a charge, and for another charge they supply the---" 'gas' wasn't in the local vocabulary, "the stuff to burn to heat it. When you want a bath, you, ah, turn on the mechanism that allows the water to flow into the tub." 'Tub' required circumlocution, 'large, low container.' "Then you lie in the water and wash."

'Now that's a strange way of doing things. Here we use steam. We heat up rocks, and pour water on them, and everybody goes in to get clean."

"Everybody?"

"Well, not everybody at once, of course! The building will only hold so many. Usually it goes by family, but there's usually room for one or two more any night."

A suspicion crept over Alison. "Men and women together?"

This got her another look. "Of course."

"I can't!"

Moralei gave her a stern look, like the curer administering bad-tasting medicine to a child. "Girl, so long as you're a guest in my house, you'll stay clean. Or do you want to move out to the barns?"

Alison said no more about it.

They went past Samishak's field later on that day, and Alison saw some weeds were drooping.

'Magic,' She thought to herself. *'Someone brought me here somehow, something the locals call "magic" because they don't understand it. But this, even I don't understand this.'*

Some boys, carrying long sticks, were apparently in charge of some animals who were foraging in and around the surrounding forests. The animals were about four feet tall, hornless, with a hoof divided in three. It was recognized by the 'language-teacher' as a djasa, used for milking, and occasionally for meat and leather.

There was a smaller sort of animal, usually wandering in more closely bunched herds, known as raxler. They had two-part hooves, and though the females were milked, the main purpose of the raxler was to be sheered for its wool.

There were birds around as well, which seemed lo be semi-domesticated. They had the general shape of a cassowary, though Alison admitted to little knowledge of birds, and they were slightly smaller than the cassowary as well. Their local name was sordigut, but the language-teacher didn't seem to know them.

"Are they wild?" She asked, feeling foolish for having to ask.

But Moralei chuckled. "Oh, yes. They gather around because of the bits and scraps of food they pick up. And these ones have taken to nesting right near the village. They have to be kept out of the fields, particularly right after sowing, or they'd eat the crops before they had a chance to sprout."

"You don't magic them away?"

Moralei's expression told her she'd just asked a stupid question. "Why on earth would I do that? They're so willing to hang around and be ready for the eating. Chasing them off would be foolishness. Long as we don't kill too many at one time, so they get don't the notion this is dangerous territory, they'll keep hanging round. Another bit of food when the crops are low."

That night Moralei said, "Come along, we're going to the bath-house."

"I can't undress in front of all those people!"

"Why not? They'll be undressing in front of you?"

"Because---." She couldn't force herself to explain.

"So." Moralei stared at her closely. "This deep trouble, it still holds you?"

Alison glared at her. "You're telling me to get over it?"

Moralei shrugged. "Stop letting it rule your life, for sure."

"Stop letting it rule---! You don't know what you're talking about!"

"No exact words, no. But you go around with every muscle in your body shouting 'I carry the weight of the world wherever I go!' Hard to miss. Only thing I can say is, I can't fix it, no one can fix it. You've got two ways to go: Be the broken bird all your life, or take charge of your life and deal with it on your own terms."

As psychotherapy went, it was terrible. Psychotherapy was supposed to be non-directive, to help the person see the way to deal with the problem for themselves.

As advice, it was even worse.

"Seems so easy the way you say it!"

The wise woman shrugged. "Most of life's difficult. We all of us have our troubles and our burdens. Seems to me the thing to do is to see just how much of the burden you really need to carry all your life.

"For now, though, come along to the bath-house."

Moralei kept a light hand on Alison's arm all the way, and Alison had a feeling that if she tried to get away, that hand would take a firm hold.

It was worse than she'd expected. Not only was all clothing taken off at the door, but the talk was all ribald joking. The sort of talk that went on here was known as 'bath-house talk,' and was recognized as not fit for other occasions.

Even though the main part of her mind accepted that this talk meant nothing to the local people, whoever, whatever had brought her here hadn't adjusted her own notions of what was right.

It was one of the hardest things she'd done, Alison decided. Though she picked a dim corner to sit in by herself, staring at her own toes most of the time, she felt as if all eyes were on her. Though the few times she looked up, no one seemed to cast more than a glance in her direction.

Some plants that were considered 'weeds' when among the farmers' crops were actually good for medicines. Just as boys back home grew up learning to distinguish the makes and models of cars, so children here knew every plant in their world, at each stage in its growth.

The medicinal ones they would bring to Moralei, with a little ball of earth around the roots, and she would set them into small plants and encourage them to grow. Very few of them refused to do so.

"I'm Chief Curer of the village, mostly because I got a bit of plant-magic as well. A lot of people have some plant-magic, but some jobs need a bit more than that.

"As for the Curer business, most families have a list of medicines and remedies that get passed down among the family, and they're usually willing to share them. I pick up a few others from time to time, brought by visitors from other villages, or by merchants passing through.

"I have a bit of good luck with my remedies, too."

"You mean you use magic with them?"

Moralei chuckled. "Only magic I got is a bit of skill with making things grow, or not. Don't really do spells with my herbs, but people seem to get better with them."

"Placebo effect." The words were specifically in English.

Moralei's brow furrowed. "What's that?"

"It doesn't translate, exactly. It is that doctors back home have discovered that some people will improve, even if the pill they're given is nothing more than sugar.

"This means that when they test medicines to see if they have an effect, they always have one group taking a sugar pill instead, and even the researchers don't know which person is getting what. To be considered a proper medicine, the drug has to be more effective than the sugar pill. I'm making the process seem more simple than it actually is, but that's roughly it."

Moralei nodded. "Curers have a saying. 'We don't cure people; we just make it easier for the body to cure itself.'"

The village was small enough that Alison came to meet all the three men who'd met her in the forest the first day. Daro, the leader of the trio, was friendly, and Flan would give her a friendly wave and a smile as well. She was still sure she didn't want to be anywhere alone with Flan. Though she couldn't exactly trust that feeling, knowing how much it was coloured by the events of that first day.

She fell into the position of 'assistant Curer' in the village. She also discovered that she had a nickname, 'Corner Girl,' from her habitual position in the bath-house. It wasn't her favourite nickname, but she had to admit she'd been called worse.

She came to be on good terms with Old Kangasa, learning what his job was by listening and watching what went on in the village. His authority over the people was based on consensus, and was not used to enrich himself, or have people work for him. He was recognized as a "Good" Elder because in all his time, only two families had chosen to go somewhere else rather than agree to one of his occasional suggestions. Furthermore, he had could mediate disputes between people, and between families, without leaving a permanent rift in the village.

On the other hand, Moralei warned Alison of two families, "Be careful about mentioning any member of one family in the others' hearing. They're still a little sensitive from the matter of the raxler three years back."

Alison wanted to ask further about that, but she was still too new in the village, and didn't think it was her place to be nosing out all the gossip.

People are people, though, and the people of Strick's Bolg were no exceptions. Quarrels happened, often over little things, and sometimes even came to blows. Alison was present at one such situation; Moralei had said, "Take a dose of this painkiller up to Orfolo; He's still having trouble from the gash he gave himself with the hoe yesterday."

She was just coming up to Orfolo's garden when she saw Orfolo stand up and swing a fist into Kiambil's face. Kiambil went down, surprise on his face, then came back up, roaring. "You blasted Slasher, I'll show you!"

Alison stopped still, but suddenly people were all around the pair, pulling them apart and standing between them when they attempted to get at each other. There was a lot of shouting around of people trying to calm the participants, and Alison got the gist of the affair; Kiambil had been badgering Orfolo, calling him "Slasher," and every time Orfolo made a move—he'd been hoeing his potatoes—saying such things as "Oop! Count your toes, Slasher? Still got enough fingers?"

Finally, Orfolo had had enough.

Which had been the time of Alison's arrival.

Old Kangasa had come, at as much of a rush as his old bones would allow, and took the situation in, then began talking. Alison knew that, in most circumstances, he would not decide immediately, claiming he needed a night to think.

The next day, in front of as much of the village as cared to gather, he would lead the men through a long rambling discourse on how much they had meant to each other, and what it meant for the village to divide against itself.

This time, though, he didn't give himself the night to think, but launched into his oration immediately. At parts of the speech, various people would at least nod, perhaps even going so far as to say "Yes, yes!"

'Local equivalent of "You preach, Reverend!"' Alison thought to herself.

At last, the two men themselves nodded their own agreement. Finally, the Elder asked the important question. "Will you stay as friends then, or will you leave the village?"

The Kiambil muttered, "I will stay," followed a moment later by Orfolo's grumble of assent.

"Good," Kangasa said, giving each of them a measuring look. "Let it be so."

That was usually the end of such a dispute, and no more was said. People went back to their business. Kiambil moved off a little from Orfolo and found a task to busy himself with. Alison delivered Moralei's medicine and noticed that Orfolo was still tense. It would be a while, she figured, before those two would be at ease in each other's company.

There were no clocks nor calendars in the village, though there were limits set by the season as to when plowing and planting had to be done. As an assistant-Curer, though, Alison's duties were a little fuzzy, and so long as she was not too far away when Moralei wanted her, all was well.

So she took her time heading back, studying the various plant-life, occasionally trying to compare it to some similar thing back home. Of course, even back home, there were plants she didn't know, or didn't know at all well. Someone was always discovering some new thing in the jungles of Papua New Guinea, or in the Amazon---.

She heard a movement behind her and saw Orfolo striding out of his house with a spear in his hand. Her first thought was that it was a bit late in the day for hunting. Then she realized he was striding toward Kiambil. By the time she recovered enough from her stunned shock to yell, Orfolo had rammed his spear through Kiambil's chest.

Death was almost instantaneous; there was no question of a wild, unaimed blow. Orfolo had aimed for the heart, and hit.

Then the shouting started anew. This time, though, while Kiambil's relatives tried to get at Orfolo, who was standing there, stunned at what he'd done, Orfolo's relatives were around him, protecting their kinsman.

Spears were coming up, now, and axes, though no one did more than a tentative jab or feigned strike.

Other people, less closely related, tried to come between the two parties. They carried no arms, so as not to inflame things the more, being concerned for the good of the village.

Kangasa was fetched again, and he came, huffing and puffing with haste. He surveyed the scene, and grief was clear on his face.

"Ah! A bad thing, this!" He glared at Orfolo for a long while. "Orfolo, you must go from the village. If you wish, you may come back when the moon has waned and become full again, and see if there is a place here for you."

Kiambil's family were not satisfied. "No! Blood for our blood! Blood for our blood!"

Kangasa turned a severe look on them. "'Blood for our blood,' you say? And next Orfolo's family will shout 'Blood for our blood,' and the village will drown itself in a never-ending river of blood!

"No, Orfolo will leave here. Any who hinders him must first strike me. Am I heard?"

There was a dull muttering from some quarters, but Kangasa escorted Orfolo to his house, where he collected an axe, a spear, and a bag of food. Orfolo was not yet married, so there was no wife or family to accompany him. Kangasa saw him off to the edge of the forest, then returned.

He returned and spoke to the small group of people standing there watching. "Tomorrow we must hold a spirit-feast, to lift the spirit of murder from the village."

When Alison got back home, she asked Moralei, "Has Kangasa got enough authority that they'll just let Orfolo go like that?"

"He has as much authority as the people will allow him. Orfolo had better go far and fast and stay hidden. Kiambil's brothers will probably be after him before sundown."

"You mean..."

"Sometimes the slayer would go off and perhaps come back at the appointed time. He might even find a place in the village. But there are some cases, such as this one, where there's too much anger."

"What about Orfolo's brothers? Will they go out to help Orfolo?"

"Probably not fight alongside him, more likely just go out and try to mess up his trail, make it harder for anyone to follow Orfolo. Even that could lead to trouble out there in the bush. It could still destroy the entire village."

Alison remained silent.

The next day—next evening, actually — there was a large communal feast at which attendance was as near to compulsory as managed in a society where compulsion was abhorrent.

Kangasa spoke with a great deal of fervour, much of his speech being as a prayer to the Supreme Deity, Sannat, asking that Sannat would lift the spirit of murder from Strick's Bolg.

Kangasa also spoke to the people.

"We are much greater together than we are apart, and dividing into factions will destroy the village. As surely as if you set the buildings afire, killed the livestock, and plowed up the growing crops."

The speech was accompanied by a lot of mumbling from the crowd, and though most seemed to agree with the Elder, other, less peaceable voices murmuring as well.

A djasa had been killed for the feast. This was served with some of the store of potatoes—despite her knowledge of the local language, Alison found it hard to think of them as anything else—which were baked as well.

Sufficient bread was available also, each household having supplied a loaf or two.

Even Kiambil's close relations contributed to the feast. Apparently, they could see that it was for the good of the village, though it kept them off the murderer's trail for an extra day.

Later that evening, Alison asked Moralei, "Do you think it helped?"

"Helped? Yes, for sure, if only that some people could actually do some thinking before they went chasing off after a killer. It means that many people are at least thinking about the good of all above their need for vengeance. Or their need to protect their relatives."

She was quiet for a moment. "Next few days will tell the tale. If we see too many hunting parties going out, we may be in trouble yet."

Alison was left to consider the problems of administering justice in a small, isolated village. Who made laws? Well, apparently the king issued edicts, mostly to do with taxation. But how was justice, whatever you called it, locally administered and enforced?

The most serious crime, murder, which they'd just seen, involved not just the killer and his victim, but the families of each. Just as, back home, any murder almost always brought the family of the victim to demand vengeance, so it was here.

The difference was that here, all that kept the village from seeking vengeance was whatever moral suasion the village and the elder could bring to bear.

Custom frown on seeking an eye for an eye; it was recognized as harmful and divisive. However, there was no force locally to prevent people from seeking vengeance.

The notion of jails was ridiculous; the village couldn't spare people to guard the jail, let alone to feed someone who couldn't contribute to the welfare of the village.

Capital punishment? That left the family of the executed murderer with a grudge against whoever had passed the sentence, as well as against whoever had carried it out.

She shook her head. The village was run by rules and customs that had developed over years, likely centuries and more, and the situation was so far different from anything she knew that no suggestion she could think up would fit the state of affairs.

Besides that, it was very difficult to change a traditional society overnight, and no one would thank her for trying.

Chapter Four

It was three nights later, somewhere after midnight, and both Alison and Moralei were sleeping. There was a sudden rapping on the door, and a voice called out, "Koowa! Moralei! Talbon's time has come! Moralei! Are you awake, Moralei?"

Moralei sat up. "Yes, Kemilo, I'm awake. So is half the village, by now. Give me a second to get dressed."

She looked over in the darkness to where Alison was awake again. "Babies don't pick a sensible time of day to come. Go back to sleep; I'll slip back in when I'm done, try not to waken you."

Alison muttered an agreement that she'd heard and lay back again. She was thinking vaguely that this was a very interesting society, where someone could recognize the voice of someone else through a closed door. No, she realized, that came of having a small enough neighbourhood where everyone knew everyone else. She barely stayed awake past the time when Moralei gently closed the door.

Sometime later, she woke just enough to know that the door had opened and closed quietly. It woke her up just enough to think vaguely that Moralei hadn't been as quiet slipping back in as she'd hoped to be.

The first thing she was aware of was that someone had pulled off her blanket. That disturbed her sleep, but what actually woke her was the hands on her breasts. For an instant, she was back in that horrible night, that man with the knife.

This was not that night, though.

Since that night, Alison had trained to protect herself. She trained in several martial arts which concentrated on the use of crippling, incapacitating, and even killing blows.

It was also drilled into them that running was little use, unless you'd crippled that man first. Also, there might be a situation, such as here, where there was nowhere to run. You had to concentrate on staying calm as possible, until he laid hands on you, when he was well within your reach. *'Men have longer and stronger arms. But in order to assault you, it would mean they have to get within reach of you!'*

She was nowhere near calm, though she tried to pull herself out of her panic, striking almost wildly. She jammed the V of her thumb and forefinger up at the man's throat. It wasn't anywhere near her full power, but the man pulled back, gagging.

That gave her an instant to collect herself, though calmness was still some ways off, and jab two stiffened fingers at his eyes. He pulled his head back, and trained reflexes shot her fist straight to his already battered throat. This time, he rolled off onto the floor, gagging horribly.

She pulled herself up, and in the dimness could make out Flan's features.

All the training that had taught her to deliver the blows and kicks had not prepared her to watch and hear someone die after she'd delivered one of those blows. It was not a quick process, either. With his smashed throat, Flan could not scream or shout, only thrash around, gargling and clawing for air.

It wasn't until he went still that Alison realized she'd been screaming for some time.

Suddenly, the door was flung open, and two other men, Daro and Samishak, came rushing in. Daro had his spear and Samishak a torch.

"What happened?" Daro demanded.

That brusque question washed over Alison like a bucket of cold water. She pulled the blanket around herself; nudity was not taboo here, but she wasn't from around here. "What the hell do you think happened?"

She realized she'd spoken in English and started over again. "What do you think happened? I woke up, and he was all over me, so I had to fight him off. I killed him, and it wasn't fun at all."

"You killed him? What with?"

"With my bare hands." It was with difficulty that she refrained from saying,

"Want me to show you?"

"Bare hands?" There was doubt in his voice.

"Bare hands. I've had training in defending myself bare-handed."

"He didn't stumble and injure himself?"

"No! He came here to — to rape me — and I fought back."

"This is bad. Flan's family will be upset."

"Flan's family will be---! Listen, I was the one who was attacked!"

"But Flan is the one dead on the floor. That is what will be important to Flan's family."

Alison suddenly understood; with all his questions, Daro had been attempting to allow her to shift responsibility for Flan's death. While she, from the world of law-courts and pleas of self-defence, had let her mouth insist on an accurate version of facts.

She wasn't sure whether Flan's family would have seen much difference in the way of responsibility; he'd come into her bed, and he'd died. Intentional blow or a fall, Alison was still the only other present, and that was probably enough.

"What now? I take a spear and head off into the bush?"

Daro looked doubtful. "No. For one thing, you are the wise woman's guest, and no one would want to offend her, not if they think clearly. On the other hand, people rarely think clearly in a situation such as this."

He looked over his shoulder. A crowd was gathering outside, and some form of the story was likely being passed around.

He looked back at her. "You stay here; Samishak and I will take Flan out. No one will dare violate Moralei's hospitality, at least not for a day or so."

She nodded; her mind went back to that classic scene in the old western movies of the town marshal in front of the jail, facing down the lynch mob.

But for all Daro's willingness to help, he still had to live in the village, and she was an outsider, with no relatives to take her part.

"That Flan! He was a good enough fellow most times, but every once in a while...." Moralei was scowling. "So you killed him barehanded, eh? More to you than a first look shows, seems like."

"Not something I'm proud of. I'd be less proud, though, if I'd let him go through with it."

Moralei nodded. "Well, if we're really lucky, we can come through this without destroying the village, and with no more deaths. You're going to have to stay inside with me until we can work this out."

Alison nodded. "Makes sense not to be flaunting my presence in the eyes of everyone, particularly Flan's relatives. I'll spend some time working on herbs."

Moralei gave her a grim smile. "Yes, you do that."

It was not possible to stay inside all the time, no matter how much she wanted to. Perhaps it was her imagination, but she felt eyes on her every time she went to the outhouse, though no one seemed to look at her outright.

Kangasa came to visit her, ostensibly to hear her side of the story. "You did not invite him to come? Even possibly without meaning to?"

It took her a moment to calm her anger enough to produce a sentence in the local language instead of English. "So the woman must be to blame all the time, then? No, I did not invite him in. He came sneaking in during the night while I was asleep. All I did was to defend myself. Surely everyone knows what Flan was like!"

"Yes," Kangasa replied gravely. "All know very well what Flan was like. His family, though, they say he was never that bad. They say that if you'd slapped him and told him to stop, he would have. But you did not slap, you struck blows, and from the indications you struck to kill, or at least injure seriously.

"My concern, you see, is for the welfare of the village. Flan's family are not a large group, thankfully, but set against that group, you are less important. Your only tie here is the guest-right Moralei has given you, and even that will not last forever.

Alison looked at Moralei, who looked as though she'd bitten into something sour. "He's right, Alison. I'll stand by you and protect you as much as I can. If Flan's relatives hold fast to their anger, though, sometime, somewhere, someone will come after you with a spear or dagger.

"My status here will give you protection. But set the respect of my status and ability against an anger that grows bitter the longer you are in our presence, and you can read that path yourself, can't you?"

Alison went cold. Despite her rage at the unfairness of it all, she could see that both Moralei and Kangasa had to live in the village. While Alison had no one, no family to offer protection to her. In fact, the most helpful thing, from Kangasa's point of view, was to chase Alison out of Moralei's house and let someone put a spear through her.

When she looked at it from the village's point of view, it was hard to blame him, but she still harboured some resentment.

"You'd prefer me to walk out there and let someone kill me, wouldn't you?"

Kangasa looked down. "The spirit of murder may take a firm hold on a village, whoever is killed. Who's to say that the death of an outsider would be the end of it?"

She caught in this the feeling that the spirit of murder, a separate entity by itself, was what caused people to murder each other. While it seemed a foolish notion to her, it was still very real to the local people. Each death, it seemed, strengthened that spirit. The Headman would try to prevent more killing, but he still might see one last death as less likely to lead to more.

Anger boiled over. "You tell them," she said. "You tell them to remember their precious boy, Flan. Remember that he came on me asleep and unaware, and he died. Tell them to think about that!"

She knew it was just rage talking, but words seemed all which were left to her. Kangasa looked at her, a little reproachfully, and she couldn't read Moralei's expression at all.

❀

The New Land, with its small villages in widely spaced cleared sections of the forest, went by below Royin. He'd checked his course this morning, and should come in sight of the right village soon. He'd heard that the New Land had produced its own set of customs and traditions, including a distrust of outsiders, particularly, they said, "City People." They were also a bit in awe of 'City' magic, but that could change in an instant to violent antipathy.

He'd brought some trade-goods, nothing fancy, just good iron hoe-heads, axe-heads, and the like. As for any sort of magical demonstration, he'd wait to see what the situation was. It just might be that an unasked-for magical demonstration could turn an annoyed populace into a hostile one.

He went back to general consideration of the balloon as a means of travel. The benefits were obvious, but there were also problems. It required a lot of power to go against a headwind, and even fighting a crosswind could be difficult.

They might be limited to certain seasons of the year. Though a man who was able and willing to pay for constant charging of the spell-boxes could even ignore those limits.

He considered weather-control spells

for a moment, but rejected the notion. It was possible, of course, and had been done many years ago. Among the things that had been discovered was that bringing rain to this place took it away from that, and the same with bringing clear weather.

Worse still, after some years of fiddling with the weather, there was a five-year-long series of terrific storms, causing widespread damage, as well as famine, because crops were washed out in many places.

More efficient motive-power spells might be the answer. Perhaps something that took advantage of the motion of the wind, turning that motion in another direction? Not for the first time on the journey, he regretted the unavailability of the Household Library.

Alison could feel the tension in the air. She understood—she'd had no visitors since Kangasa—that there were no few people in the village with some sympathy for her. Unfortunately, that sympathy was not enough to bring them to the point of pulling the village apart over one person with no local ties.

Moralei's face grew grimmer every day, until at last Alison said, "Why don't I just leave? Slip out some night and make my own way to the City?"

"Don't be ridiculous! That would be tantamount to sending you out to die, even if Flan's relatives weren't on your trail in half a day. There're nasty things out their in the woods, even without considering the thought of outcasts from some other village, living rough, and only slightly better than beasts themselves. No, I'll hold things the way they are for now. It's still possible that they'll calm down. It's not a simple thing to violate the vine-house."

Despite Moralei's seeming confidence, Alison knew the situation couldn't last. In the end, the wise-woman's guest-right would be violated, and some part of the village would find themselves in fear of Moralei, rightly or wrongly. Would she use her powers to cause certain persons' crops to wither instead of the weeds? Would she poison certain people rather than heal them?

Who exactly would she blame? The precise individuals who killed Alison? Any and all their families? Perhaps even the ones who had not stepped forward to protect her?

Well, it would only be Flan's family. The whole family had some share in the 'guilt,' though the Elder might cobble together a 'peace' for many, if not most.

Even so, the village would likely be destroyed by her death, as it had not been by Kiambil's.

"But I didn't ask that lout to come in and attack me!" She muttered.

Moralei looked a question at her. Alison shook her head. "Nothing. Or at least, nothing useful."

❁

Melungtal looked at the wall of his bedroom. He'd thought the matter through for three days and finally had come to a conclusion. It wasn't that he loved the Rosthanites; the God knew that if another Blue-Blossom Wizard arose, it would likely be there. On the other hand, there was just too much likelihood of the Project, as it now stood, coming back against Saljashin.

No, he couldn't go along with that.

He muttered a phrase. A spot on his bedroom wall grew black, deep, deep black.

It wasn't so much a distrust of Hadjalloni as a concern for the whole Watcher organization. Their procedure was to declare a person Suspect, on whatever evidence. Declaring them Suspect seemed to be the equivalent of declaring them Guilty. The Suspect was taken away to a dungeon, where he or she was held until next Cleansing Day. The Suspect was then brought out and blasted to bits—by the so-abhorrent magic—in front of a crowd of cheering citizens.

Melungtal had developed a minor spell, not detectable—he hoped—by the clumsy sledge-hammer methods of the Lower Watchers. But something he could use in a prison cell. As it happened, though, he didn't need to worry about that.

He stepped forward. The black spot had grown to about thumbnail size, which his calculations said was large enough.

He was in blackness, a whirling, vertiginous sensation such as he'd never imagined. Then he was on hands and knees on solid ground again, vomiting as if he might cough up bits of his innards.

After a while, he could consider his surroundings again. He was in a wooded area. *'Good. Couldn't exactly test that out. The Watchers would have demanded explanations, and the spell was of use pretty much only for escaping. Explain that to a lot of suspicious minds.'*

There were limits to what he could take along on this escape; his small knife, an eating-knife, his clothing, and that was about it. He had also brought along his mind and all that was in it. It was said that a certain man could be called, if one were at a certain place in the forest.

Some of the younger, more romantic souls said that if you passed his trial, he would give you your heart's desire. The older and more cynical said that if you paid him well, he could supply just about anything you needed. While he didn't consider himself to be particularly cynical, Melungtal found himself more among the latter group. The mysterious summoning, from a particular place, was most likely a means of keeping the Watchers off the track.

He himself was on a path, and he knew his destination lay on the path, but backward or forward was another matter. His escape spell had been, or at least according to the theory should be, accurate within about three hundred feet. It was only a matter of walking a small distance one way along the path, then retracing his steps back, and a ways back beyond where he'd started.

He was sufficiently experienced that he didn't expect his theory to actually prove out in practice, at least not the first time.

Shortly, he came on a small stream that crossed the path, with a thick, gnarled old tree on its bank. 'Tis was the place,' so they said.

He put a hand on the tree-trunk and said, "I need help. I need help. I need help."

It felt a little like one of those things from the old stories, with the formula needing to be repeated three times. However, the three repetitions made it less likely for someone to accidentally trigger whatever spell was present.

There was a long wait, with nothing happening save the birds singing in the bushes, the insects making their own noises, and the breeze rustling the leaves.

A sudden flame burst out on one of the limbs of the tree, about the height of Melungtal's face. Though the flame seemed to burn brightly, it neither harmed the tree nor put out any heat.

Melungtal regarded the fire. "Ah, yes. Here we are."

A long, bearded face showed in the fire, compacted to fit into the small space. A voice spoke. "here we are indeed. Ah, yes, Melungtal siTalrun, one of the 'Legitimate' Wizards of Saljashin! Very interesting that you should come."

"How did you know me?"

"Just because I don't put up a shingle in the city does not mean I know nothing of what goes on there. And it's much better for my reputation if you have no idea what my sources of information would be."

Melungtal could think of two ways of taking that statement. "I'm alone, if it concerns you."

"Oh, yes, I can see that, too. No, don't be surprised; it's my life at stake, so I have more spells at work than just this fancy little thing.

"So, what can I do for you?"

"I need help to make my escape."

"Escape? That is very interesting. One of the Magicians that Saljashin allows to work, and you need to escape. Yes, we must discuss this. Wait there."

The fire went out.

Melungtal took a seat, leaning against the tree, and waited. He never claimed to be a man of extreme patience, but he had various problems, magical and non-magical, with which he could occupy his time. One main thing was, just exactly what was his aim?

By himself, without the resources of the Kingdom of Saljashin at his disposal, there was not much he could do to carry out the Project, to render it safe. Even if he could, he doubted he could get a hearing in Saljashin now. No, all he could expect was to be declared a Suspect, and Cleansed on next Cleansing day. His works, the works of a Suspect, would be destroyed. "Except," he thought cynically, "the work on the Project, which no one would think of destroying."

The only place he could think of that might allow him the resources was Rosthan itself. No, nobody in Rosthan would be willing to work for their own destruction, but when the project turned to maul Saljashin, Melungtal just might have the means for its salvation.

It wasn't likely that Saljashin would let him come home, not even if he brought the means to save them from their mistake. That was not a thought he wanted to dwell on; he was making himself a perpetual exile, and even Rosthan would not really make him welcome. Who would, bringing the news he was bringing?

He sighed. A world destroyed or life as an outcast; which notion was least undesirable?

No, the decision had been irrevocably made from the time---.

"Peace to you."

The long face he'd seen in the flames was leaning over him. It was attached to a body clothed in an outfit that was not exactly rags, but was long past any claim to newness.

"Peace to you as well."

"If you'll follow me, we can go to my house where we can talk more comfortably."

"Certainly." Melungtal got to his feet, avoiding any semblance of a scrambling rush.

"So, you keep track of all that goes on in the city?"

The bearded face smiled. "You'd be surprised at the kinds of information some people will exchange for a love-charm."

"Or a curse?"

That got him a sideward look. "My experience says that two kinds of people want to buy a curse. First sort are those who can't help bragging to someone that they've done it. Even if that someone is a trusted friend, that's no way to keep a secret.

"Second sort is the sort that'll give you up the moment the least suspicion falls on them. And when you think of it, the number of people with some reason to curse a particular person is limited, so that often as not everyone knows who's to blame. Of course, there're ways to get around that, but I won't talk business secrets with you."

Melungtal nodded. "Sorry. I withdraw the question."

The other looked at him, smiling sourly. "After you get me running off at the mouth longer than I ought. Quite well done, too."

"So, what should I call you?"

"Call me Slider."

"Just Slider?"

"You'd prefer something like Slider the Magnificent? I thought you were grown up."

Melungtal nodded again. "My apologies, Slider."

They walked on in silence for a while, and though he said nothing about it, Melungtal was certain that the route was long and circuitous.

Finally, they came to what seemed a rickety charcoal-burner's shack. Slider glanced at him. "What d'you think?"

"Looks very much like the sort of place a man might live if he were attempting to remain inconspicuous."

Slider bowed. "True. But if you thought that, how long until some shrewd

Watcher shows up with the same notion in mind? Well, never mind that for now; come inside."

The inside of the house was as unremarkable as the outside. A rickety-looking wooden table, and two three-legged stools. There was also a window, at present covered by a roughly trimmed piece of hide.

Slider noticed Melungtal glancing around. "Wouldn't do to disguise the outside if the inside gave me away at first sight. Don't you worry, I have most of what I need readily available. The rest, well, it's just a bit harder to get at.

"And no, I won't tell you anything you couldn't guess at; I didn't get to live this long by nattering to just anyone.

"So, you need to escape? Why?"

"For reasons that will make me willing to pay you very well."

"Aha! My own beliefs back at me! However, I can speculate. You are being pressed by those higher-up to consent to something you'd rather not. Rather than see it go ahead, you are leaving.

"Of course, your departure will only delay things slightly, so there must be more to it than that.

"Unfortunately, I can't accept 'none of your business' as an answer, particularly not from one in your position. While it's unlikely that the Watchers would press someone of your superior status into service to trap old Slider, I don't wish to mess with possibilities. What's your story? Or do I toss you out into the forest to find your own way?"

Melungtal hesitated a moment, but Slider had the upper hand here. "I've been working on a special project, one aimed at destroying Rosthan. They want to put it into action immediately, while Rosthan lacks any powerful magicians.

"The way I see it, though, there's too much possibility of the thing turning round on us yet, and I don't want to take the chance. So I'm escaping."

"To where?"

"To Rosthan."

Slider's brows rose. "Rosthan? How---interesting."

Melungtal could well guess the kind of things the other was thinking. "Would you trust the Watchers to keep any sort of deal they might make, Slider?"

Slider shook his head, a little regretfully, it seemed. "No," he admitted. "No, I suppose I couldn't. Not when I've been sliding out of their traps for nigh on ten years."

He made no apologies, which for Melungtal was a mark in his favour.

Slider continued. "We can get you well on your way, at least. Much depends on what you have to trade. You being one of the 'Legal' Wizards, I won't accept gold or silver. What I'll want is some spell or spells to make it worth my while."

Melungtal nodded. "I'd expected as much. I have this little thing that brought me out of the city to the forest."

"How nice. Its limitations?"

"I regret, I have not been able to test it fully. There are physical effects, though. Using it to move yourself outside this hut would leave you slightly giddy at the least. My move from my rooms in the city to the forest left me vomiting on my hands and knees for what seemed a very long time. To move from here to Rosthan would probably kill you."

"I see. Does anyone else know of this?"

Melungtal clapped a hand to his forehead in a dramatic gesture. "Oh, dear! You know, I completely forgot to have it inscribed in the Records! How incredibly remiss of me!"

Slider gave him a sour look. "So, you've been planning this for some time, have you?"

"Essentially, since my predecessor was listed as Suspect and I was invited to take his place. It seemed to me almost certain that, at sometime or other, I'd be listed as Suspect too.

"And while Hadji has only put me under house arrest, I'm fairly sure I'd have been Suspect within six months, at the very latest. For a Wizard, there's always something that could be used as evidence against you."

Slider nodded. "Sure you wouldn't like to join with me? We could do pretty well together."

Melungtal shook his head. "Sorry. I've got something that has to be done."

Slider nodded. "And of course, having a partner in my line of work more than doubles the risk. No, in some ways it might have been nice, but....

"So now we deal. For something like this, which you yourself have confessed is next to untried, I can't offer much. I can get you supplies and a couple more gewgaws that'll help you to the Serad River. From there, you can make your own way down the Serad to Gagapeng."

"And I, of course, am an unworldly Wizard who has spent all his time in the workroom, and doesn't know the price of bread in the marketplace. No, you'll have to do better than that. For something that has the potential of this, I'll want to get all the way to Gagapeng. At the very least, I'll need the funds to get me there."

After a bit of bargaining, much like haggling in the marketplace for allom, they reached a bargain. Melungtal threw in a few other minor spells, in exchange for which Slider would give some money, and a few minor spells, as well as names of people along the way who would give money in exchange for those spells.

Slider also provided a few little disguise-spells. "Nearly indetectible by magic," he said. "And this thing," he held out a pale blue marble. "Look at it from time to time. It'll turn pale green if the pursuit is getting close."

Melungtal nodded. A man who'd held the position he'd held would not get away easily. The Watchers would hunt for him with all the resources at their disposal. The faster he moved, the better his chances of getting away, and it would be best for him to be on his way immediately.

"You know they'll track me here?"

Slider grinned. "Indeed, they will. But neither you nor I will be here by then."

Melungtal returned the grin. "Sure you

wouldn't like to join me on the journey to Rosthan?"

"Sannat's toenails, no! You'll find out when you get there that you're just another petty wizard, unless you can get one of the Wizardly Households to adopt you. You'll most likely live out your days selling love-charms in the Marketplace,"

"Oh, my! I suppose I should get some love-charms ready, then."

Slider gave him a sour look. "Laugh, then. You'll find out when you get there."

Hadjalloni, for all his calm outer demeanour, was fiercely angry. He'd bent over backward trying to treat Melungtal well, even put him under house arrest rather than listing him as a Suspect immediately. And Melungtal paid him back by breaking out and running!

What's worse, the spell he'd used to get out of his rooms had not been registered in the Records. That meant that Melungtal must have had this escape in mind all along. And what other magic might he have developed on the sly?

Hadjalloni looked out the window at the battered plinth, and his anger grew.

No, magic could not be trusted, and neither could the people who dealt in it. How trustworthy were the people presently working on the project? Could anything be done to assure their trustworthiness? Suppose he were to gather all the families of those working on the project, to keep them safe from the general public who distrusted magicians?

He massaged his chin. That would work, but only for a time. People who dealt in magic would be quite capable of leaving their families to suffer while they sent off to pursue their own ends.

He rang a small bell on his desk.

Shortly, the door opened, and a servant stood there.

"Fetch me Captain Yanomma."

"Yes, Sir."

Captain Yanomma must have been on his way, for Hadjalloni found himself left alone with his thoughts only a short time. There was a rap on the door, and the servant stuck his head in. "Captain Yanomma is here, Sir."

Captain Yanomma was a short, blocky man, with a red face and ears that protruded from the sides of his head like jug-handles.

"Sir."

"You have a report for me?"

He did not need to specify which report. There was only one matter which was attracting the attention of all the Watchers.

"Only a preliminary one, sir. We have strong reason to believe that he met with the man who calls himself Slider. Slider is---"

"I know very well who he is, Captain! I am seriously concerned that we have let this Slider slip through our grasp for too long. However, my primary concern at present is with Melungtal."

"Yes, Sir." The Captain continued, showing a little more nervousness. "Melungtal has dropped out of sight after meeting with Slider. I have to assume that means Slider has provided him with some means of assistance. Our best efforts at detecting him show three brief sightings. He seems to be moving north-westward."

"Seems to be moving north-westward, captain?"

"Yes, sir. Each of the three detections lasted only for moments. Long enough to fix a general location, but not long enough to say if they were real detections, or just something set to throw us off the track."

"I see." Hadjalloni frowned.

"One more thing, sir." The captain hurried on. "Each of the detections happened at a spot where a tree grew, overhanging running water. It's possible that the magic hiding him is weakest at such places, just enough for us to see him briefly."

Hadjalloni eyed him. "Or it may well be that a spell has been set off, with such places as focus, to draw us off the track."

"Well, yes, sir, that is a possibility."

"You've had agents out to ask at all these places, of course?"

"Yes, Sir. The first one, that is. We have no agents very near to the other two places, but we have sent over some of our nearest people. The difficulty is that he may be disguised, and disguised in a manner that no ordinary person could see through."

"You're telling me he can't be caught?" Hadjalloni put an edge in his voice and watched the resulting nervousness in the Captain.

"No, not that, sir. It's just that with one such as Melungtal, with his resources, such as the spell that took him out of the city. Well, the matter is a little more difficult than trapping some poor hedge-wizard."

"Such as Slider, who has evaded us all this time? Captain, I think you'd better get yourself out of your office and into the field, and not come back until you've brought me Melungtal."

"Yes, Sir!"

Chapter Five

It looked like any other village of the New Land, but Royin was not navigating solely according to direction and distance from Gagapeng. His spells of finding had already told him this was the village where the woman was, the woman Tangral had brought, the cause of all this trouble.

No, be fair, Royin. It was Tangral who was the cause of the trouble. The woman was a victim, same as all the rest, but she might be a means of undoing some of the trouble.

The smells reminded him that villages, particularly villages here in the New Lands, did not have the advantages of waste disposal plants which Gagapeng had. There seemed to be quite a crowd around one of the houses. What could that be all about? Probably a village meeting called to discuss some local problem.

A more important question, to Royin's mind, was where should he land? Pretty well every stretch of cleared land was planted to something, and he'd get a better reception if he didn't crush their crops.

Aha! There was a small patch where some runty-looking djasa were grazing, the herdboys more intent on what was going on in the crowd round that cabin than what their charges might be doing.

By now he had had sufficient experience with the balloon that he could bring it down with something close to precision.

The djasa, half-wild that they were, noticed his arrival first, and scattered away from underneath him. The herdboys, armed only with sticks, fled as well, but they fled toward the crowd of adults.

Landing the balloon required slacking off on the spells which held the thing up, and gradually strengthening the spells that attracted it to the ground. The final steps of the procedure took up so much of his concentration, he could only pay attention to his surroundings once the basket had bumped down onto the ground, and the bag, half-deflated, wobbled above him in the wind.

He looked up and saw that most of the villagers had left the gathering around the cabin, and were advancing on him. At least half of them were holding spears.

He held up his hands. "I come in peace."

For a moment, he thought they were going to ignore his declarations of peace, and put a spear through him for his troubles. Then an older man, carrying a staff instead of a spear, spoke. "You come in peace. Yet you drop from the sky like a bird of prey, scattering our djasa. A strange way to come in peace."

"I apologize. I came down in the middle of the djasa to avoid crushing your crops. I will make restitution."

One of the villagers, holding a spear, whose anger Royin suspected had some cause other than the scattered djasa, spoke. "What will you do for restitution, City Wizard? Cast some flashy spell to impress the dumb yokels, then fly away back in the sky?"

"I wouldn't do something as cheap as that," declared Royin, abandoning his notion of doing just that. "I have something here that will last longer than any spell I might cast." He bent down into the basket and carefully brought up an iron axe-head.

Despite his slow and deliberate motions, the big man's spearhead was in his face as he straightened. "No weapons, friend. See, I bring my hand up slowly. Only an iron axe-head, nothing strange, nothing magical. I offer this as a gift. I am willing to pay some agreed-on restitution, in such goods, to make up for the scattering of the djasa."

The older man spoke sharply to the spearman. "Sorenaya! Let us not allow the spirit of murder to slaughter any guest that comes to Strick's Bolg."

Royin caught from that comment he'd arrived at a tense time in the village. Did "slaughter any guest" mean what he feared?

Then someone flung open the door of the cabin around which the people had congregated, and a woman stepped out. No, it wasn't the woman he was seeking, but when she spoke, she spoke to him. "Good, good, the City Wizard comes to repair the mess he made! What sort of foolery were you up to in the City, then?"

It took him by surprise, but he recovered quickly. "Not my doing, lady. I'm only the one picked to come undo the damage so much as possible." Let them think he was some underling, not the person presently in the position of the one who'd caused the trouble.

She was not mollified. "You have no idea of the trouble that has come to this village, have you? If your fancy wizard's trick had not gone awry, she would never have come here."

She looked around at the spear-carrying men, and she seemed to have as little good to say to them as to him. "No, you fools. I do not say that you should point your weapons at him instead of her. I say that you should let him take her off to the Wizard's City, get her out of our midst."

She seemed to hint that whatever the City Wizards did to "her" it would make up for whatever she'd done here. He was about to protest that they had no intention of harming her, when the woman looked straight at him again, and seemed to shake her head slightly, a gesture of negation, as though she knew what he was going to say.

He said nothing.

Her speech seemed to change the attitude of the crowd a trifle. They did not trust him and did not like him, but they were willing to deal with him.

The woman, the local wise woman, it seemed, came up to the basket to look at him. "Get back, all of you! I want to talk to the City Wizard in private."

The people moved back, not very far, but far enough that she could be sure of being unheard as she said in a low voice, "Can you return her to her home?"

He considered lying, only momentarily, then said, "No. The one who brought her killed himself in doing so. Worse, he killed or rendered incapable anyone in Gagapeng who might have been able to do so."

The wise woman's face showed a moment of stark anger, but she went on in a calm voice, "You mean no harm to her?"

"None."

"Best you don't, City Wizard!" He wondered for an instant what she might really be capable of doing, then she was speaking again. "Old Kangasa will dicker with you for the damages. Don't let him have the coat off your back and your shoes as well, but be as generous as you can without seeming a total idiot."

She moved off and spoke a quick sentence to the man with the staff, who then approached him, "This matter of the scattering of the djasa, it is a serious affair."

In his mind, Royin sighed. It looked to be a long session.

Indeed, it was. After an extended, wearing time discussing various matters from the difficulty of rounding up scattered djasa to the respective value of iron in the City and in the New Lands, they came to an agreement.

They decided Royin should give over five axe-heads and three hoe-heads, for which the villagers would accept that restitution was done, and toss in two small skins of wine and some dried fruit.

He'd originally hoped to buy more food here in Strick's Bolg *Who was Strick? What was a Bolg?*, but this was not the time for that. He'd have to land at some other village on the way back. *'And try not to scatter their djasa!'*

At last, the wise woman went to her door and softly called what seemed to be a name. A woman came out, the woman Royin had seen so often in his searches.

There was a murmuring among the crowd, and Royin caught the repeated term, 'Corner Girl!' For some it was said in anger, for some it seemed simply curious.

Climbing into the basket in that once-fashionable dress required her to show a good deal of her legs. Royin looked away, but the picture still stuck in his mind.

When he looked back at her again, she was giving him the eye.

"You plan to get us out of here?"

He'd been facing down Royal Messengers and high-ranking members of Wizardly Houses for weeks, but this woman flustered him.

He responded with sarcasm. "Yes, Lady. At once!"

He cut off the spells holding them down, increased the spells, putting hot air into the balloon and lifting it. The balloon jerked up into the air. Royin set the course for home.

"So you've rescued me. I hope you don't have any illusions about me throwing myself into your arms over it."

He gave her a look. "Not at all. I don't know what I rescued you from, except that you got yourself into trouble back there."

"I got---! Listen, what happened back there was that I was sound asleep, and this man climbed into my bed. I killed him. Unfortunately, his family thought they needed revenge. You came along as they were trying to work up their courage to storm Moralei's cabin and haul me out."

"Oh." Given her obvious state of mind, it didn't seem safe to say much else.

Her anger was still up. "And you're likely thinking the same as everyone else, that I invited him into bed, then changed my mind. You just go on thinking that, if it pleases you. But I didn't invite him in, and if you see or hear anything you think is me inviting you, keep in mind what happened to him."

"Right." He was a little annoyed himself, in particular, because he hadn't really been thinking about her like that. "You've made the point, pushed it home, and nailed it firmly into place. I will only ask that you make a note of the fact that this basket is very small, and we're going to touch by accident from time to time. Please be assured that it is only an accident on my part, and do refrain from killing me. If only because I'm the one controlling this apparatus and keeping us from spreading our innards all over the landscape."

Alison tried hard to be civil, though she had many things on her mind. For one thing, had Flan's attempt undone all the progress she'd made at recovering from the first attack so many years ago and so far away?

For another thing, she didn't think she deserved any blame for the way things had come out in Strick's Bolg, and despite all Moralei's efforts to get her out safely, she still harboured some resentment toward the village.

Furthermore, she was in enforced close quarters with a man she didn't know, a man who'd just pointed out that without him, she couldn't keep this little balloon in the air, let alone move it anywhere.

No, the entire business was not conducive to a good mood. Worse, the fellow had only said what he'd said in reaction to her snappishness.

"My name's Alison," she said, and was instantly annoyed by the truculent tone of her voice.

"Your pardon?" He turned from where he'd been staring intently at the forest in front of them.

"I said, my name's Alison. I expect if we're going to be together for any length of time, we ought to get acquainted."

"Oh, yes, indeed." He smiled very warmly, considering their previous exchange. "I am Royin Gredion's child. As I told your hostess, I'm out trying to put to rights some of the damage done by my late predecessor."

"You can send me back?" She saw his face, and the flare of hope died.

"I'm sorry. My predecessor died in the process of bringing you over, and the effect of his spell killed or incapacitated every other wizard of equal capability."

"So just exactly what were you intending to do to 'put things right?'"

She wasn't sure exactly what the change in his expression meant. Guilt? Why?

"Let me ask you a question, Alison. Have you any idea why Tangral brought you here?"

"No. Why?"

This time she was sure she saw disappointment in his face.

"I'm sorry. Part of the problem is that I don't know myself. He told no one, and he kept his exact reasoning to himself. I have a general notion that he brought you here as part of a particular purpose. That is, I know generally what he was working toward, but I have no idea where you fit.

"What did you do back in your world? Perhaps he chose you for your abilities."

"I'm a botanist. What could he want from me here? All the plants here, with one or two exceptions, are plants I've never seen."

"I wonder, then...." his voice trailed off.

"You wonder what?" The snap was back in her voice.

"Ah." He refocussed his eyes on her. "This is only a guess, mind you, based on what little I know of the man. I suspect he brought you over in order to get information about plant-life in your world, so he could produce a plant for the Accession Day Gift."

"You're only confusing me. Produce a plant? Accession Day Gift?"

"Oh. Sorry. Was there no one in the village that did plant magic?"

"Oh, that? Yes, Moralei killed weeds, helped plants grown, and things like that."

He nodded. "I see. Well, in Gagapeng, we have more powerful wizards. Much of our work is in adjusting plants to perform better, or to produce previously unknown products. So what I see in general is that Tangral had intended to have you describe some plant or plants from your world, then he, starting from some plant in our world, would produce whatever you described for the king."

"The king."

"Yes. Our Household has been the Wizardly Household for the King of Rosthan for ages. As such, it is our duty to supply a gift for the anniversary of the Accession of the King. The King prefers a gift that can demonstrate the Power he commands, therefore it has to be something striking."

"Strikingly useless?"

His face went serious. "Alison, up here in the air, in this balloon with me alone, such things are nearly safe to say. Don't even hint that you think them on the ground, in the City. Even to me, since someone may possibly be listening. Surely you don't speak so frankly about your own king?"

Alison gave an instant's consideration to the standard lecture on the benefits of democracy over inherited kingship, but held herself back. Given the sort of thing he'd just said, he'd probably be incapable of understanding the concept.

"Ah---no," she said.

He nodded. "I'm going to land in that village there." He pointed at the haze of smoke rising above the forest. "We need a few things for the trip, and Strick's Bolg was not the place to hang around and dicker."

He landed without scattering the djasa this time, nor flattening any crops. However, the villagers were frightened by the visitation, and their fright came out in annoyance just short of hostility.

They were not so much on edge as the people of Strick's Bolg, though, and no one threatened to spear him when he reached for one of his iron axe-heads.

When they saw the ironware he had available, they took out their annoyance by hard bargaining.

A tall fellow, slender as a grain-stalk, did the bargaining for the village. "Iron is a fine and useful thing," he agreed. "But at this time of year, with the crops barely started, food is very important, and any mouthful sold now may mean hunger, perhaps starvation, later on in the year."

"Of course. I am a mere wizard, knowing nothing of these matters, save that most of my life's work is with plants of some kind or another. Do you think I know nothing at all about growing seasons, and what will and will not be available? Your flahas, there, will ripen in another week or so. Even if that were all you had to live on, it would last you for a few weeks until the allom were ripe."

"Fine, fine, a City Wizard knows all the vagaries of farming, based on his city experience, where nine-tenths of what he grows is grown under magic that keeps the worst of the weather from affecting them.

"I tell you, though, I who have farmed here for fifteen years, that it is no minor risk to sell so much food at this time, no matter how fine your iron tools are."

Royin recognized this all as bargaining tactics, meant to raise the price of the food. Not wanting to use up all his store of trade goods in one place, just in case an emergency should come up later in their trip, he cast about for something he might do to hold on to a little more of his iron.

An opportunity wasn't hard to find. He pointed to a large, erratic boulder in the middle of one of their fields. "Would it be worth anything for me to move that rock out of the field?"

"You're that strong, City Wizard?"

"That's exactly the point; I'm a wizard. I believe I could move that thing out of your fields, giving you that much more room for crops. What do you say to that?"

The long, lean man frowned. "And what will it cost us?"

"Suppose I ask only a payment equal to what you've already given me?"

"Agreed, then." The village spokesman

still appeared to doubt Royin could do what he promised.

Royin nodded. "Good, then. Make me a small fire here."

Shortly, there was a small fire burning. By this time, the crowd which had drifted away during the bargaining had returned, drawn by the promised sight of a real Wizard working.

Royin took one of the loaves of bread they had already bought, broke it apart, and tossed it in the fire. There was a collective gasp from the crowd; food was not so plentiful, they could afford to burn a loaf of bread.

Royin spoke a few phrases and pointed at the rock. A soft red glow settled over the rock, then turned green. Slowly, but determined, the rock lifted free of the soil, clods of earth dropping free of it as it moved up. Royin turned slightly, pointing toward the edge of the forest.

Ponderously, the boulder floated over in that direction, settling finally with a crackle as it crushed the underbrush. The glow faded.

There was an excited chatter of voices; the Headman turned to Royin. "So. You did as you said. But on the other hand, you used up some of our firewood to do it. I think that would be half the agreed-on value right there."

Royin raised his eyebrows. "Very costly firewood you have here. I'll allow you one tenth part of the value."

"A quarter."

"One fifth. Any more than that and I return the stone to its place." *'Just a hint as to what sort of thing you might be fooling around with here.'*

The headman showed no sort of fear, though Royin suspected he was more impressed than he let on.

They came away from the village with sufficient food and drink for the rest of the journey, as well as two warm djasa-hide robes for when they went higher.

A little later, with Alison's questioning eyes on him, he tossed out a loaf of bread for the spell to recharge the ebony box.

"What was that about?"

He was a little surprised that a non-Wizard would ask about magic; in his experience, mostly they tried to ignore it, for fear something nasty would happen to them.

For their part, the wizards did little to discourage this attitude, partly so as not to be bothered with foolish questions, and partly, he had to admit, to bolster their reputations.

But she had asked, so he answered, "I was casting a spell to replenish the magic that keeps us up and moving."

"By tossing out a loaf of bread?"

She obviously knew nothing at all about magic. "Any use of magic at all requires some sort of sacrifice, if only a drop or two of blood. The larger the sacrifice, the more power available."

"Oh." She sounded surprised, almost shocked.

"Magic works differently in your world?"

"Magic? Ah---we don't have magic, just technology."

"So do we. It has its limitations, though."

"So that business with the rock back there, that was really magic? Not just some kind of technology I don't understand?"

"Yes, it was magic. Of course."

She was looking pale now. "There's no 'of course' about it, for me. You can do anything with this magic?"

"Not hardly. You can't make a plant from nothing, for instance. And contrary to the stories you might hear, magic can't allow you to force anyone into doing anything they don't want." He didn't bother to mention his society had produced several plants which could be distilled, boiled, powdered, or whatever to give much of that effect.

"There're a whole list of things we can't do, and another long list of things that are forbidden."

"I see." He wasn't altogether sure she did see. They continued their flight in silence for some time.

❀

The caravan master looked Melungtal over, up and down. "Well, you don't look like a bandit."

He was a broad and muscular sort, showing hair on arms, legs and chest wherever his clothing didn't cover him. He was also suspicious, suspicious of everyone and everything. "You a Suspect?"

"No." *'Nobody's told me that officially yet.'*

"Hm. You seem uncommonly eager to get on the road. You sure you're not a Suspect?"

"Now how in the world could I prove that? By not casting spells?"

"You wouldn't be afraid to go to the local Watchers' Detachment and have them declare you not a Suspect?"

"Of course I would, and so would any sane person! They get a name on their lists, they go to work proving that person is a Suspect. And if you had any sense, you wouldn't suggest that. What d'you think would happen if I went to the local Watchers and said, 'Caravan Master Gurbtal wants an affidavit swearing that I'm no Suspect.' Then they'd have your name on their lists, too. You want that?

"No, never mind, forget it. I'll save my money for some caravan-master who isn't such a fuss-budget."

Gurbtal waved a hand. "Just a minute! Don't be so hasty! I'm sure we can make an agreement. You can't blame a man for being careful, can you? Not in these times."

Melungtal smiled. He could have gone on to verbally beat the man over the head for excessive caution, but he had what he wanted, and no sense utterly ruining any relations he might have with the caravan-master.

"No, I suppose not. A man has to be careful. What sort of terms do you offer?"

It took another few minutes to agree on a fee, and what said fee would include.

At the end, when the agreement was made, Gurbtal lifted a monitory finger. "When we get into bandit-country, I take precautions. Anyone acting suspicious at that time is dealt with rigourously. Anyone attached to the caravan, no matter how much they've paid, is under my rule and law. My decision has no appeal.

"Will you live with that?"

"Oh, yes, I'll live with it. I just want to get to Gorwal on the Serad."

Hadjalloni frowned at the message. All indications were at least some of the reported detections of Melungtal were false; for one thing, new reports had him appearing at two different places in the country, at distances he couldn't have covered in the time between reports.

Now, too, Captain Yanomma had reported careful questioning, revealed no traces of Melungtal passing through one of the other places. There was a possibility that Slider—fry his liver!--had developed and provided a means of disguising a person's magical essence as well as their physical features. That should be looked into. He jotted a note to have their own magicians investigate the possibility of such a thing, and how to counter it.

"Will there be any reply to Captain Yanomma, sir?"

Hadjalloni considered the matter. "Yes. Have him go directly to Gorwal on the Serad. If the Suspect is fleeing to Rosthan, most routes go through there."

The man waited a moment, in case there was anything further, then answered, "Yes, Sir."

Hadjalloni sat back for a bit, thinking of the impossibility of stamping out magic, of the necessity of using magic itself to control the misuse of magic. As the case of Melungtal demonstrated, magic was a nasty, subtle thing, eventually corrupting even those who started with the best of motives.

Yet he could not, dared not, make that declaration to anyone in authority, to anyone, really. It would result in people of any ability at all avoiding working for the Kingdom, knowing at some point they would be declared Suspect.

❀

Royin brought the balloon down to a landing in the courtyard of the Pengwa Household. It was full daylight; his landing would cause a great deal of talk, but the amount of spell-juggling needed to bring the thing down in darkness to a precise point was so close to the edge of his capability that he preferred not to risk it.

Even so, a mob of goggling servants, junior students, and children gathered pretty much at the exact spot where he intended to land.

He came down anyway, muttering to himself, "If they have at least the sense of a djasa, they'll move. If they don't have that much sense, they don't belong in Pengwa Household in any capacity."

He knew with a fair degree of certainty his fellow Masters were watching from somewhere inside where the crowds couldn't see their consternation.

He considered, momentarily, offering the king a balloon-ride as an Accession-Day

Gift, but no, that was too dangerous. Further, he'd have to make the balloon able to accommodate a whole Company of Royal Guards, plus, like as not, several of the king's chief hangers-on.

As matters turned out, everyone had sense enough to get out from under the balloon, though one doddering old retainer was pulled away at almost the last instant.

"Here!" Royin called to some of the servants. "I'm going to collapse the bag over on that side; catch it and fold it neatly!"

He gave orders for others to unhook the basket, got a couple of the baby-wizards to take charge of storing the ebony box. By this time, various upper servants and persons with some sort of authority took control of the crowd, moving them off to whatever duties had been interrupted by the sudden return of the Grand Master.

Alison took one of the hide robes and used it to get herself out of the basket without flashing too much leg.

"Alison," Royin said, "would you please come with me? My two fellow Masters will be waiting in ambush for me inside; best to get all the introductions and explanations over and done with."

The other two were not waiting just inside; they were making a point of their relative unflappability, Royin supposed.

They did a good job of that, too, coming casually down the stairs to meet Royin and Alison going up.

"So you've finally gotten back," Ormant said. Faral hung back a step and was silent.

"Yes, I'm back. I've brought with me Alison McHarg, the person Tangral killed himself to bring over."

"Oh, really?" Ormant eyed her. "Was she worth the trouble?"

"Worth the trouble Tangral caused? I don't think anyone or anything could be worth that. Worth going out to Strick's Bolg to pick up? I'd say yes."

"Who's Strick? What's a Bolg?" Ormant shook his head. "No, never mind. Like as not, even the villagers themselves would need half an hour to explain it. As for her being worth it, you'd have to say that, wouldn't you?"

Royin merely smiled. "Yes, I would. In this case, it's true, if only because she gave me reason to test that balloon. I think we have something there, though we may need to do some tweaking on it here and there."

"Something to do what? Scare cattle and farmers?"

"Think about it, Ormant. This is a prototype. We could make bigger ones, sell or rent them to merchants to take their goods from this place to that in nearly a straight line, without regard to the way roadways lie, or rivers run."

"Huh! Well, I suppose that is one thing. But you were off after the Accession Day Gift. She's it?"

Royin shook his head. "No, not as such. Best guess I can come up with is that

Tangral had intended her to describe some plant or plants from her world. Then he'd reproduce the plant for the king, with special attention to how he'd come by it. That sounds a bit ad hoc, but no one knows what Tangral was thinking."

"I don't think Tangral was thinking at all. I mean, to do something that big without shields. Well, I don't think we want to fight that one out all over again on the stairs, and I should give you a chance to get cleaned up again before I tell you all the news. And you'll have to show up to meet with a deputation any time now to demand to know what Pengwa House is turning loose on them this time."

Royin grinned. "Nice of you to allow me time to clean up. Get hold of a servant, will you, and have Alison escorted to the Guest Quarters. And I think she'll want a bath, as well."

"Are baths private here?"

Royin looked at Alison. "Private? Yes, and no. The city's Communal baths, and the Household baths, are for socializing as well as bathing. For just cleaning up, without the gossip, a person can have a bath in their room. Except for the servants, of course; they use the Household baths at set times."

"A private bath is what I want. No more Corner Girl for me."

"Corner Girl?"

"Never mind. Just show me to my room."

"Just a moment." Royin quelled his annoyance. She'd just spent a long time in a farming village where there were no servants. He called to one of the servants who were always somewhere within call. "Dolameng! I need a bath in my quarters, and the Lady Alison here needs a bath in the Guest Quarters. Please see that she gets to her quarters, and arrange for the baths."

"Yes, Royin-sir."

Royin turned back to Alison. "Alison, be careful who you ask for anything, directions or the like. In this Household, we have servants to see to most things. You can distinguish them by the yellow sash.

"And of course, any child or teenager, even if they're not a servant, should have the courtesy to help you ask for what you need."

She seemed a little annoyed, but that was unfortunate; she had to know polite manners here. It might even be she was annoyed with herself for having made the gaffe.

He turned to head off to his room.

"I'll just walk along with you, Royin. There're a couple of things I've done that you should know about."

"Sounds ominous, Ormant."

"Only if you think I've stepped on your authority with what I've done. I've been making inquiries in the marketplace for magicians to join us. Not the illusionists and sleight-of-hand artists, of course, but people who actually have some ability."

Royin frowned. "That's something I ought to have thought of. All the more so, considering I was adopted into the Household myself. Did you have any luck?"

"Four that I think will be worth the trouble. You're the Grand Master, though, you have the final say."

Royin nodded. "Fine. I'll trust your judgement in the matter. Go ahead and make the offer, and track down anyone else you think'll do well in the Household. Just let me know about anyone you're thinking of making an offer for."

"Right."

Royin took as leisurely a bath as he dared, expecting all the time to have a servant interrupting him apologetically to let him know that a Royal Messenger was at the door with half the army behind him, demanding explanations.

The expected interruption came just as he had actually reached the state where he was feeling, regretfully, that he should leave the bath and its comfort.

"Royin-sir? The King's Messenger is at the gate. With soldiers."

"Thank you, Daivalma. Tell them I will be down presently."

After that, he hurried. It was one thing to display dignity and high rank by keeping people waiting. It was another to inflame the king, who was doubtless already upset.

The King's Messenger was, of course, upset.

"I apologize for the delay," Royin started off by admitting a fault, and hoping to placate the man at least a little. "I had just come from a long trip, and was cleaning myself up. I thought it better not to greet you as filthy as a street beggar."

"I see." The man did not appear to be noticeably placated. "Grand Master, There have been more strange things happening in your Household grounds. The king is concerned as to what these may portend, and what dangers will arise from them."

Royin nodded. "Given recent events, the king might well be concerned. You may assure him that this was but the test of a new technique, one that required little magic, and that was well-shielded."

"I see. I know little of magic, though, and cannot find your reassurances reassuring."

"In that case, there is little point in trying to explain the relative lack of danger. Suppose I say, instead, that this is a test of a means of flight, and a means of flight that may be made available to all. Rosthan's merchants could have a significant advantage, being able to fly their wares from here to, for instance, Lunchmachor, in the space of a week, rather than several weeks."

"And Pengwa House will make considerable money from this, of course," the Messenger smiled tightly.

Royin shrugged. "The method was a discovery of Pengwa Household. Certainly we would profit, but the kingdom would profit as well."

"Of course. There is one other matter which has been put off for far too long. We demand that you open Pengwa House to our inspection, now, today, so that we can be assured that you have indeed suffered as badly as any Household in this disruption caused by your late Grand Master."

"Certainly. You and the king's representatives may come in and investigate as much as you wish. We will not allow Wizards of other Houses to poke and pry around to find our secrets."

"Nonsense! If we have no wizards to explain to us what we might see, we might as well trust the inspection to a troop of blind men! They will come in."

"If it is the king's will and desire, we can only bow to it. We do so under the most grievous protest, however."

"Protest all you wish. The king has desired it to be done, and it will be done."

"So be it. I will accompany you, of course."

"As you wish."

Chapter Six

The job was not done in one afternoon, nor even in two days, nor three. At the end of the fourth day, the King's Messenger and soldiers, accompanied by Wizards of the other Households, had seen every part of Pangwa House, from roof to gardens.

Royin had considered amusing himself by trying to steer the search past some particular room, claiming it to be only a storeroom for old pots, which would cause them to be more determined to search that room. They would then find that it was, indeed, a storeroom for old pots.

He decided against such an amusement as unworthy of a Grand Master, though, and did no interfering, merely watching the search. He did sometimes find occasion to remonstrate. "I'm sure that the King, when he desired you to search, did not desire you to smash every pot in the House. Look at things, peer into them, even dip fingers into them, but please leave them whole."

The King's Messenger had given him an exasperated look, but said to the soldiers, "Be a little more careful, will you? Breakage could come out of your pay, you know."

He couldn't hide Alison, nor her obviously foreign appearance. When the search party looked into the room assigned to her, he merely said, "This is Alison, a woman from one of the Eastern Lands beyond Saljashin, come to give us the benefit of her knowledge of plant-lore."

If he had admitted Alison's true origin, he knew, the King's Messenger would have insisted on taking her away, to have some of the "unbiased" Wizards test her for every kind of potential danger. She was a guest of Pangwa Household, and therefore due protection from that sort of thing.

✺

Melungtal was happy to see the last of Gurbtal's caravan. The man had taken his claim of absolute authority over his train seriously, to the point where those who had merely paid for passage with him found themselves required to help with the various caravan chores, feeding animals, and setting up and breaking camp. Anyone who protested was told they could travel alone, if they wished. Since lone travellers were prime prey for bandits, everyone complied. Everyone, that is, except for those few who paid an extra fee to be free of chores.

Not that Melungtal objected to doing work, it was the manner in which it was introduced. There'd been no mention beforehand. Just the first morning on the trail, Gorwal had pointed to him with the coiled whip he carried, and said, "You! Go help feed and water the animals!"

Melungtal had looked up at him in amazement. "You paid to join the caravan. You agreed that on the trail my word goes. Now, I'm telling you to go help feed and water the animals!"

There didn't seem to be much use arguing with the man, so he'd gone off to help feed and water the animals.

Melungtal was a patient man, but this trip had been a severe trial to his patience.

At Gorwal on the Serad, he went looking for a boatman. Despite the distrust between the two nations, there was still healthy trade going back and forth between Rosthan and Saljashin. Boats were carried along the stream to Gagapeng—and other towns—and were poled laboriously back, laden with cargo each way. It was easy to find a boatman willing to carry him, for a price. All which was required was sufficient coin.

His bargain with Slider had provided him with coin, not in abundance, but sufficient, if he spent it carefully. He had few skills, save magic, with which to earn anything more on his journey, and using magic before he had gotten out of Saljashinite territory, well out of it, would be dangerous foolishness.

❊

Alison was uncomfortable, not physically uncomfortable, but socially uncomfortable. Back in Strick's Bolg, she'd been a guest, but had been able, if only in a semi-skilled manner, to help Moralei.

Here she was, a guest once more, but a guest on the level of her hosts, leaving her nothing useful to do. She had no ability to use magic, and botany here was highly developed. Most of the magic had to do with causing plants to grow in some specialized manner, producing some particular seed, sap, blossom, stalk, or whatever.

'I'm sort of like a computer specialist of 1980 being jumped into the year 2000 without having had the chance to live through all the progress between. I know a whole lot of theory, but almost none of the practical applications. I can't even read the language!'

She looked down at the book in front of her. She'd been working at remedying her lack of literacy. The writing system, unfortunately, had been developed for some language of long ago, and no longer exactly represented the sound-system of present-day Rosthanite. It was a bit like a Turk, used to the alphabet developed for Turkish, trying to learn to read English. Even worse, since the letters of the local alphabet bore no relation—of course—to the Latin Alphabet. So many of the letters had different pronunciations, depending on what letters went with them, and sometimes apparently for no discernible reason. Which meant words had to be memorized, though she had to admit there were a few general rules about pronunciation.

She had to depend on Royin to explain things to her, which was made worse by the fact that he was, apparently, in charge of the whole Household (clan?) and was very busy dealing with the ramifications and results of the late Grand Master's actions.

She wasn't about to take advantage of her status as a guest by insisting he help her with every little thing which came up.

A Royal Deputation had searched the House from top to bottom to ensure Pengwa Household had suffered as badly as any from the cataclysm, and that this was not some sneaky trick to destroy the other Households, leaving Pangwa supreme.

She'd been introduced to the deputation as a person from a far land, here to advise on botanical matters, but in fact, as she knew very well, she was useless.

One of the younger men, who were termed 'baby magicians' took Alison for a tour of the Household. She was almost certain he'd done it under instructions from Royin, and her mood on the tour varied from 'am I supposed to remember all this?' to 'what are they hiding from me?'

Every time she found herself thinking the second, she tried to force herself to believe they had no ill intent toward her, despite the fact they insisted she was here for good.

She tried not to think about that fact, if it were a fact too long or too hard. For it became too easy to miss things back 'home' to work her way into a depression, brooding on the notion she'd never see home again.

"Just a minute! What's behind this door here?"

"Oh, that's just the Garbage Room. Nothing interesting in there."

But that brought to Alison's mind Moralei's comment on how the 'City People' handled their sewage.

Besides that, it was one way of asserting herself, of not just accepting the explanations people here gave to her. "I'd like to have a look."

His expression was mainly exasperation, but he opened the door.

She wasn't sure what she'd expected, perhaps a bunch of flashing lights and extremely magical-looking things, but there was nothing like that here. It looked like a swamp, more than anything, with bushes of smaller and larger sorts growing in it, as well as smaller plants and grasses. It was open to the sky, allowing the plants to get all the sun they needed, save round the sides where the walls sheltered it.

The scent was mostly flowers, though if she tried hard, she could catch a faint whiff of human waste.

"The plants do it all, then?"

"Yes, of course, Alison-lady. All the plants here have been bred to take their part in reclaiming waste. The Masters have also seen fit to include a low-grade spell to subdue the worst of the smell."

"This is fascinating!"

"This place? All it does is take waste

and grow on it. Every once in a while, we have people go through and clip back the branches, then compost them for the gardens."

She gave him a look. "You have any idea how many cities have no way of dealing with their waste but throwing it out the window and hoping the rain'll wash it away?"

He shrugged. "Maybe in Saljashin, but not in Rosthan."

"I passed through a little place in the New Lands where they didn't have this stuff." She waved a hand at the room full of plants.

He shrugged again. "The New Lands. Well, yes, they couldn't afford it just yet. A lot of them may not even know it's possible."

She was on the edge of talking about the necessity of taking care of waste so as not to cause disease, but she held back. Rosthan was ruled over by a King, whose only care about the farmers in the outback was they pay their taxes on time. He might be led to see that a healthy populace would mean more taxes, but he would also likely see anything which required him to spend money as a bad idea, with a result seen only in the long term.

For crying out loud, they still considered diseases to be caused by "noxious vapours." How likely was it that a person from a strange place, and a woman to boot, could convince them that the "noxious vapours" could be dealt with?

"Okay," she said. "What's next?"

❀

"We can't wait any longer." Hadjalloni was quiet but determined. "We have people hunting Melungtal, but it's nowhere near certain we can get him before he gets to Rosthan. We can't allow them any time to make preparations against us. I know all the Wizardly Households have been rendered ineffectual, but I still wouldn't bet against them being able to manage something, if only some kind of last-minute counter-attack."

"Yes, sir." The man who'd taken Melungtal's place was a competent enough wizard and had an extreme respect for the authority of the Watchers.

"There will be no problems?"

"Well---No, sir."

Hadjalloni did not like the hesitation. "Something disturbs you?"

"No, Sir!"

"Good. Go see to it. It's time the life-twisters of Rosthan were put down."

"Yes, sir!"

❀

Captain Yanomma's message was simple and annoying.

"There were a few traces of him at Gorwal on the Serad, but too few for any real tracking. We're certain that he took passage on a boat. No one recalls anyone of his description, but he was surely wearing some sort of magic disguise. I am continuing to follow."

Hadjalloni scowled at the paper. Yanomma was obviously an incompetent, likely only pretending to follow the trail. Well, when he finally came home, he would be listed as a Suspect.

❈

"The training is going as well as could be expected, though not as well as we'd like. I don't think it's possible to do as well as we'd like. Two of the older students have been passed and qualified as Junior Masters, on the understanding that they spend a good deal of each day studying."

Ormant looked up from the paper in front of him and went on. "We now have five, three men and two women recruited from the marketplace. We're starting to get people coming to the door and asking to be taken on. Depending on how far down we let our standards go, we can probably get a few more."

"Any problem working the recruits into our Household?"

Ormant's face twitched into a near smile. "Biggest trouble is teaching them Household manners. We haven't been able to let them back out on the streets yet. Our reputation is still low, and having someone out there wearing our colours and acting like street dregs isn't a good idea."

Royin nodded. "From all I hear, our reputation is getting worse; unless something good happens, or something bad takes their minds off us, in a few days we're going to see our servants stoned in the Marketplaces."

He laid a hand on the table. "The Accession Day gift is going to be less than spectacular this year. We have a young woman able to describe all sorts of strange and wonderful plants, but we have just about nobody to really do anything about it. I'm going to make a try to produce something, but I don't know if our Royal Master will be impressed."

"Has she understood she's never going to be able to go home again?"

Royin shrugged. "I don't know. She's been told about the situation. She seems to understand, but I'm uncertain."

"What was old Tangral thinking, anyway?"

Royin shrugged. "That anyone, anywhere, would be happy to serve as part of one of his plans? I'm becoming less and less impressed with our late Grand Master. I have a feeling he wasn't operating with all his faculties. I wonder if we ought to have some system in place to let us remove a Grand Master if he shows signs of instability."

"Then you'd have all the Masters spending their time politicking, rather than working."

"True. Well, I'll give some thought to the matter, anyhow."

Royin did his best to visit Alison every day, sometimes for a long while, sometimes just for a brief moment snatched between all the other calls on his time.

During the longer visits, much of his time was spent explaining his society. "Bloodfeud? Not in the cities. It still happens from time to time in the smaller communities farther from the capital, despite the king's edicts. The New Land? Well, that's far enough from Gagapeng that the king is satisfied to simply collect taxes, but it'd cost too much to keep garrisons out there to make sure all his decrees were followed."

"I see," she said. "Listen, about this business of adapting plants, how does it work? You can't just take any plant and magic it to do what you want it to. Or can you?"

He shook his head. "It has to be done in stages. You take a plant, most times, one that already has a tendency to produce what you want, then you spell it to---to nudge it toward what you want. On a very few occasions, you can get exactly what you want the first time. Mostly, though, you have to successively nudge each generation for several generations. Once you've got what you want, the next thing is to get it to breed true."

"So. You need something from me to make a spectacular plant for the king. But you have to get it within the next few weeks; how could you possibly manage all the generations until you've got something which breeds true?"

"That's another part of the magic. You can press the plant into growing from seed to maturity in a very short time. You lose a lot that way, of course. Each generation pushed through will have at least ten in a hundred samples, which have problems ranging from stunting to total throwback to the original version to dying at the leaflet stage, and half a dozen other problems."

"Can you do the same thing with animals?"

"Plants are easier to work with. With animals, any significant hastening of the growth is likely to cause malformations. That means a longer time before you get to the stage of breeding true.

"And before you ask, working with humans is forbidden. I don't mean no-one ever does it, but if they're caught, they're punished.

"There's quite a trade in spelling children in the womb to come out healthier, stronger, and so on. Some of the people casting the spells aren't even charlatans, and some of them have some success. It's frowned on, though.

"If there's a stillbirth or a deformed child born in the upper levels of society, it's likely someone's spell went awry. You also hear stories of an occasional wizard in the lower quarters being lynched; chances are he was accused, rightly or wrongly, of messing up the spells on someone's child."

"The nobles aren't so vindictive?"

"Oh, they are, they are! Their vindictiveness usually takes the form of a quiet killing, though."

"Back to the Accession Day Gift. What happens if you don't have something ready for that?"

Royin laughed. "Oh, there's always something we can use for an Accession Day Gift! It's just that it may not be as flashy as we could desire. I have a feeling that nothing we could do this year is going to meet with the king's unalloyed approval. Not with what Tangral's done to us."

He suddenly realized what he'd said. "That isn't for repeating to anyone else. It's one of those things that pretty well everyone knows, but if someone says it out loud, people have to take notice."

"You needn't worry; you've been keeping me away from anyone outside the House." He could hear the bitterness in her tone.

He wished there was some sort of magic to give her a complete comprehension of the situation. "It's very touchy. If it comes out that Tangral had successfully brought you from an outside world, there'd be enormous pressure on the House.

"It'd put you in personal danger, too. The king would see you as something strange, something he didn't understand. He wouldn't know for sure whether or not you presented a danger to him and his kingdom, so the most likely thing he'd do is have you killed."

"Really?" He could hear a tinge of disbelief in her voice, for all the experience she'd already had in this world. Sannat's toenails! She'd barely gotten away from Strick's Bolg before her best friend had come to the end of her ability to protect her guest from death in revenge for a self-defence killing.

"Really. The only protection you have here is Pengwa Household and its reputation. Tangral has ripped the Household and its reputation to shreds. I've been dealing with matters as though that weren't the case, and trying to rush the building up of our strength, our wizardly manpower. If the king takes a notion to push us, though, we'll likely fall apart."

"I see," Alison said, and he thought she did see, at least to some degree. The Household Servants weren't that good of actors, and something of the House's situation must be coming through to her.

"I'd appreciate it if you could stay quiet, accept that your situation coincides with ours, or at the very least, that it coincides with ours, better than to that of anyone else in this world."

He could see that was pressing her too far, and cursed himself for a fool.

"All right," she said, but he had a feeling her agreement would only last as far as it took her to discover some way which seemed to suit her better.

Alison had some reservations. There wasn't a wizard left in Gagapeng with the power to send her home? Well, that was Royin's story, and everyone she met agreed with it. Except she had met with no one save those under Royin's authority.

She paused. Now, that thought could lead in several directions. Why would Royin want her under such a delusion?

Of course, she knew only bits and pieces of this society, this city. She knew the subtleties, traditions, and drives of the village of Strick's Bolg better than those of Gagapeng, and she had to admit she knew only a fraction of the things a teenager of the village grew up knowing.

Might she just be too suspicious?

Not that she had no reason for suspicion! Look at Strick's Bolg; she'd thought she had been getting along quite well, then all of a sudden she was the focus of a blood feud.

What didn't she know about Gagapeng?

She opened up one of the books she'd been using for reading practice. She'd memorized the alphabet long ago, all thirty-three letters. The big problem was working out how the letters were pronounced when they were put together. She could do a lot with context, of course, and was getting better at that.

Despite that, she was constantly making lists of words which she needed someone to pronounce for her. Most of the servants were functionally illiterate. She was allowed to talk with some of the older students, most of whom were helpful, save for a snobbish few who seemed to feel if a person of her age hadn't already leaned to read. They obviously lacked the intelligence. For those students, the fact she had no magical ability at all only made matters worse.

She never complained, but one thing she had to say in Royin's favour, he somehow found out about these things, and the worst offenders were sent to apologize. That, of course, just made them less willing to have anything to do with her, but at least they weren't actively sabotaging her efforts.

There were some of the usual student-type jokes, such as just this morning, young Haldam had tried to tell her that the word she was asking about was the word for "excrement." The first part of the word could just possibly give that sort of pronunciation, but the pronunciation of the second half would have required the violation of several "rules," exception-ridden though the rules were.

She called him on it. "Are you sure? Any way we handle them, those last letters give us one too many syllables."

His square, young face attempted to radiate assurance. "No, this is one of the words where the rules change. This 'eot' here, it goes silent."

She fixed him with a look. "Hmm. What happens when I use that word with Royin, and tell him where I got the meaning from?"

A more accomplished jokester would have assured her he was right, and would have put together some kind of explanation for Royin later. Haldam was not quite that secure. "All right, then, it means 'historian.' Almost had you, though."

"Not even close, Haldam."

There had been an occasion, early on, when she had nearly been taken in, but a snicker on the part of the student had given the game away.

She never told Royin about any of these incidents, of course. She could have, but she wouldn't have him fighting all her battles for her.

She considered the books made available to her, in light of her suspicions. Actually, they had given her access to everything in the library, if she wanted it, though the librarians had noted certain of the works were probably too abstruse for beginners.

Just to be sure, she'd checked some of these books. Abstruse? Like a junior high school student attempting to work their way through Newton's Principia Mathematica (rendered into suitably obscure English).

On the other hand, she couldn't read well enough to make out the system by which the library catalogued its works, and they needn't go to any great trouble to hide things from her. Not right now, at least.

Given the size of the collection, she could hardly believe they'd culled the library of all works which might tell her things they'd rather not have her know.

She concentrated on the "suggested" books, at least for now, and occasionally wondered if her background and the things which had already happened to her in this world were making her too suspicious of all men?

The boatman's wife had a small baby, who seemed to spend most of the night and day crying. In the confines of a riverboat, there was nowhere one could get away from the sound.

Melungtal told himself he ought to have been more particular in taking passage on a boat, but word had been going round the town of Gorwal on the Serad that they were expecting a special deputation of Watchers. He wasn't sure they were after him, in particular, but good sense told him they were.

He hadn't thought to ask the boatman important questions, though, like "Does your wife have a child who cries incessantly?"

After a few days, he was less forgiving of himself over that lapse.

On and on they went along the long grey river, with the crew occasionally adding a push from their poles to the speed of the current, always on the lookout for rocks, sandbars, logs swept down from the higher reaches of the river, and other such obstructions.

And the baby continued to cry.

"If you want my opinion," Alison said, "that's one of the most pitiful roses in existence."

The smile Royin gave her held a trace of embarrassment. "Perhaps so. But it's the only rose in existence in Rosthan. That being so, there's nothing to compare it to. I think, rather than spend another week trying to improve on it, we should put a spell of preservation on it, and present it to the king. The scent is right, is it?"

"Oh, yes, the scent is right. Perhaps a little intense, but it should do."

She paused. "Sorry. I can't seem to say anything good about anything without putting in a dig."

He shrugged. "If I'd been taken out of my own world into another, where I had no proper skills to support myself, no family to help me, and put in danger of death as well, I suppose I'd feel upset at everything too."

She was very close to snapping at him, not to be so darned understanding, but she held her tongue in check.

Chapter Seven

The boat pulled into the wharf at Gagapeng. The river smelled here, smelled of all the refuse which people dumped in the water. Melungtal wondered whether the famed Rosthanite spells which kept the city smelling fresh were simply not equal to the task of keeping the water clear.

The baby stopped crying as the boat touched the wharf. Melungtal's first thought was, "Has the child cried itself to death, then?"

He frowned *'Not a kindly thought at all, Melungtal.'*

Time to go see what the Kingdom of Rosthan was like. No, not exactly. He had his first introduction to the kingdom of Rosthan some days ago, with every village and town having its own wizard or wizards. One had even shared the trip with him between two villages on the river. He'd been shocked at first over how openly the little fellow declared his profession, and boasted a little about certain wonderful spells he'd come up with, though he'd been cagey about their exact workings.

Melungtal got used to this after a bit. He himself, however, was still hiding his abilities. Melungtal had to expect Hadjalloni would have agents out after him with orders to kill him when they found him. He portrayed himself as a merchant, of limited means, travelling to Gagapeng to claim an inheritance, which could enable him to support his business back in Saljashin.

This gave him a reason for being somewhat secretive about his background and motives; he had to make sure the competition did not get word of his movements.

He pretended to be impressed at the minor workings the magician was so proud of. His mind insisted all the while that Watchers were about to come up at their elbows.

'Melungtal, old fussbudget, you're three day's travel beyond the borders of Saljashin, well into Rosthan, and the Watchers won't be after mere magicians. They'll risk the causing of an international incident for runaway High-ranking Saljashinite wizards, nothing less.'

Out on the river, passing small towns, Melungtal had been aware of a constant feeling of uneasiness, with magic so open and freely practiced.

Here in Gagapeng itself, though, it seemed almost every third person used at least some sort of magic. Sometimes the magic was as innocuous as driving rats out of grain storehouses, something Melungtal knew his home city of Lunchmachor could have used.

On the other hand, the nature of magic was such that it could, and did, have other, darker uses. Practitioners of these forms would naturally not be so public.

He pushed his way through the busy streets of Gagapeng. All the forms of magic which forced the will of one person on another, those could possibly culminate in the rise of someone such as the Blue-Blossom Wizard. How much difference was there between offering a love-charm to make a particular man or woman desire you, or pressing several people into your personal service?

As far as the Watchers of Saljashin were concerned, it was a matter of pure luck that it wasn't always happening. Melungtal had wondered about that for some time; though he'd never wondered aloud. If something was only being prevented by pure luck, it ought to happen at least once, especially here in Rosthan.

He hadn't asked on his trip through Rosthan, partly not wanting to draw attention, but mostly, he had to admit, for not wanting to sound like too much of a stereotypical Saljashinite. He suspected the Wizards of Rosthan were vigilant in their organizations to watch for such things, if only for their own good reputation.

Now that he was here, he could see to attempting to connect himself with one of the larger Households. Slider, as part of his bargain, had given him some hints along the way. He would be best to present himself to Pangwa Household, as the Household which supplied all manner of services and advice to the Royal House of Rosthan.

"From what I've heard," Slider had said, "all the Magical Households are recruiting even more than they usually do. You might as well try for the top; with your training and your ability, practically any of them'll take you on."

❀

Gagapeng was full of people rushing about from here to there, taking only an occasional glance at the Saljashinite wandering more slowly among them.

The languages of Saljashin and Rosthan were similar enough he could understand and make himself understood. The difficulty was getting anyone to stand still long enough to talk. Finally, though, a wall-eyed carpet-seller paused long enough to answer Melungtal's query.

"You go over that way two streets, maybe three. Turn right, and keep going. You'll see it, eventually. Dirty, great wall around it, like a City in the City.

"They won't be staying so high and mighty much longer; they did this thing that killed all the magicians in the City, killed 'em dead as rats in a rain-barrel. Made a mistake, though, killed off all their own magicians too.

"Pangwa House isn't very popular in Gagapeng these days."

The carpet-seller's directions were not very precise, Melungtal found. He followed them until he found himself in a blind street. The back wall of the premises before him was battered and stained, missing some bricks, and two large cracks, top to bottom, showed a part of the wall was close to falling away. It was in no way likely to be a part of a Wizardly Household, nor any other establishment with claims to quality.

He worked his way back along the blind street to where it crossed the next street and paused. After a bit, he was able to catch the attention of a man bound for the Market-place with a pair of long jugs of wine lashed to a rack on each side of a small rukala.

"Can you tell me how to get to Pangwa House?"

"Pangwa House? Who'd want to go to that ill-omened place?"

"I would. I have business there."

The man looked him up and down. "Hm. Well, if you're determined to go, I won't hold you back."

Melungtal was beginning to feel his temper fraying. "Yes, but will you tell me how to get there?"

"Oh, that!" The wine-seller pointed with his weathered jaw along the cross-street. "Yes, two streets that way, then turn left. Hard to miss there, even from a distance. Peace go with you. Come on, Ourdh, we've wine to get to market."

Melungtal was about to ask a few more questions, to be able to definitely identify Pangwa House when he saw it, but decided not to. It seemed the general run of opinion was that the less one dealt with Pengwa Household, the better, so perhaps he ought to see what he could accomplish by himself.

Following the wine-seller's vague directions, Melungtal found himself in sight of a large building, but a street or more to the right of where he ought to be.

With that building as a guide-mark, he made his way through the surrounding streets and finally came up to a street apparently jammed end-to-end with people.

He tapped the man in front of him. "Excuse me, sir, is that Pangwa House?"

The other, a blocky man in well-cut clothing, frowned as he turned. "Yes, it is. And you'll have to wait like the rest of us."

"Wait?"

The other gave him a superior glare. "Of course, ninny! All the rest of us are waiting for the chance to get taken on as Wizards of Pangwa House. Where on earth are you from that you don't know that?"

"I'm from Saljashin, and I have an important message."

"Huh! Of course you do! And I'll wager you think you're the first who's tried that one? You just wait there behind me. You'll get your turn."

There didn't seem to be many choices other than waiting or causing a riot among several classes of Wizards and would-be Wizards. He even briefly considered that second option, but it was most likely he'd be discovered for the one who'd caused the trouble, which would only add to his difficulties in getting a serious hearing.

He waited.

About the middle of the afternoon, a voice called out from the still far-off doorway of the house. The voice had obviously been magically augmented so as to be heard at equal volume down the street. "We have taken in all the applicants we will take for the day! You may return tomorrow if you wish. No one is to loiter about this street overnight. If it becomes necessary, we will clear the street, and you may not like the method we use. Go, now!"

The man in front of Melungtal drew in a deep breath, then let it out, and apparently the ending of the rivalry of the queue rendered him slightly less unfriendly.

"Well, that's it for the day."

"But I have to get in!" He realized as he spoke that he sounded like a fool, but he couldn't stop himself in time.

"Look, fellow, I assure you that you won't get in today. That fellow wasn't joking about clearing the street; I got caught by it myself the other day. People were jammed in so tight behind me I couldn't get out, and suddenly there was this terrible stench, all the worst smells you could think of, all mixed together. There was one or two crushed in the rush to get out after that."

Melungtal had a feeling it hadn't been so much people behind this fellow which had held him in his place, but it was also very likely that the people of Pengwa House would use drastic measures to clear the street, if need be.

He turned to go. "Do you know of a place to stay?"

"Somewhere near here?" The other chuckled. "Yes, but it's full up, like everything near here. Come along if you want, and I'll show you, but I doubt there'll be floor-space for you."

He moved briskly along giving out occasional comments such as "The late Grand Master of Pangwa House certainly caused a disaster for most of the Wizardly Households of Gagapeng, and though I'm not one to rejoice over another's tragedy, it most certainly has provided the best opportunity I'm likely to find for a while."

Or, "It may be a risk connecting oneself with Pangwa House, the way their reputation is just now. But I still say they're going to come back from it, and most likely the stronger."

The Inn, Afmogus' Wine-barrel, was indeed full, with room for no one else, so Melungtal went off in search of other accommodation. He had noticed an interesting thing; the innkeeper's wine had a spell on it to preserve it. Probably wouldn't keep it good more than an extra day or so, but that was worthwhile for the innkeeper.

It also meant someone in the houseful of wizards was paying for his room with a wine-preservation spell. This was something for Melungtal to keep in mind if he had to stretch his stay for very long.

He had to walk quite a distance before he found an establishment which still had room for him.

In the course of that long walk, he saw many different styles of architecture; he'd never paid attention to such things before, but now he did, for want of anything better to occupy his mind. It was clear the city of Gagapeng had developed and grown over many years.

He went back to Pengwa House again the next day, as early as he could manage without walking the streets in the dark. Despite this earlier start, he was far enough back in the already gathered queue he suspected he wouldn't make it to the door today either.

He held his place in line, though; there was no telling how slowly or quickly the recruitment process would go, and it might be possible that a large number would be summarily dismissed. It was certain, though, he wouldn't get in if he didn't stay.

Having found out yesterday how the process went, he had no need to talk to anyone in the line, leaving him alone with his thoughts.

Perhaps it was his mood, but most of the people around him appeared surly and unwilling to talk, anyhow.

As it worked out, he could work himself within ten feet or so of the doorway before a Household servant appeared and announced the end of the day's quota. Melungtal couldn't help but feel discouraged at the waste of another half-day.

He went to the Marketplace, a loud and boisterous place. Though he'd had no experience in hocking his magical skills, he was able to remove a few warts, cure a rash, and earn a few coins to supplant his funds.

A servant-girl gave him a strange look when he claimed to be unable to make a love-charm to cause her chosen man to fall in love with her. It seemed it was an every-day occurrence for wizards here in Rosthan to interfere with people's lives.

Not that the matter was impossible; rather, it was a case of his having fled a certain aspect of Saljashin, but not everything. Love-charms and such were taught to the Wizards of Saljashin, if only to demonstrate the theoretical fear of the return of the Blue-Blossom Wizard was more than theoretical.

No, to be specific, he thought the risk of destroying Saljashin, perhaps the whole world, was too great in the course his masters had set.

Where was the sense in destroying Saljashin merely to prevent the return of the Blue-Blossom Wizard?

On the other hand, though the serving-girl would have paid him a nice little fee, this was too close to the work of the Blue-Blossom Wizard for his liking. He was reluctant to interfere with people's wills just yet. Sannat grant he never found himself willing to do so.

✤

The next morning, instead of walking through the streets, he used his escape-spell to bring himself to the back doorway of Pangwa House right at dawn.

He came through, leaning against a wall and trying to hold his stomach down. It wasn't as bad as the first time, but the distance hadn't been as far as the first time, either. Quickly, he was sufficiently aware of his surroundings to realize he was a bare two feet from the doorway, in the middle of a small group of people, all of whom were shouting at him angrily.

Melungtal wasn't sure what might have happened then had the door not opened. A man, not a servant, stood in the doorway.

The man pointed a finger at Melungtal and spoke a little phrase. A soft blue glow settled on the small crowd, though Melungtal noticed that on his own skin, the glow was mauve.

"You, there!" the man shouted. "Come up here! You others stand back and let him come. Stand back, or I'll close the door for the day! That's better. Come on, you! I can't wait all day!"

Melungtal forced his stomach into submission, came forward on unsteady feet. "Sannat's Toenails! Are you drunk, too?"

"No. Sorry. The spell's just a bit disorienting."

The wizard looked at him. "Hm. Disorienting, is it? Can I assume you know more than just one spell?"

"Yes, I do." Melungtal was starting to feel a bit better. "I need to talk to someone in here. I have a special message."

"Oh, really? Well, we'll see, in a moment. Right now, one thing we have to do is make some tests. We know for certain that the other Households would like to slip someone inside Pangwa."

"But..." Melungtal went quiet. No matter what he said, he was going to have to do their tests before anyone of any importance was going to talk to him.

He sat still while they set several spells on him, spells which made his skin tingle, spells which made it itch, which made him feel extremely cold, which made his hair stand on end.

Finally, the young man stood in front of him again. "All right. Unless one of the other Households has produced some really fancy Spells of Concealment, you're most likely safe. You're from Saljashin, which is unusual. You don't seem to hate us Rosthanites, just have a bit of suspicion about us."

Melungtal listened to all this; all the way along the journey, he'd known he would have to restrain his suspicion of all Rosthan if he was going to get a hearing, and apparently, he had been at least partly successful.

"Of course," the fellow went on, "being a magician of your potential, you probably never did have much feeling for Saljashin. They kill your kind over there, don't they?

"So, just a few more tests, then, to see what class you come into."

Melungtal decided it was best for him to go through the process of recruitment before insisting on speaking to someone regarding his real reason for coming. It seemed to him the better he passed the tests, the easier it would be to ask for—and receive—an interview with someone in power, so he went through the tests, with attention to all safety precautions, but as rapidly as possible.

After all the tests were done, the young man looked at Melungtal with considerable respect. "You are well qualified, aren't you? You'd be surprised at some of the people who want to join us. Barely enough magic to extinguish one weed at a time, or to make one plant grow a quarter of an inch, and they think we'll accept them immediately. But you, I think the Grand Master is going to want to speak to you."

Chapter Eight

The Grand Master was entirely too young for that title. By now, Melungtal connected Hadjalloni's desire to attack Rosthan with other facts. The previous Grand Master of Pangwa House had attempted a powerful spell, one which ran wild on him somehow, and killed all the higher magicians in his Household, as well as in all the Wizardly Households within a wide area of the city. Those it didn't kill, it incapacitated.

Because most of the powerful Wizards were within one section of the city, and within a certain radius, the only magicians of any power left in the city were ones who had not belonged to any Household, either because they hadn't been taken on, or worse, because they had been cast out.

Further, this left Gagapeng vulnerable to the attack which he, Melungtal, had been working on. Furthermore, Hadjalloni, seeing an opportunity, decided the attack should be launched now, with no waiting.

Melungtal's own feeling was the late Grand Master had been a colossal fool for not having used appropriate shields.

The present Grand Master surveyed his guest. They were in a comfortable wood-panelled inner room, one in which the present Grand Master seemed to be a tentative occupant. "So, you're the wonder from Saljashin?"

"I wouldn't call myself a 'wonder,' save in comparison to the Wizards who are left in Gagapeng. But I'm sure I can be of benefit to you."

"I'm interested in how someone like you came to be produced by Saljashin."

"I was chosen at an early age and trained rigourously. The training was always concerned with making sure I should not become a second Blue-Blossom Wizard; I'm sure you know something of our history.

"I was set to work on a project which had as its aim the destruction of Rosthan, as the nation which was most likely to give rise to another Blue-Blossom Wizard.

"From the time when my predecessor was declared Suspect and executed, I have been the head of that project, and just recently I was removed myself, though not yet declared Suspect."

The young Grand Master's eyebrows rose questioningly. "And after so many years of working toward our destruction, you come to us for refuge?"

Melungtal had long ago given up on the notion of saying his true reason for defection. "You may think you know what it's like being a magician in Saljashin, but let me explain.

"Anyone who shows any potential for magic is constantly watched. Some few are taken on and officially trained. Part of the training is being forced to watch, almost weekly, as one of one's fellow students is ripped apart by magic because he has been declared Suspect.

"'Suspect,' of course, means any sort of behaviour the authorities don't like. You eventually come to realize the chosen suspect was declared, not so much for what they might have done or said, but to be an example for the survivors.

"Even becoming head of an important project, such as I was, is no real safety. It merely means that the Watchers will see you as a greater danger of turning yourself into a Blue-Blossom Wizard.

"I was removed from the project because I thought it was still far too dangerous to Saljashin itself to be used safely. The next thing which would have happened is that the Watchers would have declared me Suspect, so I fled.

"It seemed to me that, with my knowledge of this project, Rosthan would be most likely to protect me, so I came here."

"I see. What is the nature of this dreadful project, then?"

"Simply put, it consists of several plagues turned loose against you at once, as well as several forms of blight and fungus to attack trees and crops."

Again the eyebrows rose. "Hm. How do these plagues and blights distinguish between Rosthanite and Saljashinite, or between Rosthanite and Saljashinite crops?"

"A good part of the development consisted of spells to prevent these plagues and blights from flourishing within particular territory. Part of my objection to their use was not enough work had gone into stabilizing the diseases. I felt there was altogether too much chance of wild forms coming back on us, destroying not only Rosthan, but all nations."

There was more than a touch of anger in the Grand Master's voice now. "So you have come to give us what, a two-days' warning of what's coming? How generous!"

Melungtal shook his head. "The truth is, I can't say how much warning you might have. I can tell you, though, how to do the counter-spells, and give you most of the details of the plan as it stands. All this should allow you to catch up without going through years of development."

Melungtal realized the interview had long ago gotten away from any control he might have had over its course. He only hoped that this too-young Grand Master would allow his good sense to outweigh his anger.

"Fine," the Grand Master said. "And you bring us all this at the time when Pangwa House is short of trained wizards, and will have serious difficulty trying to counter your project on the necessary scale. Sannat's toenails!"

"Will not the other Wizardly Households take a share in something such as this, which affects them all?"

"You don't know the Households, do you?" The Grand Master considered the matter. "Well, I think I'd be best to try to take this to the king. He can, if he will, give orders to the Households. How quickly the Households will be to jump to obey such orders is another matter altogether."

Hadjalloni watched the wizards. The first thing they had done, some days ago, was to kill several djasa, then stand, holding hands, upon a map of Saljashin. As he understood it, the spell must be repeated every day for three days in order to be sure of covering the whole country.

Today, they had set up a massive iron bowl of grey-green powder, which, he understood, was held in place by a simple spell.

They had killed two more djasa, and then stood, chanting, around the bowl. "Rise up, rise up, move as the river moves, move as the wind moves, move to Gagapeng! Rise up, move, descend upon the town of wizards.

"Rise up, move, descend, and do your work!"

As they continued to chant, a chant which would go on for hours, the powder rose straight up in a long grey-green streamer into the sky.

As the Wizards had explained it to Hadjalloni, somewhere up there the streamer would bend and move toward Gagapeng. The original intent, many years back, had been to cover all Rosthan, but the massive amount of powder required for such a surface area would be an extreme danger to Lunchmachor itself. They had settled for massive plagues in Gagapeng, which would by nature spread to most of the rest of the nation in the end.

In any case, Rosthan would be destroyed as a nation.

Saljashin would still have to be vigilant, since Rosthan would likely produce more Wizards. On the other hand, knowing this disaster had been produced by Wizardry, the people of Rosthan might well decide on their own to stamp out Wizards.

He brought his mind back to the present. First, wait to see how well this project succeeded.

They had told him the very soonest any effect might be seen would be a week and a half from now, and they had also assured him that would be the most fortunate circumstances.

It would be best to keep these present magicians working on the project, continuing to refine it, and producing better antidotes. Melungtal and his successor had expressed fears about the project. If those fears came to pass, and some form of the disease, or any of the diseases, came about, which was not amenable to the controls the Saljashinite Wizards already had, swift action was going to be necessary.

He set his mouth in a firm line. They would have to be watched, too. The seduction of magic was insidious.

He spent a moment thinking about Melungtal. Could he have gotten to Gagapeng? It was a long and dangerous way. Even if he had, though, how quickly would he have been able to find anyone to listen to his story?

Everyone knew about the attitude towards Wizards in Saljashin. If some Wizard, albeit a Wizard of capability, appeared in the streets announcing that Saljashin was preparing doom and destruction for Rosthan, who in officialdom would listen to him?

How exact was Melungtal's memory of the work done on the project? That, unfortunately, could not be minimized; as head of the project, he knew enough of it, and enough of the details. It was likely someone could reproduce it from what he had in his memory.

The only salvation was that, given the restriction on the use of writing-materials in the project, he would not have been able to copy down any significant amount of it to take with him.

Hadjalloni shook his head slightly. There were too many variables. All he could say for certain was Rosthan would be very late in making any attempts at protection. Furthermore, they were very short of high-quality Wizards there. And if this latest minor item were true, all the Wizardly Houses in Gagapeng were at odds with each other, too.

If they didn't pull themselves together swiftly, more swiftly than it seemed likely they would be able to, the project would succeed, at least to the point of rendering Rosthan a negligible threat.

Captain Yanomma had not yet reported back, which meant he had most likely failed to catch Melungtal. The Captain had also probably worked out what his failure meant; demotion at the very least, most likely listing as a Suspect.

Hadjalloni spared a moment to think of the Saljashinite agents in Rosthan. Unfortunately, it was not possible to protect them from the attack on Rosthan. What good would it do, anyway, when Rosthan was shortly going to become a desert where little or no food grew? It had never been possible to send them messages warning them to leave; one such message getting into the wrong hands would undo all the good Hadjalloni's careful planning had done.

It was even possible such news would drive the Rosthanite Wizards to unite, permitting them that one last little faint possibility of pulling themselves out of disaster.

No, it was unfortunate for Saljashinites presently in Rosthan, but Saljashin must be protected from the return of the Blue-Blossom Wizard, in whatever form he might come.

Alison hadn't seen Royin for two days. There was a rumour among the servants that someone had come to Pangwa House from Saljashin—near as she could make out a nation to the east—with some kind of seriously bad news.

Solitang Melapis'-child, a slender young man just out of his teens, what was known in the Household as a "baby wizard" came into the canteen and approached Alison's table when she waved him over.

"Have you seen Royin in the last few days?"

Solitang shook his head, grinning. "Big troubles, I hear. I understand he's been trying to get a message through to the Royal House, and the King is acting like we're not here. Our Grand Master wants the King to order the cooperation of all the Wizardly Households of the city.

"They're saying the Saljashinites have come up with some kind of spell to destroy all of Rosthan."

She nodded. "I've heard that one, too, though I'll admit I still don't know enough for it to have meant a lot to me. You think there's something to it?"

"There's always something to servant gossip and town-gossip, though sometimes not the actual truth. You have any more words you can't figure out in that thing?" He pointed to the big book she'd been carrying, still intent on making sure there wasn't something in it someone didn't want her to know.

She gave him a look. "Speaking of things that sometimes don't have a lot of truth in them. Not just yet. Thanks, anyway."

The next day, Royin appeared in the canteen, looking worn and discouraged. "Well, Tangral really did it to us. Has anyone told you about Saljashin?"

"A little bit. State to the east of us, highly antipathetic to magic and wizards?"

He nodded. "There's a bit more to it

than that, but that's the important part. They had a Wizard turn up, very good with hypnotic drugs, called himself the Blue-Blossom Wizard. Used political skills as much as anything else, if you ask me. He ran the nation for some time until an uprising of some sort got rid of him.

"The whole thing left them with a hate for magic and wizards. Since we in Rosthan use magic for so many things, even common, everyday things, they worry about another Blue-Blossom Wizard showing up among us."

He shrugged and continued. "Apparently, despite their distaste for magic, they've been working for years in an effort to destroy us.

"The man most recently in charge of that effort has made his way here to warn us. Not so much as he decided he loves Rosthan, apparently, but so much as he's afraid they haven't got it fully developed, and it may turn around and destroy Saljashin too, possibly even the rest of the world."

He ground the heels of his palms into his eyes. "I've been wearing myself out trying to get the Palace to take note of it. I can't get anyone over there to pay attention. It seems the general feeling is that this is something Pangwa Household has dreamed up to improve its battered reputation.

"It also seems nobody's told the king yet. I've talked to Messengers and Ministers, and they've promised me my message will be taken to the king in due time."

He snorted. "Huh! Due time means three weeks, maybe more. According to Melungtal, we have as little as three days."

"Melungtal?"

"The fellow from Saljashin. He says they have decided to rush their attack because they heard about the disaster Tangral caused. They expected they'd be best to attack while we had few strong Wizards to deal with the thing. That rush was part of what drove Melungtal to desert."

"How much can Pangwa House do by itself?"

"That's one of the problems. We can only do so much. We have no hope of protecting all Rosthan, not even all Gagapeng. If we protect only Pangwa Household, then when the thing hits, sure as smoke flies upward, everybody'll blame us."

"What sort of "thing" is this?"

He shrugged. "It's apparently a pair of attacks in one. One aspect of it is a set of plagues to attack the people, the other is a set of blights to attack most of the food crops."

"But they're keeping these from coming back and attacking their own territory. How?"

"They've developed a set of spells to protect them. Just before they set loose the active part, they'll be covering their own territory with the protective spells, which won't let the plagues or the blights have a chance to start."

"And you can reproduce these protective spells?"

"That's where the problem lies. Yes, we can and we are reproducing this spell, based on what Melungtal's told us. We don't have enough Wizards capable of handling enough power to take care of the entire country. Even with the help of all the other Households, it'd be tricky. The other Households won't agree to anything we suggest, though.

"Our only hope would be to get the king to issue a decree to all the wizards, and for that, we have to get a message through to the king immediately, something which seems unlikely to happen."

He shrugged. "We've been working hard, covering Pangwa Household, and we have it fairly safe. When people start dying, though, word of our attempting to warn the king is going to get around the city, and Pangwa House is going to find itself in the centre of a massive riot."

She nodded. It wouldn't be the first time in anyone's history such a decision was taken by a half-knowledgeable population. Pangwa House, in the person of the late Grand Master, had caused the original trouble; the panic surrounding an outbreak of plague would do the rest.

"Do you plan to evacuate the city?"

His eyebrows went up. "Have you been listening at doors where you shouldn't be?" He grinned. "No, don't bother getting angry; I suppose anyone with any sense has been thinking that way lately.

"Yes, we've been slipping people off for a long time. Some of the older servants, with a few younger ones, to take care of them. We've been sending them off to the farming colony at Nalagang Bay.

"Trouble is, a mass emptying of Pangwa House would likely start the riots ahead of time, and we quite possibly wouldn't survive to get to the gates of the city."

"What about your balloon?"

He smiled, tiredly. "I'm a bit ahead of you there. I've had a couple of advanced students making flights, taking copies of all the basic books out to the farming colony. The balloon can only carry so much, though.

"We're building a bigger one, though, but we're still concentrating on the old-fashioned wagons. We should be able to get most of our people out."

Royin looked around the Council Table. Everyone was looking as weary as he felt.

"Well, does anyone have any good news?"

"We've recruited a lot of wizards." Faral said. "A few of them could be sitting here instead of us."

Royin's mouth went into a stiff line. "That's going to be more trouble down the line. Some of them already know something about how the Households work, and in a while, a few months or perhaps years, they're going to think they know enough about the history and customs of Pangwa to be able to run things, and run things better than we do. About that time, we may have to deal with a lot of unrest."

"There's no procedure allowed for to vote us out of office." Ormant said. "Grand Mastership goes to the highest-class living master. I don't think there's even a procedure allow for abdication."

"If you look through the records," Royin said, "assassination has happened a time or two. Mostly it's been covered up by reference to 'severe illness,' but it's happened."

"You sound calm about it."

Royin shrugged. "I think I have two to five years before that really becomes a problem."

"Anyway, we have to make a decision on whether or not we're going to protect the Palace, even if they won't grant us permission."

Ormant shook his head. "We've talked about that. We'd have to lower the protective spells we have on the Palace first, and that'd cause all the alarms to go off over there. Can you imagine the excitement over in the Royal House if they thought we were attacking them? I don't think it'd help much if we told them, 'Don't worry, it was just us, your loyal wizards of Pangwa Household, putting some protective spells on you.'"

Royin looked at Faral, who spoke. "I agree with you on this one, Royin, but just barely. Protecting them even though they haven't allowed us to consult with them on the matter is just barely better than letting them go hang because they won't allow us to consult.

"They'll be upset about the lack of consultation, but they'll be even more upset when the real attack comes and they start dying. Maybe this way we can keep them inactively hostile to us rather than actively attacking us."

"I still say we're being too nice to people who will not be grateful," Ormant declared.

"All right. We'll start the protective spells on the Palace immediately."

"And Rosthan is finished?"

"I'm afraid so, Faral. Pangwa Household has been put in a position where no-one will take our warning seriously. Worse still, when the plagues and blights hit, everyone is going to blame us."

He paused. "I've given orders for the production and testing of several larger balloons. We'll be able to use the speed in communication to keep Pangwa Household alive, though I think it's going to be vastly different from Pangwa Household as we presently know it."

Ormant frowned. "What are we without the city? Without the King? Just another band of wandering wizards, looking for a home."

"But we'll be alive. We could put barriers around the Household Grounds, but how long can we hold them in place? Particularly if the blight makes it near impossible to live in this area? And the king, like as not, will send his army to demand answers of us; best we move somewhere else."

Ormant drew in a deep breath. "And we can't protect the entire city, with our limited resources. So I suppose investing some of them in something which may have a positive outcome, keeping the king from being actively hostile, might be the best idea."

Royin nodded. "Thank you. We'll start on it this evening."

There was a rap on the door, and a servant stuck his head in. "Royin-sir, the Grand Master of Falandar Household would like to speak to you."

Royin looked at the others. "Falandar? What could that be about? They're actually one of the smaller Houses, but we can't afford to turn down even the least bit of help. If you two will wait here, I'll talk to him and report back as soon as I'm done."

Pipakalat Lenbagat's-child, Grand Master of Falandar House, was slightly corpulent, and seemed a little ill-at-ease in the more expensive clothing which became his suddenly acquired situation. He was clearly trying to keep worry off his face and out of his voice, but only with moderate success.

He spoke right up with what was on his mind. "Grand Master Royin, they're saying you've had word of a coming attack from Saljashin."

"That's true. We've been trying to convince everyone to help us, but no one trusts Pangwa any more."

"Hm." The Grand Master of Falandar did not say, by word or facial expression 'We have reason,' but the words seemed to spring, unsaid, into the slight silence. "Suppose we do. That is, suppose Falandar House puts some trust in your warning. Is there anything that can be done?"

"I believe so. I doubt it will be possible to save all Rosthan, not even all Gagapeng, but we can save something. The same man who brought us the warning from Saljashin also brought us most of what we need to know to prevent it. The difficulty is that we, that is, Pangwa House, do not have sufficient Wizards of sufficiently high calibre, to do all the work that is needed."

"So. What will you charge us for this knowledge?"

Royin hesitated only a moment, then said, "We offer it to you for nothing, or at least for future considerations to be negotiated at that time."

Pipakalat looked suspicious. "For nothing? Can we expect it to be worth more than we pay for it?"

"You know how they think of Pangwa House in the city these days. To have even one Household willing to do business with us is no slight advantage."

"We don't want it trumpeted about that we're on your side!"

Royin shook his head. "It wouldn't be to our advantage to merely have another House hated and distrusted as we are. It would be more of an advantage for us for you to quietly give us aid and assistance when you can."

The Grand Master of Falandar hesitated, then said, "We aren't rich."

"No. We are, comparatively, but it does us no good if no one will sell to us."

"I see. I assume you've thought of the situation in the city when the plague hits?"

"Yes, we've been thinking of that quite a lot."

Pipakalat gave Royin a look. "Yes, I'm sure you have. And you have some plans for escape, I assume?"

"Yes, we have plans. We'll pass on some suggestions to you, if you wish."

"For a fee, I suppose."

"For nothing you can't afford. It's not in our interest to stand by and see all Rosthan, even all Gagapeng, destroyed, you know."

"So you keep saying."

"We've got Falandar House on our side," Ormant said. "Is that supposed to be an advantage?"

"It's better than it was, Ormant. You know the troubles we've had with our servants being recognized and occasionally stoned in the streets, with no one willing to sell to us, save at inflated prices, sometimes not even then. We'll need to buy a lot of things, very noticeable things, for our evacuation of the city. At the least, Falandar House can do some silent purchasing on our part."

"And you've given them everything, for no cost at all?"

Royin frowned at him. "I'm sure you heard what I just said, Ormant. That little benefit, the ability to make purchases without the matter coming to the wrong ears, is worth a whole lot of gold. And I did leave the price open to negotiation, so we may make a bit of gold too. On the whole, I think we'll come out ahead in the bargain."

Melungtal chewed on the end of his pen. He had, some time ago, reached the end of the portions of the project he knew by heart. He was thinking, not for the first time, how nice it would have been to have brought a little notebook of jottings and reminders with him.

He snorted. *'Notebooks! The way writing materials were controlled on the project, you know very well you were lucky to have brought yourself away, let alone anything written.'*

Even so, it wasn't really the diseases and blights as produced by the project which were the trouble. It was those that weren't sufficiently stable yet, which could lead to natural changes occurring, with all the consequences that entailed.

No matter how good the wizards of Pangwa Household were, they were at a disadvantage without as full a knowledge of the progress of the project as possible, from the very beginning.

Anything he could give them was an advantage, of course, but he had come to the project late, and even he had had to consult the records frequently just to be sure of what had been done before.

So now he was scribbling away here, bringing little bits and pieces out of his memory, and hoping he could make something coherent out of them.

He knew his reputation in Pangwa House was not the best. He'd been one of the people to have produced this horror, and he'd brought warning to Gagapeng was not a complete amelioration. Indeed, when he came to think about it, he found it hard to forgive himself.

That long ago time as a student, when not doing your best, could lead to being condemned as a Suspect, the more recent time when not putting all your efforts toward the destruction of Rosthan could lead to the same consequences, all seemed far away.

Was there nothing he might have done to prevent all this? No Suspect got to make a public declaration of their beliefs; few of your colleagues would listen to you, for fear the Watchers might see them as Suspect themselves. Furthermore, most people in Saljashin were convinced that Rosthan was exactly what they had always been told it was, the great danger of the return of the Blue Blossom Wizard in some guise.

Should he have tried to slip out and be a Slider? How had Slider reached his present status? How did he learn enough to survive, to be able to continually slide out of the grip of the Watchers? And how would Slider himself survive when the plagues changed and altered, attack Saljashin?

He sighed, and wrote another phrase, stared at it, reread it, and sat for a moment with his eyes closed, hoping to recall a bit more, a few words on either side of that phrase.

The thing was, he hadn't become another Slider; he hadn't gone the least bit against the Saljashin authorities until he himself was facing the fate of a Suspect.

Hadji seemed to have tried to give him a little leeway, not calling him Suspect immediately, perhaps even hoping Melungtal would ask to be reinstated. An indication of the Chief Watcher's respect, he supposed. That respect would likely have lasted only another day or two at the most, though.

Should he have gone to some other nation?

He could have, he supposed, but Rosthan had been the nation most likely to take action, and most likely to have the kind of people who would take action. That had meant Rosthan was the place to go, despite the disaster which had struck down so many of her Wizards.

Yes, Rosthan was the place to come, even if his welcome here was not as open as he could have wished.

He set down his pen and stood; his new masters would strongly prefer to have him stay here, bent over his pen, nor could he fault them for that attitude, considering the horror which might already fly through the night sky.

On the other hand, he had already done the important part, written out the antidote spells to the plagues and the blights, written out all he clearly remembered of the notes of the project, to the best of his ability.

He didn't fool himself that everything was faultless, save for the antidote-spells, which he had had the occasion to study and even write out several times while he worked on the project.

A capable wizard, going through his notes on the project, would probably spot many of the flaws which he was too close to the matter to see, and at least, they would be better off than they would have been with just a bare warning that the attack was coming.

He felt he required some exercise, avoiding thinking too much about whether or not he deserved it.

He'd been introduced, very briefly, to the Household Canteen, almost as if he weren't worthy of visiting it, but he understood food and drinks, beer, wine, or fruit punch, were available on his signature, and that it was a place of free discussion.

Coming from the Watcher-dominated society of Saljashin, such freedom seemed unlikely.

The wall decorations of the canteen, however, consisting of impossible fruits and vegetables, plants which might be forced into being, but would not likely bear seeds.

Other decorations showed very carefully drawn pictures of impossible constructions, scenes an artist could only render by using tricks of perspective or perception; not at all the kind of thing which would be on display anywhere in Saljashin.

In fact, certain drawings of this sort were occasionally passed around surreptitiously among the trainee-wizards in Saljashin, with the threat of being declared Suspect always in the background.

Further, his impression was it would be the sort of thing that the present Grand Master of Pangwa Household had not yet grown out of, though to give him credit, he seemed to press himself to grow up to the stature required of him.

Several young people were nattering back and forth, including one young, well-dressed woman who held a place marked in a book. Part of Melungtal's training had included at least a degree of Rosthanite work, though too much interest in Rosthanite writing could be Suspect.

The book this woman held would have been Suspect in Saljashin, if only for its very abstruseness, which hinted at a search for hidden knowledge.

He wasn't sure just how much hidden knowledge the young woman sought, but it seemed she didn't exactly trust the explanations the young men were giving her, or at least the one young man speaking.

He listened a moment to the youngsters trying to explain it, youngsters who ought not yet to be studying that book or its like.

What had been wrought in Rosthan? Were they so pressed for Wizards they were thrusting young men and women into this sort of thing?

Actually, it was a bit beyond him, too, and he considered for a moment saying so.

One of the young fellows looked at him. "You there! What do you think this means?" He demanded.

Melungtal shook his head. "I don't know that one."

"You don't know that one? Where are you from? It's one of the standard works of Magic."

The young man paused. While Melungtal was considering ways of avoiding getting into things, the fellow went on. "You're that Saljashinite, aren't you? The one who came bringing prophecies of doom and destruction?"

Melungtal shook his head. "Not something I want to get into."

"Huh! I suppose not! Everybody knows how badly you people hate magicians. So what have you been up to over there? Plotting and planning how to destroy Rosthan?"

Melungtal shook his head again, noticing the third young man had slipped quietly out of the Canteen, clearly seeing trouble coming. Trouble that he, the Great Wizard from Saljashin, had been totally blind to.

How far and how fast had the story of his presence travelled, not to mention several versions of the reasons for his coming?

It seemed less and less like a good idea to have left his study.

The young woman saved him. She slapped the book down on the table-top hard enough to get the attention of both, then said, "If you're trying to show off to impress me, Loniswal, you're doing it the wrong way. Bullying a foreigner who's already nervous about being in a strange country just strikes me as juvenile. Stop pushing him and back off."

Loniswal brought his head up sharply and looked at the young woman. For a moment it looked as if he were going to say something, but only snorted "Huh!" and strode away.

Melungtal looked at the young woman, saw her smiling at him, a smile carrying little mirth. "That's me, Alison MacKarg, useless woman or causer of cataclysms, however you look at it. I'm the one the late Grand Master of Pangwa brought over, wanted me so desperately he broke all the rules, and because of that, destroyed the chief wizards of Gagapeng, which means most of the best wizards in Rosthan.

"And nobody knows what to do with me."

"You aren't a wizard?"

She laughed. "As magical as this table-top, here. Probably less so because it's likely that some magic went into making the table."

"But you're studying that book?"

She gestured with the book. "This? When he brought me over, the late Grand Master gave me the ability to speak the language, more or less, but I can't read a word of it. Couldn't, I should say because I'm learning it, though not as fast as I'd like.

"They encourage me to read as much as I want, in the hopes that they can figure out why I'm really here; the only reason they've come up with so far just makes Grand Master Tangral look that much worse.

"And because I'm a suspicious sort, I insist on reading a few they say are 'too abstruse' for me."

She gave him another look. "In case you hadn't guessed, I don't necessarily trust everything they tell me."

He smiled. "Not much use my agreeing with them, then? I find that book too abstruse."

She gave him a sharp look, then relaxed slightly. "I suppose it'd be too much of a complicated scheme to just happen to have the wizard from far-of Saljashin meet up with me and assure me that this book won't tell me anything anyone doesn't want me to know?

"Truth is, I might as well be trying to read one of the books in the Ancient Languages for all I'm getting out of this. Maybe I should have you go through the library with me to find some works that might be useful?"

She shook her head. "Sorry. Forget it. From what I hear, you're far from useless here."

This brought back to Melungtal the memory of his guilt at the desertion of his duty. He shrugged. "Walk a mile into flames, why not two? Suppose I come along and give you a few suggestions, then get back to work?"

Her smile this time was real. "If word of this gets around, young Loniswal is going to be red and green and steaming at the ears. Let's go."

Royin surveyed his gathering of wizards. Most of them were men who'd recently been taken on; not yet formally adopted, but well on the way. The single one of whom there was no question of fitness was the Saljashinite, Melungtal. Ability was only part of the fitness, though; the man could well have taken on the Grand Master's role, if mere ability were all that mattered.

One thing still bothered Royin. Melungtal had spent all those years working to develop the set of processes and spells which would destroy Rosthan.

Then suddenly he ups and runs off to warn Rosthan. Not so much for the love of Rosthan, it seems, as for his concern, the attack could run wild and destroy Rosthan, Saljashin, and just about everything else. Royin had a suspicion if they'd had all the knots out of the thing when old Tangral had done his disaster, Melungtal would have been just as happy to have let fly....

Well, he'd already spent too much time getting down to business.

"All right, Masters, you've had time to study the matter at hand. We're about to put a protective spell on the Royal House. We've worked out all the parts and all the requirements, including sufficient shielding for the work.

"We'll want to go to work immediately, with no stops or hesitations. Does anyone have any questions?"

There was a silence, then one of the fellows, Kalangas from Pelang, spoke up. "Uh... Everyone knows how the king feels about us, Grand Master. When we lower the shield to put this spell on them, won't they just be the more suspicious? Perhaps even hostile?"

Royin frowned at the man. He'd either been denied a family name, or had lost it, thus having to call himself 'from Pelang.' That wasn't necessarily a reason to dislike or distrust him, but when he came up with a question like that, at this time...

"When I say that we have made a decision, I mean that the Grand Masters have made a decision. *'No matter how thin the board of Grand Masters might be.'* I suppose the question is, Kalangas, do you accept the decisions of the Masters of Pangwa Household?"

Kalangas' eyes slid away from Royin's gaze. "No argument, Grand Master. I just...." His voice trailed off.

'You just asked a troublesome question at the wrong time, Kalangas. Did someone put you up to it, or are you just being naturally awkward?'

"All right. Are there any further questions, then? So, let us begin."

As the wizards moved to their positions, Royin considered it might have been a good thing for Kalangas to ask his question. It had forced Royin to bring out the Hammer of the Master's Decision. Any other question regarding the reasons for doing what they were doing would risk going against the Master's Decision, and unless there was some conspiracy going on which was more serious than Royin thought possible, no one was going to ask anything more.

❖

Alison noticed Royin was looking more than usually tired this morning, as he came up to her table at the Canteen.

"Don't want to push myself on you, Alison, but we've just done something that's likely to have important consequences. I'd as soon you didn't have to find out from all the rumours that'll be going around."

"Sit down," she said, "and tell me about it." In her mind, she was wondering if they might have decided to do something with her. Or about her.

"It doesn't really have anything to do with you, personally, save that it concerns every member of the Household." It almost seemed he'd been reading her mind, but she was concerned about her future, and he knew that very well.

"Just last night, we took steps to protect the Royal House against the attack from Saljashin. That required lowering the magical shields we had over the Royal Household, something they'll notice over there.

"Given our present relationship to the Royal House, we can expect them to react with suspicion, at the very least.

"You'll likely hear all sorts of rumours, such as that we're attacking the king, that we're trying to take over the kingship of Rosthan, and so on. The truth is, we're just doing our duty, trying to protect the Royal House, though given our lack of credit, the king might well choose not to believe that."

As Royin spoke, he had absently fingered the little book Alison had been reading. He looked down at it, then up at her. "Are you finding this a little easier to comprehend?"

Alison felt herself flushing. "Yes, a bit. Melungtal pointed it out to me."

She saw Royin's eyebrows rise a bit before he spoke. "He did, did he? Good for him, then. I always thought you were trying to push yourself too far, too fast."

"But I insisted on suspecting everyone of hiding something from me." For all her care at watching what she said, the admission seemed to jump out of Alison's mouth, and she felt herself flushing even more.

She forced herself to look up at him. "I guess I've always been too suspicious, haven't I?"

"Considering the situation you're in, yanked away from everything familiar, with no chance to agree or disagree, for a reason that no one seems to have more than a vague notion of, only assurances that no one means you harm, I'd say that suspicion was a reasonable frame of mind.

"Then add to that the business that happened in Strick's Bolg, where you defended yourself and still found yourself on the wrong end of things, well...." He let his voice trail off.

She forced herself to smile. "Be careful. Any time now, you're going to push me to my other reaction, to be mad at you for being so damned understanding."

Before he could respond to that, Alison hurried on to a less dangerous topic. "This book. Right here, at the end, is what seems to be a spell for making things seem larger."

"Ah, yes, the Magnification Spell. I know about it mostly from history. A fellow was about to start a woodworking shop and wanted a spell to enable his craftsmen to assess the grain of a piece of wood easier.

"So someone produced the spell for him. Trouble was, his craftsmen had all been trained in the old-fashioned way, doing things by eye, and had little use for this newfangled thing.

"So the enterprise went on, though I believe it folded later on due to some unwise business decisions. The spell is kept around as an example of something that the Wizard in question ought to have talked the customer out of bothering with. Nobody's ever found a use for it."

"I see."

Chapter Nine

The Royal Messenger was upset and fearful, which made him hostile.

"The King demands your presence immediately, to explain the most recent doings of Pangwa Household!"

Royin nodded. He'd expected no less. "Certainly." He looked around. "Ormant, you are in charge while I'm away. Take all necessary measures."

Ormant nodded in return. "Yes, Grand Master."

The military escort formed round Royin, and they marched off. Taking their cue from the Royal Messenger, they were as rude as they dared be.

They took a circuitous route through the city, to display as widely as possible the arrest of the Grand Master of Pangwa House. Nothing specifically had been said about an arrest, but Royin knew that was a mere technicality. They prevented the people from throwing stones, or any other solid missiles, but only objected to the throwing of other objects if the objects came too near any part of the escort.

Royin kept calm. It was uncomfortable, but he could stand it. He was certain the king was not yet at the point of playing some sort of game which ended in the death, accidental or otherwise, of the Grand Master of Pangwa House, before he, the king, could confront that Grand Master and pronounce a death sentence.

As for the possibility of a death sentence, that was something which Royin hoped to prevent, by one means or another. He had taken some precautions before the Royal Messenger had shown up at the door.

They marched through the outer Palace, and on into the presence of the King. All the way along, various people watched the progress of the once-mighty Grand Master of Pangwa Household.

The courtroom was decorated with fine statuary and expensive jeweled carvings, all the better to demonstrate the power of the king. The king himself, in his robes of state, sat upright on his throne. He was a dark-complexioned man and strongly built. His face was tight with anger.

"So, Grand Master of Pangwa, what have you done to us now?"

"With respect, great king," Royin said, "we had received word of an attack on you by the Saljashinites. We sent word to your servants, requesting leave to pass the news, but for whatever reason, we received no response.

"Yesterday evening, we decided to take action, rather than waiting longer, and thus being held to account for the destruction of the king and the capital."

The king sneered. "And you were successful, of course, since I am still alive? How nice. And there is no way we can prove you wrong, is there?"

"Great king, it is unfortunately not so simple as that. In our limited state, we were able to preserve you and your Household, but unfortunately, we do not have the power to save the entire city. Sometime soon the plagues will hit, and it will be bad. If you were to order the other Wizardly Houses to assist, we can ameliorate the situation greatly. If not, the result will be tragedy."

"The result will be---! Grand Master, what have you done now?"

So, Royin realized, it had come to this. The king had heard what he wanted to hear, not what Royin had said. As far as the king was concerned, Royin and Pangwa Household themselves had attacked the city, in an effort to impress, or possibly threaten, the king.

He pulled himself up. "No, great king, I believe you misunderstand. We have the information that will enable us to save most of the city, but we require assistance."

"I think not! Recent history shows that Pangwa Household cares for little but the welfare of Pangwa Household. Enough of your threats and extortion, Grand Master! In fact, enough of you, yourself! Guards!"

"Wait!" Royin's voice, magically augmented, stopped everyone for a moment.

In that moment, Royin held up his right forefinger, and a three-foot-long green flame flared at its tip. At the same moment, everyone present, save for Royin himself, sneezed violently. The guards stopped and looked at the king.

Royin spoke again. "I may be a fool in some things, great king, but not so much of a fool to put myself in your hands without some safeguards.

"The man I left in my place at Pangwa House has orders, if I do not return, and return safely. He will then break down all the magical protections around your Household. If you will not help us, then do not hinder us, and we will save, unaided, as much of the city as we may."

"You are threatening me, then!"

"Great king, I make no threats. You still rule the land of Rosthan, and I will do my best to prevent the destruction of the city and the nation from enemy attack. As far as I am concerned, there will be peace between our Households, if only because the lack of peace makes it difficult for me to carry out my task.

"Now, to prevent any possible misunderstanding, might I request an escort of your troops to my home?"

The route back home was shorter, and the trip was less disturbed. When they reached the main door of Pangwa House, the Royal Messenger in charge of the escort seemed almost on the verge of ordering one of the soldiers to put a spear through Royin, but apparently good sense won out.

Ormant looked at the state of Royin's clothing and said, "Trouble?"

"We've been in trouble since the night Tangral decided to do his work without appropriate safeguards.

"All that happened today is that it's been pushed home to the king that he and his Household have become steadily more dependent on one Household, Pangwa, for all wizardly protection. We're going to have to make preparations to evacuate the rest of the Household from the city, and if necessary, to stand off the king."

"Stand off---! Sannat's flaming toenails, what've you done?"

"I insisted on trying to protect as much of Gagapeng as possible. It just may be that I tried a little too hard, but if you don't mind, we can fight that out later."

"Royin---!"

Royin whirled on him. "Listen, Ormant, I made decisions. Way back at the beginning of this mess, I made the only decisions I could see that wouldn't end up with Pangwa Household broken up and scattered among the other households, unable to use our ability to try to make up for what Tangral had done.

"Right now, we've come to a point where everything's coming down on us, and every minute we spend debating the past is another minute taken away from planning for the immediate future.

"After the storm has passed, we can enjoy all the recriminations we want. Right now, we have things which must be done. Can you accept that?"

For a moment, the matter stood on a knife's edge. Whether Ormant would accept Royin's ruling as Grand Master or rend the Household irreparably by rejecting Royin's authority in the face of immediate danger.

Finally, Ormant nodded. "All right, we'll go your way. But don't think this is forgotten, Royin."

"No, I won't think that. Let's get down to preparations."

❖

Pipakalat Lenbagat's-child was nervous. "You're pressing for Falandar's Household to move forward on the agreement. Isn't that a little hasty?"

Royin looked at him. "Meaning you've heard about the latest business between Pangwa Household and the Royal Household? And you're feeling shy about even the thought of being connected to us?

"You know, this attack from Saljashin is coming, one of these days, however much you and the king and the rest all doubt it. You've read the copies of the Saljashinite material, haven't you?"

Pipakalat looked as though he were swallowing something extremely sour. "Yes, I've read it. Parts of it I've read twice and three times. It's scary, for sure, but---."

"But what? It came to you via Pangwa Household, with our reputation attached to it? Tell me, do you think we put together something like that, including making sure that it read as if a Saljashinite had written it, just to frighten people?"

"I don't personally, but many people are saying that Pangwa Household is about to make a push to replace the Royal House."

"Come, Pipakalat, follow the steps that I would have to have taken. I'm the Grand Master right now. I'm the one trying to push this thing. This means I'd have had to have someone start the thing off for me, or else I did it myself, hiding my own real identity.

"I'd also have had to arrange for Tangral to pull that trick of his, and almost kill me in the process, Or else I arrange some skillful thing by myself that killed or incapacitated everyone, meaning some kind of exact formulation to kill or incapacitate everyone, but not damage myself too badly.

"All this to carry out some kind of extortion scheme."

He paused, then leaned forward. "Wouldn't it have been much more simple for me to provide the plagues and all, let them cut through the population, and suddenly, in a great effort, destroy the plagues and announce myself as the saviour of the nation? Wouldn't it?"

Pipakalat leaned away from him and took a deep breath. "You---you make an excellent case, Grand Master."

"I have to do better than that. I have to make a convincing case, and start moving now, either today or as close to it as possible. I'm risking my House and all to try to stop this thing, and I'd really like to give my people some infinitesimal chance to save their lives as a reward."

Pipakalat took another deep breath. "All right. I'll push it through Falandar's

Council of Masters as soon as possible. I wish I could give you a solid guarantee, but I'm going to have to twist some arms and make some speeches. Better than that, I can't promise."

Royin nodded and smiled, a smile that showed more confidence than he felt. "You'll manage, Pipakalat."

A day and a half after Royin's confrontation with the king, one of the younger wizards on shift watching the Spell of Detection called out, "It's here! It's here!"

His Supervisor, Borilil from Tsolaki, responded to the young man's call. Borilil was a little paunchy, and somewhat sour at the discovery that he was required to put in a probationary period with Pangwa Household before he could be put in the kind of supervisory role he felt he deserved.

"What now?" He looked at the Spell of Detection. A landscape view of the city magically projected on a blank wall. A fierce orange pillar stood over the Royal Household. "Sannat's buttocks! Where have you been hiding? Wait until the Grand Master sees this!"

He rang the small crystal bell would resound throughout the House.

The two stood watching then, until the Grand Master appeared. He had clearly thrown on his clothes in a hurry. Borilil gestured toward the picture before them. "This useless fellow let things get this far before calling me, sir. I called you as soon as I knew."

The younger man said nothing, only stood looking sullen.

But the Grand Master glanced from the picture to the two wizards, then snapped, "Borilil, if you aspire to be a Master, act like one! Everyone was told that the Spell would show first what looked like a small orange sandstorm, building to this within moments.

"Go pass the word to the people working the protection of the city that it's time to shift to the Evacuation. You, young man, what's your name?"

"Nambar from Achol, Grand Master."

"Do you know your part on the Evacuation Plan?"

"Yes, Grand Master."

"Good. Keep watch here for the time being. I don't expect anything to change, but if it does, sound the alarm again. Don't stay too long; the Household can't afford to leave anyone behind."

"Yes, Grand Master---, uh, no, Grand Master."

The Grand Master smiled grimly. "Don't worry, we're pretty much all confused by now. It's up to me to straighten things out as well as I can."

❀

Alison came awake in the middle of the night to hear the alarm-bell ringing. They had explained the meaning of the alarm bell to everyone. It meant everyone should assemble at one of a series of points in the House, from which orderly evacuation would begin.

She wondered if orderly evacuations in this world were any more orderly than evacuations back home.

She grabbed the few things she had to carry, including library books. It occurred to her to wonder what would happen if she lost a library book. The Household Library appeared to run on an honour system, though she suspected in her case, the honour was connected to Royin's wish she have complete freedom of the library.

There were no cards, merely a little slip of paper on which you put your name and the book's title, so that the librarians knew who had which book. If someone requested a book you were using, the honour system said you'd return it to the library as soon as possible.

"You know, girl," she muttered to herself, "for a person in a strange world, and about to evacuate a city which may well be hostile, your mind is taking some very weird turns."

Her own evacuation station was the canteen, one of several places in the House which could contain several people at once.

By the time she arrived, many people were already there; it seemed to be a mix of servants and wizards, some more excited than others.

An older wizard came in, slightly hurried, carrying something that looked a great deal like a tablet. But this world didn't have that kind of technology, though, and there seemed to be some kind of magic stylus with which he could change 'pages.'

He also seemed to have done some magical augmentation of his voice, too, for though he didn't seem to speak loudly, when he spoke, everyone listened.

"All right, everyone, calm down. Yes, we're evacuating the House and the City. Yes, there's some danger, but we've organized everything to be able to minimize the danger as much as possible.

"First off, are we all at the right place? Everyone here was told to muster at the Canteen?"

"All right," he continued. "Just to be certain, I'll call your names. When I say your name, you answer *'here.'*"

There was a long period of repeating of names and answers, some of the responses shouted out, some muttered too faintly to be heard. Alison was so caught up in listening to the names she almost missed answering to her own.

Finally, the man in charge lifted his head from the clipboard. "All right. For a wonder, no one's missing. Next thing, is there anyone here who shouldn't be? Anyone whose name I didn't call?"

"Aha, we have one! Your name? Dilata Penkara's-child? Hmm. I don't know how you managed it, Dilata, but you managed to hear 'Canteen' for 'Baking Hall.' You'd better scamper. No, don't worry, there'll be someone there for a while yet to take you in charge. Go! Go!"

He sighed. "If we're blessed enough to have one little thing go wrong, I'll be deliriously happy. Not to mention shocked silly.

"So, we begin. Parillang, where are you? Ah, there. Now, everyone take note, we have taken the precaution of putting Parillang into an orange hat and jacket. We will all be going, in an orderly fashion, through the Hallways to the Back Courtyard. Can everyone find the Back Courtyard? Good.

"Parillang will go first, and the rest will follow, counting off in sixes, with a brief pause after each half-dozen.

"When you get to the Back Courtyard, look for the orange section. We feel almost all of you can find your section, as each cart and wagon in the section is decorated with orange rags.

"If you can't find your section, for any reason, do not attach yourself to any other group. Find someone with a clipboard," he waved his "and ask where your section is."

He paused and looked them over grimly. "This whole process has been worked out by the Grand Master himself, in such a way that nothing should go wrong. Keep that in mind and think about yourself up in front of the Grand Master, explaining to him he was mistaken."

"Any questions? Please understand that the stupid question is the one you didn't ask, and therefore made a stupid mistake. And think how stupid you'd feel explaining that to the Grand Master."

No questions were asked.

He looked them over again. "All right, Parillang, lead off."

Parillang led off, and the man in charge called names and counted off people on his clipboard as they went out.

At that moment, one of the problems of making the process orderly appeared. People were scattered around the room, so on more than one occasion, a person who was called was across the room from the door, and had to hurry across. As far as Alison could see, this would only be a serious problem if any of these late-leavers didn't know how to get to the Back Courtyard. Since she did herself, and she was still almost a stranger here, it seemed likely everyone else could manage.

Her name was the last one called. The man in charge said, almost apologetically, "Alison-lady, it was thought you might not be totally familiar with the hallways of the House, so they suggested you go right before me."

"I think I could manage, but I accept your offer." She was actually annoyed, but caught herself well before she could take it out on a fellow following his orders.

He nodded. She couldn't tell for certain whether or not he was happy not to have an argument, and felt a tinge of guilt at having gained that sort of reputation.

There wasn't much chance to think of might-have-beens then, because no matter how skilled and detailed the Grand Master's plan had been at the beginning, the reality of this part of it was hallways full of people rushing along, some near panic. There was a lot of shouting, and an occasional argument escalating towards blows.

When such arguments began, there was usually someone around, one of the people in the coloured hat and jacket which marked a group, or one of the people with clipboards. That person would touch each of the prospective combatants, and suddenly they would go calm, and move along toward their destination.

'The Old Valium-Spell,' Alison thought, after witnessing the second such incident. *'Works every time.'*

When they came to the Back Courtyard, Alison found she didn't recognize it by night and torchlight, and was glad for her guide.

"We're over here, Alison-lady." It was fairly obvious which group was theirs; there was no mistaking the orange streamers for any other colour.

The guide called the roll again. "For a wonder," he said when he was done, "no one's lost, strayed, or stolen."

That had not been the case with all groups, though; there were still harassed and frightened-looking people going this way and that in the courtyard.

The Head of the orange group grabbed the ones which came nearest him, calmed them down, and pointed out their proper places.

Heads of other groups were doing the same, here and there, and shortly the situation seemed to be fairly well in hand. Alison thought it was just as well that any small children had been sent off long ago; they would have made this business even worse.

✤

"The usual great confusion, Royin," Ormant said. "Two different groups had rukasa or djasa come up lame at the last moment, had to borrow spares from other groups. Got it straightened out, though."

"Good. What word from Falandar House?"

"Just come in. They're expecting us."

"Good. I'd expected they'd show a lot more nervousness when we actually had to move. Let's go."

When he considered it, though, Royin realized there had been nervousness aplenty displayed as the wagonloads of supplies—and wagons themselves—had come slipping through the darkened streets the last several nights, moving as unobtrusively as magic could permit them to, even using a bit of magic to cut down on the noise.

He hadn't argued over the profit Falandar Household had made on the wagons and supplies; it hadn't been that heavy, after all, and Royin had paid little of it in coin. There were several spells, long-held secrets of Pangwa Household, which many other Wizardly Households had greatly desired. These were worth a good deal of gold, though privately Royin wondered how valuable they would be in Rosthan in the situation the nation would find itself in shortly.

The wagons rolled through the dark streets. Alison noticed there were no such things as street lights, and in most places, not even street-signs. Each wagon and cart was equipped with a magic light, some sort of bioluminescence, she suspected. She was also near certain each driver was very familiar with the streets.

A driver could always follow the fellow in front, and hope that the fellow in front didn't get lost himself.

As she understood, the reason for the evacuation—and the explanations given had been very rough—the expected Saljashinite attack had been detected, and in about two days people in the city would start dying. Given the reputation Pangwa House had gained over the last while, it was very likely they would be the centre of civil unrest shortly after that. They were hoping by that time to be well out of the city and on the way towards this farming colony they'd spoken of.

She didn't like the notion of deserting the city, since Pangwa Household had the only knowledge to fight the plagues, but she also realized any good they could do was severely limited by their manpower. Dying heroically by being massacred by the people you were trying to save might make a stirring novel somewhere, but trying to survive to save as many people and as much knowledge as possible was more realistic.

The phrase "Curse Tangral!" was going to become very common in the next few years.

She was still useless, too, a botanist in a world where not only plant life, but the study of it, differed greatly from what she'd known. To make matters worse, she could only claim to merely be on the way to becoming literate.

"Yeah," she muttered to herself, "Curse Tangral!"

The young man seated on the wagon beside her looked up at her. "Your pardon, Alison-lady?"

She shook her head. "Just talking to myself, Solitang. Nothing important."

Pipakalat was nervous. Royin wondered if it should be 'nervous again' or 'still nervous.'

"We have everything you asked us to get. I hope we've managed to keep it fairly secret, but you know yourself that sometimes a servant, or even Sannat help us, a Master, will gossip to a friend outside the Household."

"You don't want to join us? I think we have room at the colony for more. If not, we can expand it. Plenty of unclaimed land in the vicinity."

The Grand Master of Falandar Household shook his head vigorously. "Not me! I was born and raised in Gagapeng. I'll stay!"

"It won't be comfortable in a few days."

"Even so, I think we'll hang around."

"All right, your decision. Will your people give us a hand getting the supplies stowed?"

"Yes, we can do that."

Royin had a feeling that as far as Pipakalat was concerned, the faster the Pangwa fugitives got out of his courtyard, the better. But the man had carried out his part of the bargain so far, and he, Royin, had made his own fair share of hasty decisions since this thing started.

Royin also wondered, then decided it was none of his business, if Pipakalat were planning on becoming the Rescuer of Gagapeng; that could be risky. If people decided Falandar Household were profiting off their misery, they might react badly.

He turned his attention to pushing the loading of supplies; the sooner they were on their way, the better.

The train of wagons slipped through the streets of Gagapeng. They moved as silently as magic could make them, or at least as silent as magic could make them, and still have something left in reserve for emergency.

At this time of night, there ought not to be anyone out on any lawful business, but Royin was sure depending on that fact was not a good risk to take. They had lit the route with magical lights, lights which came on just several wagon-lengths before the first wagon, and went out as many wagon-lengths behind the rearmost.

They'd discussed the matter thoroughly, and Royin had made the other two see the significant risk involved in having the lights on all along the route until the last wagon passed through. "This way, someone's probably going to notice the light; with the lights on all the way, a lot of people will notice them for sure. We can do without a bunch of people getting in our way."

The faces of the buildings were grey in the bluish magical light, with strange tricks of shadow playing around every doorway and alley-mouth.

Falandar Household had been left behind, to cast its fate with that of the city.

Grey-blue buildings dropped behind the cavalcade: rich houses, poorer houses, shops with houses attached, and shelters which hardly rated the term 'house.'

There was a shout, more like a squawk, from one of the windows. Royin debated for a moment casting a sleep-spell, but it was likely he'd need his power later on. This one person wouldn't likely be able to wake enough people to hinder them.

On they went, rukasa puffing under the loads they were carrying. That squawk behind had turned into a full shout; Royin peeled his rukasa out of the stream of traffic and pointed in the direction of the window. A quick mutter of words was all it took, and the shout died away.

'Bad omen for the rest of the trip,' he looked around; fortunately, Ormant was watching the rear, out of sight.

On they went, through the narrow winding streets, moving at a fast trot. A gallop was too risky here, even if it wouldn't wear out the draught-animals too soon.

Sannat's toenails. Was that more shouting? "Keep moving!" he called out, unnecessary advice, as all the drivers were urging their rukasa to keep moving, moving at an increasing speed.

People were coming out of the buildings now. He'd hoped to avoid a mob, and the people as yet were mostly curious about the light and the so-quiet wagons.

They had made sure every wagon and cart carried their Household emblem, for the reassurance of the people. That could have another effect, though, to let people know just who it was trying to slip out of the city.

There was a gathering roar of voices back there; it wouldn't take long for a crowd to form, even at this dark hour, and the bluish light which lighted the fugitives way would also permit the hunters to track them.

It would have been a nice thought to think that they could outrun people on foot, but a wagon going round a corner had to slow down, and rukasa, especially rukasa hauling wagons, could not outrun a man over any distance.

Royin dropped back, and further back, until he was at the rear of the train. Loniswal and Ormant were back there, the one too young for such a position, the other too headstrong. Curse Tangral!

A stone came whirling out of the dimness back there to strike Royin's mount, who went into a dance. Royin calmed the animal, then pointed backward and spoke a spell.

There was a roar of anger and fright; he had done nothing outright fatal, just a strong burst of the horrible smell they'd used to clear the people out of their back alley.

It was only a burst; he didn't have the power to spend on something more than that, not when it might be needed worse somewhere further along the way.

"Let's go!"

The other two turned to follow the wagons. Ormant with an expression that said he hadn't appreciated Royin's help.

'Should've left it to him. He doesn't like people pushing in on his patch.' Too late for that, too late for any apologies, even if they had time.

The stink-smell wouldn't keep the mob away very long; Ormant and Loniswal would still have work to do tonight.

Rattling over the cobblestones, rushing past the houses, on they went. Altogether too soon, the mob was shouting on their trail. How soon would the noise bring people out ahead of them, in enough numbers to block their path?

Now the first of them were coming into the gate-yard, at the end of which were the great gates, shut and barred between sundown and sunup. Guarded, too, but that was something Royin had prepared for.

"Ready with the sleep spell?" Royin asked.

"Ready," responded Kalangas.

"Now!"

Kalangas cast his spell. It had none of the flashy illusions which many Wizards used to impress the locals, but it would put everybody within the vicinity of the gate into a deep sleep. This would include the gate guards, and anyone who might be near enough to hear or see something if they looked the wrong direction at the wrong time.

"Solitang, you can manage the gate?"

"Yes, Grand Master." Solitang spoke a spell, then made an upward gesture with his hands. The bar of the gate moved up and was set gently aside. Solitang made another gesture, and the gates swung open.

The convoy continued on its way.

When the last wagon and cart were outside, Royin, Ormant, and a few other young wizards took on the task of closing and barring the gate. Putting the bar in place, without being able to see it, was a tricky business, something beyond Solitang, skilled as he might be.

The mob was still coming. "Ormant! Loniswal! The sleep-spell, whatever it takes!"

They obeyed, and the first part of the mob fell asleep in the midst of their rush.

The massive gates swung shut with a bang, and the bar, a little fumblingly, dropped into place.

Royin looked at his companions, wondering if they felt as worn as he did.

"We're out."

❖

Melungtal found himself alone on a crowded cart. Shoulder to shoulder with ten other people, none of whom spoke to him, barely even acknowledging his presence.

He could hardly blame them; so far as they were concerned, he was the cause of their having to leave their homes behind. Even worse, he felt himself to be the cause, no matter how much he tried to tell himself that some other person would have headed the project if he had not.

No, it was he, not someone else, who had brought the set of plagues close enough to perfection that someone like Hadjalloni would risk using them.

The city of his fellow-passengers, likely even their whole nation, would be destroyed, and by Melungtal's work.

All to remove the potential threat of a Blue Blossom Wizard.

But the attacks he had perfected, well, not perfected, merely improved. They would not be killing only potential Blue Blossom Wizards, they would kill anyone and everyone who was not protected. Was "I hadn't thought through the implications," any sort of exculpation?

They camped on a piece of level ground about two miles beyond the last buildings that had grown up outside the walls of Gagapeng.

"So. Three wagons broken down. We managed to spread their loads, among others." Royin said. "Two others were totally unaccounted for. I'd say we had Sannat's hand on us."

"'Unaccounted for?'" Ormant demanded. "How could any be unaccounted for, with all the safeguards and trouble we took?"

Royin held his temper with an effort; they'd all been working hard, maybe too hard, over the last days. "I don't know how. You've heard the saying, 'No plan so perfect it can't go wrong?' Well, it's happened to us. Maybe one of the wagons will show up, mixed in with the wrong section. Maybe they won't. I don't like it any more than you, but going back to look for them just runs the risk of losing more people."

Chapter Ten

They spent a day where they were. Royin grudged even that day, but the fugitives from Pangwa Household did have to reorganize before setting out on the road. Their flight from the city had not gone unmarked, unfortunately.

"The mob's not a great worry," he told his Magicians. "They won't likely follow us out of the city. The Army, well, that's another matter. I can't see the King getting them out after us until tomorrow. We've assigned people to watch the gate to let us know if they come sooner. As for the rest of you, I've worked you too long and too hard as it is. From now on, we hope to be using a lot less magic."

He could foresee, but he would not say it right now, that times would come, down the road, when they'd need as much magic as they could muster, and he had a crew of cantankerous elder recruits and quarter-trained baby wizards to call on. His drilled-in respect for Grand Masters had frayed sufficiently that he could even think, with very little guilt, "Curse Tangral!"

It was just short of certain the king would send the army after them. The king was going to have troubles enough in the next few days. On the other hand, the king and court were convinced all the troubles were the fault of Pangwa Household, and might want to mete out punishment, just for the look of it, though that punishment would do nothing to halt the plagues.

There were several large towns along the way, and he also had to assume word would come to those towns, and somewhere a city garrison might try to stop Pangwa Household, and they'd have to fight their way through. There were ways of sending messages other than by a man on a fast rukasa; the only consolation was that very shortly, the people of Gagapeng would have other things on their minds than sending messages.

He clamped his teeth together; he'd just called a disastrous plague a consolation.

He scowled. Yes, they'd be called the Bringers of the Plague, and everyone would resist the Household's passing through their territory, no matter what assurances he tried to give. The irony was that he and his people were much less likely to spread the plague than were any other group which might come from Gagapeng.

He walked through the camp, surveying the situation. In part, he wanted to let the people see he was with them, sharing their troubles. Unfortunately, that little bit of encouragement was all he could do. There was too little he could do in any material sense, and he certainly couldn't respond to every request for help.

He saw Alison sitting beside a campfire with young Solitang Melapis'-child, apparently discussing that old wood-grain inspection spell. What did she find so interesting about that spell? Probably just some word-usage or other that was outside the ordinary.

He didn't bother to stop to talk to her, just gave them both a smile and a cheery wave.

Tomorrow, they'd have to be travelling.

Melungtal was still alone, even on this second day, still too well known as the author of all their troubles. He'd been bumped and pushed a time or two, but he suspected word had come down that he was under the protection of the Grand Master, and no one should mistreat him. Otherwise, he might have found himself the target of actual blows and kicks, if not a full-fledged beating.

He was careful not to respond with magic, even the least calming-spell, since to accentuate the fact that he was a wizard would only make the situation worse.

The calming spell. That was another of those anomalies of Saljashin, like the magical punishment for those suspected of using improper magic. The authorities in Saljashin still used the calming spell, one which controlled the behaviour of people by magic, despite the fact it was so close to the manner of operation of the Blue Blossom Wizard himself.

He looked back from the jouncing cart and saw smoke rising from the far-off city. It was common, when plagues hit, for people to burn plague-stricken houses in hopes of lessening the risk of contagion.

In most quarters of most cities, the straw-thatched houses were packed close together so that this practice risked setting whole sections of the city afire, perhaps even the entire city, if too few able-bodied people were left to control the flames.

"What're you staring at?" A belligerent voice demanded. "It's not your city!"

Melungtal remained quiet, knowing anything he said in an attempt to placate the fellow would simply have the opposite effect. He turned back to face forward. Again.

✦

Royin's own thoughts were about whether or not someone had set fire to Pangwa House itself. He had been adopted into Pangwa Household, but at so early an age most of his memories were of Pangwa. Even Grand Masters were not immune to feelings of loss and nostalgia. Perhaps they might be even more prone to such.

Pangwa Household might well rise again, in another place, but it would not be the Pangwa Household he'd known for so long.

✦

Alison looked back at the smoke rising from the city. She recalled reading, somewhere, about how fires were a great terror in ancient and medieval cities. With the building materials available, and no way of delivering water to a fire save by bucket, even an accidentally started fire could destroy an entire city, or most of it.

She saw tight faces all around her.

Everyone knew there was no going back. Everyone knew the city which had been their home was lost to them. She didn't have it in her to say vindictively, even to herself, "Now you know how I feel!"

Royin tried hard not to intervene in quarrels among the fugitives, preferring to get the attention of the nearest subordinate and let them handle the dispute.

"Awful lot of bickering going on," Ormant commented.

"Everyone's upset about having to leave the city, about heading off to who-knows-where. Ask yourself if you don't feel just a bit testy. Like maybe you want to try to pick a fight with your Grand Master."

He smiled as he said that last, watching Ormant's expression.

Ormant managed a smile of his own. "Fine sight, that would be, the two highest Masters rolling around on the ground punching and kicking like a pair of troublesome youngsters."

He sobered then. "We're going to have a lot of those sorts of problems too until everyone gets settled into their new homes."

"We have to get there first."

"True."

They hadn't bothered stopping at the nearest villages; the people of those villages had frequent contact with the city, if not daily contact, and the doings of the wizards and their conflicts would be common currency.

Later on, when they came to villages Royin felt would not yet have heard the news, the people he had assigned to foraging duties went out.

Ormant watched the foraging parties come back with laden wagons.

"We're doing not too badly."

"Yes. Every one we have like this is a gift. So far, the word doesn't seem to have spread to the villages about the Fugitive Plague-Carrying Wizards. It will, though. Some wizard or other will send a fire-message for the king to the largest cities on our route, or perhaps the king will send out messenger birds. There won't be much doubt what our route is."

"I suppose you, being the Grand Master, have to think of all the problems, not just how smooth the going is right now."

Royin glanced at him, wondering just what might be behind that comment.

"So, do you think you can do it?"

Solitang grinned. "Easy enough to do. Even showing the picture on the tent wall is no problem. Trouble is, they'll notice the use of magic, and the Grand Master might be upset at unauthorized magical fooling around."

"I'll explain it to him if he asks."

Solitang's grin slipped a little. "I don't think you understand, Alison-madam. I'm a 'baby wizard,' just learning the trade. If the Grand Master decides I'm too reckless to be trusted, well, given our present situation, I doubt he'd expel me, but he'd sure hold back on training me for anything new, and concentrate on training me to be reliable. And magic isn't merely something I enjoy doing, it's my life."

Alison was about to make some comment on his willingness to take chances, but she stopped herself. She still wasn't of any use here; did a mere possibility of doing something useful justify pushing someone else into something which might affect their career, might make them even slightly useless?

There was only one possible answer, of course.

"I'll talk to him, get him to approve it."

It wasn't too hard to find Royin. The difficulty was in getting close to him. Despite the fact he had delegated as much responsibility as possible, there were still problems which only the Head Person himself could untangle.

She got the feeling, talking to the people who were "blocking" for the Grand Master, that they been told to let her see him at any time, because no one asked Alison about her business.

On the other hand, the fellow in charge did say, somewhat apologetically, "You'll have to wait in line, Alison-madam."

"All right."

She waited, too, watching while Royin

dealt with this problem and that. She suddenly realized that Royin, the man, looked quite worn.

After a bit longer, she turned away. The man overseeing the line-up said, "It won't be that much longer, Alison-madam."

Alison shook her head. "I don't need to see him that badly. Make sure that he gets some rest."

The fellow smiled tentatively. "If I can."

She wandered back to where Solitang was waiting. He looked up at her. "Well?"

"He's busy taking care of the lot of us. I'll talk to him later. If you can't do anything magical, you can help me with a few more words."

❈

Forest had given way to scrub-brush, and it was on the edge of where scrub gave way to the plain that they came on the first village which refused to have anything to do with them.

It seemed like the whole adult male population of the village, with some women as well, standing in a grim mass across the trail, blocking the path of the Pangwa House fugitives. Clumps of children were watching from what seemed to be a safe distance.

Arms among the adults were mostly spears and hatchets, with a few plain staves as well.

Their leader was a grim-faced bearded man wearing the plain leather garb of a farmer.

"We've had word of your coming, Plague-Wizards! Begone! You'll not spread your plague among us!"

Royin looked at the determined face. "I'll consult with my people," he answered.

"Consult all you want. You'll not come through our land."

Royin rode back to Ormant and Faral. "They've heard of us. 'The Plague-Wizards,' they call us. We could fight our way through, one way or another, if we wished."

Ormant gave him a look. "You say that as though you had something else in mind."

"I have. I think we ought to swing aside and go past them and the village."

"Let them turn us aside? And what do we do the next time someone blocks the trail? And the next?"

Royin shook his head. "If we fight every time someone stands in front of us, we'll wear ourselves out with fighting, and eventually be overwhelmed. We're not soldiers, not trained for that sort of thing.

"There'll come a day when we have to push our way through, but the longer we can put off that day, the better off we'll be."

Ormant remained silent. Royin could see he didn't like the notion, but he didn't try to argue further.

The villagers watched, grimly silent, as the convoy swung off to the left and moved on. The children sent up a mix of cheers and jeers.

❁

Hadjalloni finished up his report, which included information coming from various sources in Rosthan. Gagapeng was a ghost city. Most reports said the Royal Household and some other parts of the city still survived. Most of the population, though, were either dead or fled to the countryside.

There was also a rumour that a party of wizards were roaming about Rosthan, spreading plague wherever they went. He hadn't bothered to include that bit of foolishness in his report.

He considered a recommendation that anyone coming from Rosthan be turned back at the border by force if necessary. No, that would only lead to them slipping in through all the back trails and so on. Best just have them quarantined until it was certain they showed no sign of the plague.

He skimmed over the report once more. It seemed, despite whatever warning Melungtal had brought, the project had been a success. Obviously, the man had warned someone; they had sent the plague to centre on the Royal Household, but it seemed the Royal Household had been almost unaffected.

The Royal Household of Rosthan was of little use, however, if its capital city, its nation, were destroyed.

Hadjalloni set the report aside. Scribes would take it and copy it neatly, making sufficient copies for all those to whom Hadjalloni reported.

Yes, the project had been a success.

❀

If it hadn't been for the presence of the Grand Master, Melungtal felt, the situation would be ludicrous. He was giving a lecture on magic to people who, simply because of who he was, would prefer not to listen to him.

But Royin had made it clear before the session started that they all, including Royin, needed to learn what he could teach, and his lessons should be treated as seriously as if they had been given by any other Master. He did not quite require them to take notes and be able to repeat the salient points of the lecture, but the point seemed to have gotten across.

It had not improved the mood of the gathering, but it made it better than a mere futile gesture. Of course, if Royin alone learned anything from it, the lecture would not be wasted.

"You will see," Melungtal said, pointing at the page projected on to the tent wall, "the two phrases appear to have the same effect. The first, though, can take effect immediately, though the second is to be preferred, for though there is a moment between its pronunciation and the effect, the effect is longer lasting.

"There are still occasions where the first is to be preferred---."

"When you're in a hurry to start your plague," muttered an older fellow in the front row.

Because of his isolation, Melungtal had not yet learned the names of all the people, even all the Masters, so he hesitated to say anything.

Royin showed no hesitation, though. "Kalangas, I believe you owe the Teacher an apology."

Kalangas sat silent and sullen. Royin spoke once more. "Kalangas, Melungtal is giving this lecture at my request. That means it is as if I myself were teaching. I trust you see the significance of that?"

Kalangas muttered, "My apologies, Master," though from his tone and expression he might as well have said, "Sannat blot you out."

Wisely, to Melungtal's way of thinking, Royin did not press the matter. Melungtal continued his lecture.

❖

Alison finally got to speak to Royin, not because she waited in line, but because he took time to come by and speak to her. He came, not when they were camped, or halted for a rest, but rode beside the wagon as it went and spoke to her.

She was extremely conscious of the presence of the other passengers, all acting as though they couldn't hear a word.

"Alison! How are you getting along?"

She put on a smile. "As well as any, and better than many, I think."

"Sorry I haven't had a chance to talk to you sooner."

"No apology's necessary. You're the one in charge, the one everyone looks to in order to solve their insoluble problems."

He grinned. "Sometimes I'd like to ride away and leave it all behind and live all alone somewhere. Trouble is, I started this, and I can't quit now."

He paused. "Do you need anything?"

"Uh---." She stopped. He'd asked, of course, but was it fair to add another petty decision to the even more important things he had on his mind?

He smiled again. "Come on, Alison. You have something on your mind. What is it?"

'All right, then.' "Could you authorize Solitang to do some magical experiments for me? Nothing big. He could handle it easily, he says, but he needs your permission."

"What spell? Or what spells? There're some things I'd prefer not to have anyone fooling around with while we're out here."

"Just that Magnification Spell. And a spell to project images onto a tent wall, maybe one or two others."

He thought a bit while his rukasa continued to walk alongside the wagon. "All right. But remember, wizards, even beginning wizards like Solitang, are an important resource for us. Don't wear him out, because I may need to use him, and with no more than a moment's warning."

She thought for a moment he was going to give her a complete lecture on how important one magician might be, but he left it at that. She was glad he did, since she wasn't sure just how much she could trust herself to stay polite if that happened.

She wondered if she was ever going to be able to react like a normal person. She even wondered if she could remember what "normal" felt like.

There were troops formed up, blocking the way to the city of Angarat.

"Well," Royin said, "It was bound to happen sometime. In the last three weeks, we've had some villages sell to us grudgingly, some a little more willingly, and we've had some turn us aside altogether. It was about time we had actual troops out to face us."

"They don't want us coming near Angarat," Faral said, speaking the obvious.

"I wouldn't be surprised if it were worse than that," Royin said. "I'd wager we're about to be required to surrender in the king's name. I wouldn't bet against summary execution, either."

"So now we do all those nasty tricks you've been having us practicing," Ormant said, almost eagerly.

Royin sighed. "I think I'd best at least talk to them first. I doubt it'll be worth the bother, but if I can avoid fighting Royal troops, I'd prefer to. Ormant, you take charge. Make all the preliminary preparations in case we need them."

As he rode his rukasa forward to parley, he wondered momentarily if, sometime when he went forward to parley leaving Ormant in charge, his second-in-command would instigate something which would leave him, Royin, with a spear stuck through him, and Pangwa Household with a new Grand Master.

He shook that off. He was the one to make decisions, so he had to do the parleying, and leaving Faral, junior as he was, in charge, would put Ormant's nose severely out of joint. Not to mention there were a lot of newly recruited Wizards, superior to Faral in wizardly ability, who probably wouldn't let his least decision go unchallenged.

He smiled grimly. That one fact, Faral's inexperience, meant Royin didn't dare stick a dagger into Ormant, even if he could bring himself to cold-blooded murder. He needed someone to take care of Pangwa Household if anything happened to him, and Ormant was the best he had.

The officer in charge of the troops was a grizzled old fellow, with a long scar from temple to cheek which added to his grim and ferocious look.

"You are the Grand Master of the Infamous Pangwa Household?"

'So that's how it's going to be, is it?' went through Royin's mind.

"I am Royin Gredion's-child, Grand Master of Pangwa Household, which has preserved the king and his Household."

'Just to get our side of the story out, for all it matters.'

The commander snorted in derision. "I am required, in the king's name, to demand the surrender of yourself and your people."

"Unfortunately, I am not permitted to surrender my people into anyone's authority."

"Not permitted?" The commander's voice held incredulity and anger. "Not permitted? Just who are you to say that you're 'not permitted' to obey the king's orders?"

"I am the Grand Master of Pangwa Household. The king has seen fit to accuse my

Household of causing a disaster, simply because we warned him of it. Because of this, I will not put my people into the hands of the king's servants."

"Instead, you put yourself in my hands? Seize him!"

Royin pointed his finger and spoke a word. There was a bang and a flash. The soldiers, temporarily blinded, halted.

"Commander, I am the Grand master of one of the chief Wizardly Households of Rosthan. Do you think I would put myself in a position where I could be so easily seized?

"I would suggest that, if you or any of your men recovers their vision before I return to my people, and has the temerity to launch an arrow, consider first what defenses I might have arranged for such things.

He rode back to the evacuees.

"They don't like us?" Ormant inquired.

"On the contrary, they like us so much they want us to be their guests for some indefinite period. They were much displeased when I informed them that we had a prior commitment."

"'Much displeased?'" repeated Ormant. "Yes, I could see that. In fact, I think they may be coming over to insist that we accept their invitation."

The troops were advancing, with archers at the flanks coming on a little faster, to be able to launch their flights of arrows before the main body came into contact.

"Wizards forward!" Royin shouted. "Faral, the shields! Borilil, kill the djasa, then help us! First, Fog and Confusion!"

They hadn't had any time to drill in military fashion, nor were wizards in general much amenable to briskly following orders. However, Royin and the rest had practiced sufficiently that they went to work with little lost time.

Suddenly tendrils of mist began to curl from the ground between them and the oncoming archers, tendrils which rapidly became a thick fog-bank. Some of the archers seemed to guess what was coming, for they raised their bows, despite the range, then disappeared in the fog

Royin cast two minor flashes, one in front of each archer contingent, then continued with the Fog and Confusion. The flashes wouldn't be quite so effective, with the fog blanketing them, but they might help.

Several arrows flew out of the fog, launched by guess more than by aim, and Royin heard several cries among the Household. Killed, wounded, or merely startled? No time to check just yet.

Then the fog was full and grey, and shouts of alarm came out of it. Two more arrows also came out, shot wildly, and nowhere near the evacuees.

"They'll be in no shape for fighting even after they get out of there," Royin said. "Let's move!"

As the party got underway, more slowly than Royin would have liked, Ormant approached him. "They'll follow us, won't they?"

"Actually, the question is, 'How soon and how close will they be on our track?'"

"So along with everything else, we have to arrange a rear-guard."

"Exactly. Anything you can think of to discourage them from following us would be welcome."

❀

By pure bad luck, one of the three arrows which had landed among the Household had struck an older servant, who had died before any significant aid could be given him. As for the other arrows, they had hit no one, but they had shocked several. Taken with the one actual death, that shock had been magnified considerably.

There was muttering among the people, who now fully understood they were set against the rest of the country.

"They won't likely do anything serious just yet, since they've all been brought up to respect the Grand Master and his decisions," Faral reported. "There's just a lot of words, muttering about what they've gotten themselves into, and talking about the likelihood of leaving their bones scattered along the track between here and the Nalagang Bay."

"That's to be expected, I suppose," Royin said. "We'll have to try to think of something to raise the morale."

Kalangas broke in. "The soldiers are still half a mile behind us, but keeping their distance. Should we do something to discourage them?"

Royin shook his head. "They're far enough back that it'd take a lot of power to do anything. We still don't have the resources to waste.

"When we camp, we'll set our alarm-spells far enough out that they can't come up on us by surprise at night."

It was definitely a paramecium. It was shaped like a footprint, with cilia around the edges, and all the appropriate parts which were labelled in biology textbooks.

Solitang had projected it onto the tent-wall. In the light of a flickering fire, it might have been hard to identify, but Solitang had cadged a small magical light from somewhere.

"What on earth is that?"

"It's a paramecium, Solitang." She had to use the word she knew, since this was the first paramecium anyone in this world had seen, so there was no local word for it.

"You say that this thing lives in water?"

"That's the simplified version, but yes."

"What does it do?"

"Swims around, eats, reproduces. It has no mind, just instincts."

"Is it harmful?"

"Not so far as I know."

"Is it good for anything?"

"Hmm. How do I explain 'ecology?' Let's just say it's part of the world as it is." She grinned. "It also makes an excellent demonstration."

"It does that. You say that everything you look at this way has to be stained?"

"It doesn't have to be, but it shows up better if it is stained. I wish I remembered my course in slide-preparation better; I'm going to have to do a lot of trial and error."

She smiled at him. "It's a lot easier having someone around who can say 'alikazam' and change the staining."

"'Alikazam?' What's that? I thought you didn't do any magic?"

"It's something from back home, too complicated to explain, and no, I still don't do any magic."

"So, then, Alison-madam, what good is this business of looking at little tiny things in the water?" He always went formal when he questioned, or seemed to be questioning, her reasons for doing something.

"Well, it can have a lot of uses. For instance, one can look at a drop of blood from a sick person, and often be able to see the bacteria that's causing it. Unless it's a virus." She continued, mostly to herself. "I wonder if this spell can be made to function like an electron microscope."

"But disease is caused by noxious vapours!"

She looked at the young wizard and wondered what she might be setting herself up for.

He went on. "That's the reason they can be so hard to deal with sometimes. The vapour has little in the way of substance, so it's hard to work with. Mostly all we can do is fight the symptoms, and hope that attacking the symptoms will carry over to an attack on the vapour itself. Even the Saljashinites, who've been working at this for so long, had to use a combination of several different spells to be able to annul the three plagues they produced.

"As for the production of the plagues themselves, I've read some of Melungtal's notes, and they're beyond me. If you ask me, I think a lot of what they did was just 'throw the dice and hope for the best.'"

"All right, let's not argue that one just yet. Let's try another approach. This can be used to see the way a plant is put together, in extremely fine detail. A lot of what your wizards do is urge plants to change in a certain fashion, and you do it all by 'feeling.' Suppose you could look at a plant, before and after you'd made the changes, and see what had happened to the inside of the plant, stem, leaves, flowers, and all? You could then have something to visualize, to see just what sort of further changes you wanted to make. You might be able to cut out several generations of breeding that way."

Solitang looked doubtful, and it suddenly occurred to Alison that she might be putting herself in the same position as that long-ago businessman, trying to get his woodworkers to do something different from the way they'd always done it.

Chapter Eleven

The village was dead, save for a half-dozen djasa and two rukasa that had not yet wandered off.

"Plague," Faral said, needlessly. "It's spread this far, this fast?"

"Definitely plague." Royin said. "It may not necessarily be one of the ones the Saljashinites sent. Nambar, go fetch me Melungtal."

"Yes, Grand Master."

They dismounted and stood looking at the desolation until Nambar returned with Melungtal. The Saljashinite wizard had a newly blackened eye; Royin looked at it, then at Nambar, who shrugged.

"He had the eye when I found him, Grand Master."

"I see. Melungtal, the first thing I want to know is whether or not you can tell if this village has been hit by one of the Saljashinite plagues. If it was, then we're immune, and we can see what we can salvage from it. If not, we'll have to consider further."

Melungtal straightened. "It should be possible, Grand Master. Let me see; I'll need about two grains of cereal to give me the power."

"We can manage that. Nambar, you get a small fire going. Loniswal, go fetch a small cupful of cereal from the supplies. Melungtal, do you need anything else?"

"No, Grand Master, that should be all."

The fire was soon lit and burned brightly. The group sat or stood around watching until Loniswal got back with a cupful of grain, from which Melungtal chose two grains, and tossed them into the fire, muttering a few words as he did so.

After that, he drew a circle in the ground and inscribed a few letters and symbols into it, then spoke another word. There was a long pause, then a pink glow settled over the village.

Melungtal looked at Royin. "Yes, Grand Master, it's one of--- uh, ours."

"So. We can safely take anything usable from it. Ormant cast the antidote spell over the whole village and contents. Faral, go call for volunteers to sort out what can be salvaged. Particularly those animals."

"Grand Master---." Melungtal began.

"Yes, I know. The antidote spell won't have any more effect, since we're immune already. But it'll make people a little less leery of taking what we can use.

"Now, I want to know about your eye."

"I stumbled against a cart, Grand Master."

"You're a poor liar, Melungtal."

"With respect, Grand Master, let it be. If you start punishing people, even a severe scolding, for anything they do to me, it'll just make matters worse."

Royin was quiet for a moment.

"All right. A bump and a bruise here or there is nothing special, I suppose. But if you start bumping into too many carts, and it starts working its way up to something serious, I'm going to have to put a guard on you and make them responsible for anything that happens to you. Whether you like it or not, you're too valuable a resource to us to be wasted."

They spent a half a day gathering what could be gathered from the village. The djasa were happy enough to come along, and the fugitives got one of the rukasa, but the other one fled at their approach, and Royin decided not to spend the time chasing it down.

Before they left, they cast a minor fire spell on what remained of the village, and left it, sending up a pillar of black smoke behind them as they trekked away.

When they camped that night, Solitang talked to Alison. "The people aren't happy about all this, Alison-madam. They think it's bad luck at the least to take anything from a plague village. Feels even worse than plundering the dead."

"I've told you before, Solitang, don't call me Alison-madam. Just Alison is fine."

"The Grand Master won't---"

"When the Grand Master's around, be nice and respectful if you wish. When it's just you and me, it's Alison."

"All right, then." He grinned. "You're trying to steer me away from telling you the bad news."

"If you insist on looking on the bad side of things, go ahead. I sort of prefer to trust the Grand Master."

She saw the look he gave her and hurried on before he could say anything that might upset her. It was altogether too well-known that the Grand Master took a great interest in her. "There are a couple more words I need help with."

"You're going to read that book to pieces, Alison-ma---, Alison."

She grinned at his slip and recovery. "See, that wasn't so hard, was it? I can't believe anybody here hasn't invented a xerox-spell yet."

"Ziroks? What on earth is that?"

"What on earth, indeed? Well, back where I came from, we had a process that could make copies of pieces of writing, of anything on paper, actually. It used electricity—no, I will not try to explain electricity right now--, and it made producing copies a lot easier."

"But we have a spell like that! We don't call it Ziroks, though, we call it the Writing Reproduction spell. It has problems, though. You have to go through the copy side by side with the original, afterwards, because sometimes it just puts in a blot instead of a letter or letters. It's worse with poor handwriting, or crabbed writing, too."

Alison decided not to bring up the problem of Optical Character Recognition in computer scanning of printed material. An idea came to her, though. "I wonder if a person took the Magnification Spell, and made the piece of writing larger, large enough to make the letters a bit more distinguishable, if you'd have better luck."

"That's beyond my knowledge. We'd have to try it, and the Writing Reproduction Spell needs a fair lot of power. I don't know whether the Grand Master would allow it."

For a moment, all Alison's previous positive thoughts about the Grand Master's decisions went whiffing away like a mist before a strong wind, then she got hold of herself. "I suppose this is one of those things we're just going to have to keep in mind for some time when we have a bit more leisure."

"It's something to think about, I suppose. Will the people who have to copy manuscripts and letters and the like be glad to have their job made easier, or mad at you for putting them out of work?"

Alison stayed quiet for a moment, thinking again about the fact that any innovation, no matter how useful, would have its detractors. How could you blame a person for being upset that his—or her—entire career had been made into a quaint hobby of little practical use in the real world? Now, if she could just invent a cure for some disease, that would be useful. All she could do, though, was suggest basic hygiene.

She looked up.

"What is it, Alison-ma--- Alison? Is something wrong?"

"I've been thinking too close to myself and my own interests, that's all. I need to talk to the Grand Master."

"I'm sure he'll talk to you, but...." Solitang sounded doubtful.

"If I can just convince him I know what I'm talking about," she said, "I think he'll be glad to hear it."

There were still people waiting to see the Grand Master, though the numbers were smaller. Most people, Alison supposed, discovered that they could untie their own knotty problems without waiting an hour or two to see the Grand Master.

He smiled when she approached, but she was sure that underneath the smile, he was wishing she wouldn't take up his time. There were too many things that needed doing.

"I have something to tell you," she said. "First of all, I have to explain some things we've discovered about disease back on my world."

His eyebrows went up. "Go on."

"Disease is caused by little things, semi-animals, you might say, smaller than the eye can see, carried in water and sometimes air, often on the backs of birds or vermin.

"Water can be made safe by bringing it to a rolling boil, and keeping it there for, um, eighty pulse-beats or more. Anything that can withstand boiling, such as metal pots or pans, can also be cleaned by boiling them in water.

"It won't necessarily prevent all disease, but it'll sure help."

"These little things; what do they look like?"

"They have several shapes, but they're all too small to be seen with the unaided eye. That's one of the things we can use the Magnification Spell for."

"Too small---! Alison, are you all right?"

"Am I all right? Listen, you---!" She held her temper with a supreme effort. A shouting match would do no good. In fact, it would probably make her case harder.

Her voice was still shaking when she went on. "Yes, I'm quite all right, thank you. I think I should have brought Solitang and my apparatus to give you a demonstration. If you need more proof than just my word, call him in and ask him if I haven't shown him examples of little things that live in the water. Better yet, let him give you a demonstration.

"I'll even make you a further offer; every puddle of water we come to, I'll take some of it, boil it, and drink it, and you can see whether or not I get sick."

"Small living things, you say?" He sounded as if he were partway convinced.

She hurried on. "Yes. It's not my specialty. I was more into trees and shrubs, but I know some of the procedures for looking for the things." She was wondering again if the Magnification Spell could be made to see things as small as viruses.

"Boiling kills them?"

"Yes."

"Nothing else can?"

"Oh, yes. Back home, drinking water is purified by chemicals in many places."

"Fascinating. There are several spells available that can wither and destroy plants; we use them on weeds. Most of them are used specifically, 'kill everything that looks like this.' We might be able to make them general, 'kill everything living in this container,' sort of thing."

He seemed to talk to himself, but at least he was talking as if he accepted the thesis that little living things caused disease.

He went on. "Of course, it is a matter of which is more costly in resources, to boil water, or to be casting spells."

He stopped and looked up at her, as if suddenly remembering she was there. "Sorry, thinking out loud. People tend to be very conventional, you know. Not everyone is going to take your word for this, and it'll be that much easier if we can at least give a demonstration to the Wizards. And to the upper servants. Maybe more, if need be.

"Would you be willing to do that?"

Her mind was trying to go through what he'd said, to make sure she'd heard it right, and work out what she'd need for a demonstration, all at once.

"Yes," she almost shouted. "I can have a demonstration ready in a day, a day and a half."

He smiled. "Good. You make your arrangements, then, and I'll set up a time, and---."

A gong sounded through the camp.

"Alarm! Get back to your section, Alison! We'll talk about this later, I promise!"

Nambar was watching the Detection Spell, which showed everything in a wide circle around them. It had been fined down to tell animals from humans, and presently showed a large band of soldiers coming toward them, with smaller bands spreading out to the right and left.

"We caught them as soon as they came in range?"

"Yes, Grand Master."

"Good. Keep watching, alert me if anything changes. Don't wait too long to pack up and get to your section; we can't afford to leave you behind. You're too good at handling that Detection Spell."

The younger man grinned. "No fear of that, Grand Master. I have no more desire than anyone else to take a spear through my brisket."

'I'm going to foster that young man, soon as I get a chance! He's too good to let go on without the special assistance a Master can give him.'

There was no time to do more than make a mental note to that effect. The Pangwa House fugitives had gotten too used to the seemingly safe conditions of their march so far. People had taken to visiting back and forth between sections, some of the far side of the camp from their own section. This need not be a problem, but for the immediate panic, the alarm added. Not that everyone panicked, but even a few were too many.

A few magic lights had been kept going to allow people to find their way around, if only to the latrine, and in the sparse light, people were rushing to their stations, sometimes just rushing away.

Ormant was at Royin's elbow. "They're on us?"

"Not hardly. We should have time to get away easily. Get the people who're on rear-guard duty; they'll probably have to discourage the army."

Ormant nodded and turned away.

Panic appeared to be the standard operating procedure, despite the many times the people in charge shouted, "Don't panic!" The atmosphere being what it was, Alison had to keep a firm grip on herself. In that martial arts training so far away, a lot of time had been spent in learning how to control panic, since panic destroyed the ability to think clearly.

Solitang was looking stressed, but Alison grabbed him by the sleeve and spun him to look at her. "Get a grip on yourself, man! We have to get to the wagons, but we have to do it sensibly. Come on, help pull up the tents; if they get so close we have to abandon everything, we'll know it!"

He helped her, though the tent was not folded as neatly as it might have been. Other people were going around, getting people to load up everything they could. One of the wagon-drivers nearby had gone into a complete frenzy and was lashing his team into motion even though no one else had gotten onto the wagon yet.

Alison glanced that way; she wasn't big or strong enough to stop a runaway team of rukasa, so she went back to her own work. She heard yelling and screaming, and a team stamping to a stop, with the driver shouting curses, so she gathered that someone else had stopped the team.

That wasn't the only case of panicked and runaway drivers, apparently, for there were several new people added to the load on her wagon when it finally went lumbering off.

'I hope we didn't leave anybody behind altogether!' she thought to herself.

"They're coming at a run, Grand Master! If it were daylight, they'd be within bowshot already!" Nambar shouted.

"Thank you, Nambar, get to your wagon, now!" Royin shouted back in reply.

"Yes, Grand Master!"

"Faral! Sound the warning, then use the Light-flash!" Royin called to Faral.

"Yes, Grand Master!"

There was a sound of a deep gong, and Royin looked down, closing his eyes. Despite that, the flash showed red through his eyelids.

Royin looked up and shouted. "Fall back ten yards!"

Royin had no illusions that all the soldiers would be blinded by the flash of light; some would have been shielded from the light, by the people in the rank in front of them, if nothing else, and most of those would not be stopped by a mere flash of light.

Many of the riding-djasa had been looking the wrong way, and were temporarily blinded, leaving their riders forced to lead them.

Royin was contemplating the fact that there would come a day when the Wizards of Pangwa Household would have to use their magic to kill, and he had no illusion about that. At present, though, he preferred to use non-lethal spells to discourage and demoralize the soldiers.

After all, the soldiers also had to forage for their own supplies, and so could not keep up a very close pursuit.

He grimaced. *'Except when they catch me by surprise with a sudden advance by night!'*

"Ormant! See to the laying down of the Stench-cloud!"

"Right."

This Stench-cloud would not be so effective as the one they had used to clear prospective recruits from the street back in Gagapeng; back there, they had all the walls and buildings to hold the cloud in one place. It would cause all kinds of difficulty, though, up to nausea and vomiting, among any people who walked into it.

There was a light breeze blowing too, which would act to dissipate the cloud.

Some trick of the spell left a faint tinge of the stench among the magicians, a musky, sulphurous stench, with a tinge of rot in it. It was not enough to have any effect on the magicians, other than to let them have a hint of what the soldiers must be getting.

There was no time to waste pitying the soldiers.

"Fall back!" Royin called. "Follow the wagons, but be ready to turn if necessary!"

From time to time Royin flashed a small version of the Detection Spell, one which showed the soldiers as only small black specks on a light blue field. They seemed to be totally disorganized now; he suspected the Flash or the Stench—perhaps both—had caught most, if not all, the officers. He wondered if the scar-faced commander had been one of them.

There were still a few individual dots rushing forward, but they wouldn't be able to keep up the pace for long. Furthermore, when they found they were alone, without orders from their commanders, and without support, they would probably break off the pursuit.

The fugitive wizards spent nearly half the next day reorganizing, with someone always carefully overseeing a Spell of Detection.

Ormant, his face a thundercloud of wrath, reported to Royin. "Lost two more wagons. Two fools started out in a panic, with practically no one or nothing aboard, and actually got away. We passed one of them just a little down the trail, overturned and wrecked. Two dead, one badly injured, and the driver unconscious, but apparently not badly hurt otherwise. I was tempted to pass judgement and sentence right there, execute him as a warning to others, but I thought you'd want to be the one to do that."

"Yes, you're right. What about the second wagon?"

Ormant shrugged. "Still going at a gallop is my guess."

Royin nodded, thinking. A rukasa, even a team, could only run so far and so fast, particularly hauling a wagon, before they foundered themselves. Most likely that wagon would end up overturned and smashed somewhere up the road.

He'd never thought the evacuation of Gagapeng and the trek to Nalagang Bay would go smoothly all the way, but he felt every loss in the pit of his stomach.

A soldier brought the message to Hadjalloni. "There's been a case of plague at Orsiya, on the border, sir."

"One case?"

"Yes sir. One case at the time the message was sent, sir."

Hadjalloni frowned. He knew all too well how plague worked; one case usually meant more to follow.

"Send in the Head of the Project."

"Yes, sir."

Anallon, Head of the Project, was nervous, and not covering it well.

"You asked to see me, Watcher?"

"Yes. There is a case of plague at Orsiya on the Rosthan border; can you discern, from here, whether it is one of ours?"

"But the border should be protected, sir!" Anallon protested. "That was one of our first concerns---."

"And maybe someone was off visiting across the border when the protection came.

How soon can you discern what it is?"

"Well, sir, I could do it immediately if you wish."

"Then do so!"

The wizard stepped up to the elaborate wall-map and found Orsiya on it. He then nicked his thumb with his small knife and squeezed a drop of blood into the flame of the lamp on Hadjalloni's desk.

He repeated a few words and watched. A pale pink spot grew on the map over Orsiya, then suddenly disappeared.

The wizard frowned. "Now, that is unusual!"

"What does it mean?" Hadjalloni demanded.

The wizard turned to face him. "If it had been one of ours, there would have been a steady red glow over Orsiya. If it were not, there would have been no response.

"This result, minor as it was, suggests that the plague is similar, but not the same as, one of ours."

"And clearly, the antidote spell conferred no immunity to it?"

"Well, no, sir."

Hadjalloni frowned. "So I would suggest that you and your people have a new project: to find an antidote for it, and quickly."

"But sir---"

Hadjalloni looked up at him fiercely. "I am assuming it will not be simple. Ask for whatever resources you think you need. Go on, now. I don't want to see you again until you have some definite progress to report."

"Yes, sir." Anallon left, almost at a run.

The Chief Watcher sat scowling at the map, at the spot where that pink glow had appeared. No, He couldn't deny that Melungtal had warned him, and that he had chosen to ignore the warning. They had some advance notice, though, and the wizards should be able to deal with it.

He pulled over a sheet of paper, wrote a few lines, then rang the bell to summon the servant.

"Take this to the Military Commander. Tell him it is to be acted on immediately."

He sat back, thinking. The order was for the immediate burning of Orsiya and all in it. Better one town than the entire land. Whether or not this succeeded would depend on how quickly the order could be gotten to the garrison nearest to the infected town, and acted on.

He sat for a long while, staring out at the empty, battered plinth outside his window.

The wagon-driver was frightened out of his wits, Royin guessed. Well, he might be. He'd caused several deaths, and wrecked a wagon. The wagon was second to the lives lost, but only just. Its loss meant that the other wagons would have to be loaded the heavier, slowing the progress of the whole march, requiring more supplies, and possibly causing more loss, even deaths, down the road.

Of course, the wagon-driver was not thinking that. He was likely thinking of the terrible kinds of punishments an angry wizard might provide; ripping his skin off while alive, or breaking all his bones, or the like.

Royin spoke. "By your actions, you have caused destruction, loss, and death. There are some who would cry for vengeance, a life for a life. I say we cannot afford to lose any more people.

"I am sentencing you to be the servant of all until such time as I declare you have paid sufficiently. You will fetch and carry and lift, and do whatever is required of you, and you will not complain.

Royin then around at the gathered people, "I lay it on you to carry out the punishment. You are not to harm him physically. Neither will you force him to do impossible tasks, or even tasks no other single person could manage. When he is carrying out a task for someone else, no one will force him to leave that undone and do something else.

"That is my say in the matter."

"I say you're too soft-hearted. You ought to have made an example of him that no one will forget." Ormant said with a stern look on his face as he sat beside Royin, watching the flames from the campfire.

"No, Ormant, as I said, we've had too many losses, and we're likely to suffer more. This way is better. Speaking of losses, are we still missing those seven people who were left behind?" asked Royin as he glanced over to Ormant, who was still watching the fire.

"Three of them came in, still scared and shaking. When the first alarm sounded, they apparently took off running down the trail, and got themselves lost. Apparently, they heard the sounds of the camp, and found their way back. We're still missing four."

Royin frowned. "Was Sizmany one of the three?"

"No. We haven't been able to detect him with any of the usual spells, either. He's either gotten himself out of range, or dead."

Royin's frown deepened. "You'd think a magician, even a baby magician, once he stopped panicking, could use a few spells to find the right direction."

"Maybe he fell over something, bashed his brains out. Or maybe he ended up running the wrong direction, into some soldier's spear."

"Yes, you're right. There're too many things that could happen to anyone, wizard or no."

❀

Melungtal looked up from his books as Royin approached him. "I hope you don't want me to do another lecture to your wizards, Grand Master."

"No, the last one didn't go over very well." Royin said as he picked up one of the books and idly looked at it. "I'm concerned about your warning that one or more of the plagues might change to something the antidote-spell couldn't touch. Is there anything you could do to prepare for that?"

Melungtal took a deep breath. "That's asking a lot. Here, on the trail, I could try to work out some possible steps, based on the changes we made, and try to work out what might potentially happen. If we camped in place for three to six weeks, and I had a few high-ranked wizards who'd co-operate freely, I might get you better results."

"Better than I'd hoped for. But we can't stop. There're likely to be more troops moving to head us off. Even this brief stop to reorganize is more than I like.

"You work as and when you can. If you have anything to report to me, no matter what, you come to me. I'll see to it that you're brought in fast."

❀

The seacoast was off to their left, mostly in sight from the trail, and they were three days away from Nalagang Bay. Loniswal was on the Detector-spell this time and raised the alarm. "Troops formed across the trail ahead of us, Grand Master!"

"Numbers?"

"I'd estimate over three hundred."

"All right. Thank you, Loniswal." He looked around. "Wizards forward!"

When the wizards gathered, Royin outlined his plan. "We won't bother trying to parley this time; they probably aren't in a talking mood themselves. We'll be going for serious fighting this time; no more Stench and Confusion. We're going to use the Poison Smoke and Panic. We'll use the Smoke we kill off vermin in grain-bins with, but we'll have to hold it in a steady cloud ourselves.

"Sannat knows we've always tried to keep serious magic off battlefields, but I don't think we can do that any longer."

Ormant gave him a strange look. "Sannat's flaming toenails, Royin! Remind me not to get you seriously annoyed with me!"

"I hope you don't think I'm enjoying this, Ormant!" He pointed off in the direction of the still unseen troops. "Those poor bloody sods up there, somebody gave them weapons and said 'Do this,' so they go do it. I'm going to kill a lot of them, maybe all of them, and they have as little choice in what happens to them as a djasa bound for the cookfire.

"Now, let's all make sure we know the spell."

When the enemy was about five hundred yards away, the fugitives began the spell. They built a bank of fog between themselves and the soldiers, then sent it drifting down. Privately, Royin hoped that the sight of the oncoming fog, obviously magical in nature, would shake the troops' resolve sufficiently so that when people started to die, most of the rest would turn and run. When they ran, hopefully, they would scatter beyond the ability of any surviving officers to rally them.

What required the power in this spell was holding it together in the fog-bank, despite the breeze that was blowing. He could feel the drain on himself, and he imagined all the rest were feeling similar.

Now the fog was too thick to see what the soldiers might be doing, whether they were fleeing or standing their ground.

The fog continued to move, and now they could see the bodies of soldiers, some fallen in their ranks, others as they turned to flee.

"Hold it steady there!" he shouted.

They held the fog in place, then watched and waited. Finally, they could see a few soldiers fleeing off inland, having cast away their weapons to run faster.

"All right, nullify the poison!"

This was another draw on their power, but he wasn't about to leave bits of the poison around, possibly to collect in hollows in the ground as traps for any man or beast that wandered there.

When they were done, it was clear that very few soldiers had gotten away. Many had died in formation, but there was a scatter of corpses off to the rear where men had succumbed to the poison as they ran.

Royin forced himself to think that at least these ones no longer posed a danger to his people.

"Grand Master! Troops coming up behind!"

"How many?" *'And where have they been hiding up to now?'*

"Two to three hundred, Grand Master."

Royin's mind, fuzzed with weariness, assessed his resources. He'd used up most of his higher wizards on the troops in front; the wizards he had left couldn't manage to repeat that feat. They could do other things, though.

"Ormant, get the wagons moving. Junior wizards to the rear! Borilil, come with me!" *'Now you'll get some responsibility, Borilil, if only because you were closest at hand!'*

He gestured at another man. "You!" Royin couldn't, for the life of him, remember the man's name. "Get a djasa from the herd, and meet us at the rear, fast!"

He didn't wait for a verbal response, but hauled himself up on his rukasa and rode rearward.

"You all know what's happening. There're troops coming up behind us. The Senior wizards have used themselves up destroying the army that was in front of us, so you'll have to deal with these fellows.

"Borilil and I will be right close to tell you what to do, so you shouldn't have any trouble.

"What you're going to do is throw Fog, Confusion, Panic, and other things at them. Yes, the same Itch you've occasionally given to each other; Everything we can think of to harass them and slow them down.

"Does anyone have any suggestions?"

"Grand Master, I know a wood-rotting spell I could use on their spear-shafts."

"How much power does it take?"

"A little more than the Itch, Grand Master."

"All right, use it. But if it doesn't have enough effect on their general morale, you'll have to go back to something else."

"Yes, Grand Master."

The tail of the train of wagons had managed to get fifty yards along the trail before the first of the soldiers came pouring over the small rise behind them.

"Everyone ready? Kill the djasa!"

On sight of the wizards, the armed men had formed themselves into ranks as they advanced. This massive wave of soldiers broke into little eddies and rills as the spells hit. The junior wizards, though they weren't capable of a bank of fog, could call up individual puffs of poison smoke, which they directed toward individual soldiers. Others threw Panic and Confusion at individual soldiers, some of whom actually ran off, despite the efforts of their commanders, while others were able to come on again.

The Itch was even more effective, if it was strong enough, since men stopped and pulled off their armour to be able to scratch.

The ranks were badly battered, though the remaining underofficers managed to keep some order.

Royin, sensing a need for something more, sent a puff of Poison Smoke around the commander's head, and saw it dissipate almost immediately. *'They've got themselves a wizard from somewhere.'*

He flashed an illusion of spectral soldiers, skeletons in armour and brandishing weapons. These were, indeed, too much for some of the soldiers on top of all the other magical attacks, and more of them broke ranks and fled.

The spectral soldiers whiffed out of existence, clearly banished by the wizard, wherever he was hiding; Royin, depleted as he was, didn't have the power to maintain the illusion against determined opposition.

He tried to think of any spell he might manage, but he'd already overtaxed himself, and rendering himself unconscious would do no good for the morale of his rear-guard.

He gave a slight nudge to some of the Panic and Confusion spells, noting the added result. The wizard with the army, still concealed, was countering some of the individual spells, but couldn't counter them all at once. That hinted at a wizard of only modest rank.

There were no archers with this force of soldiers, just men with spears and shields. Wizards, on the other hand, had no weapons, nor training in how to use them if they'd had any.

A shadow appeared overhead. Royin looked up, and saw a balloon. It was different from his original model; the bag was an elongated shape, and the basket was larger, able to carry several people.

It hovered over the soldiers, and dark objects fell from it. Then there were a series of bangs and flashes. Illusions, he could tell, but they had their effect. The soldiers had come on despite the annoying spells, despite their comrades dropping out all round them, but this flying thing, and the noise and lights, were too much.

Royin slid around on his rukasa. To avoid falling off. He clung on to the beast to keep himself upright.

The balloon drifted over to land next to them, and Royin saw in the basket the grinning face of one of the junior magicians who'd been sent to Nalagang Bay earlier.

"Welcome, Grand Master."

"You timed that nicely...." Again, his weary mind refused to recall the fellow's name.

"Not exactly, Grand Master. We'd spotted the soldiers coming, and those other ones between us and you. There was some discussion as to what, if anything, we could do to help, and they finally decided to send us. By the time we were halfway here, though, we could see that the main body of troops had been dispersed, but there were still those last ones coming up behind you.

"So we did our demonstration on them, and it worked better than we'd hoped."

"Well done."

"Thank you, Grand Master. What do you think of the balloon? We built it according to your suggestions."

"Seems to do very well." answered Royin, hiding a satisfied grin as best he could.

"Would you like to come aboard, Grand Master? We can have you to Nalagang Bay almost before you know it."

Royin actually considered the offer for a moment before good sense prevailed. "Thanks for the invitation, but I have to see our people safe home. I'll be wanting to try her out sometime soon, though."

"All right. By the way, from aloft, I've been able to spot three columns of troops moving this way."

"How fast are they coming?"

"Ah---at a guess, Grand Master. I'd say they'll arrive at Nalagang Bay the day after you do."

"Thanks. Get back to Nalagang Bay as fast as you can, and have them start getting ready. I think we'll have another fight before we're done." *'Sannat grant it's just one more!'*

Hadjalloni looked at the map. Three more towns reported plagues. There were no marks on the map, but his mind still saw the ugly pink Anallon's spell had put there temporarily.

It was not possible to order the towns burned; one of them had been the town from which the soldiers had gone to destroy Orsiya, suggesting that they had, by some means or another, brought the plague back with them.

Hadjalloni considered having Anallon in for another progress report, but decided against it. Best they should keep on working, without interruptions. They didn't need the Chief Watcher looming over their shoulders to encourage them.

Neither was this the time to push them harder by taking some junior member of the team and condemning him as a Suspect. While it would push the others to work harder, there was always a short time of confusion and dismay after an execution. They didn't have enough time.

Hadjalloni pulled over a sheet of paper. He was going to have to write a report on this, and there was no denying his own culpability. He was the one who had rushed the project into operation, despite Melungtal's warnings. Hadjalloni was the one who had brought this on them.

He looked out the window at the scarred stone plinth. He had done as he thought best, but he had been mistaken. What would be the cost of his mistake, not to himself, but to the nation? Would they be able to save anything at all?

Hadjalloni calmed his mind and began to write again.

Chapter Twelve

Nalagang Bay was still some distance away, so Royin arranged Alison's demonstration for one evening when they'd finished travelling for the day. He didn't command attendance; the mere fact he was supporting it meant it was politic for everyone to come.

Alison had lectured to students, and to others in her own field, but there was no denying this was a tough audience, not to mention the lecture was being given by firelight at night. There were a few in the crowd who looked as if her every word was vital knowledge, but Alison was sufficiently familiar with the situation to be fairly sure those wizards were more interested in impressing Royin.

She put herself into Lecture Mode and started out.

"Solitang, the first slide."

The footprint-shape of the paramecium showed up on the tent wall. "This, back where I come from, is known as a paramecium. Such things as this tend to grow in pools of stagnant water. They're too small to be seen with the unaided eye, but using the Magnification Spell, I am able to increase the view of them to make them visible. These hairy-looking things along the edges are known as cilia, and it uses them for swimming."

In the best High-School Biology fashion, she noted the various parts of the paramecium, along with their function. The people who wanted to impress Royin were very impressed, but among the others, the most positive expressions were no better than mild doubt. There were some who looked interested, but skeptical.

Alison carried on with slides of various bacteria. She knew it didn't help her cause any to be unable to connect these with any specific diseases. On the other hand, she'd managed to get samples from the mucus of a few sick people, and could point out the bacteria she was certain was causing a local flu.

In those cases, she preached her sermon while knowing what she was presenting was little more than a guess, and without taking blood-samples from many people to give a broader statistical distribution, she could easily be wrong.

Some of the theoretically Senior Wizards, the ones who had joined Pangwa Household back in Gagapeng, wore determinedly antagonistic expressions,

expressions which said loud as words, "We came out here tonight to listen to this?"

Having lectured to tough crowds before, Alison knew very well the worst thing she could do would be to show any hint of discomfort.

It was clear these people, even more than Solitang, were wedded to the "noxious vapours" theory of disease. It occurred to Alison the Saljashinite Wizards, if they'd worked longer on their plagues, might have been forced to discover germs themselves.

That didn't help her here, though.

Advocating the boiling of drinking water was obviously silly, though she thought perhaps some of them considered it possible that boiling would drive off the noxious vapours.

When she finally wound up with a call for questions, nobody spoke for a long while.

Finally, one of them spoke up. "I must say, Alison-madam, this is one of the most interesting demonstrations I've ever seen put on by one who has no magical ability."

It took her a moment to understand that he was suggesting, in a roundabout fashion, it was all illusions.

'Hold on, girl! Letting yourself get mad will do no good at all. Dig up more proof for next time.'

There were no questions at all, which meant they'd dismissed her whole demonstration out of hand.

The trek continued the next day, and Alison spent much of the time thinking about what she could have done better, or perhaps even just differently.

The Grand Master pulled his rukasa up beside the wagon.

"Well, Alison, since you gave your demonstration, I've been going around and talking it up. A lot of them still don't believe you. It's too new, and..." Royin's voice trailed off.

"And someone they don't know from somewhere they don't know is telling them all this. Even the demonstration might be a skillful illusion, though how I, or even Solitang, could manage an illusion they couldn't detect, I don't know.

"Even when I invited Borilil to do the Magnification Spell on a drop of water taken from a random container, they didn't believe it."

She paused, frowning. "Actually, I expected there were some people who would just refuse to believe. I don't think I expected so many, though."

He grinned slightly. "Well, there are some people who have taken right to it, almost to the point of enthusiasm. I'd be happier if all of those were really behind it because they believed, and not just because the Grand Master had expressed his opinion."

Alison grimaced, "Yes. Those. Well, I'd like to do some actual experiments, have someone drink purified water, have someone else drink unpurified water from the same source, and see who gets sick. But you can't play around with people's health like that,

"I wish I knew more about bacteria. I suppose even if I did, I'd find that many bacteria here looked different from those back home."

"I think you're pushing yourself too hard and too much, and you're going to wear yourself out. Spend some time just thinking; nobody's thought about this before, and it won't matter if you take time figuring out what to do with it."

"Except---." She stopped. *'Don't bother complaining about uselessness; he's heard it all before.'*

Instead, she changed the subject. "We get to Nalagang Bay tomorrow?"

"Yes. Then we have to think about what we're going to do about the armies coming after us. We're none of us trained as soldiers, but we have to hold them off. Considering how that last fight went, I'm going to have to think of better ways to use our magical resources."

❀

Nalagang Bay itself was a beautiful, curving expanse of blue water. The town, though, was a disappointment when compared to Gagapeng, or any of the cities they'd passed along the way. It seemed to Alison it was five times as big as Strick's Bolg, perhaps bigger, though it was nothing like Gagapeng. The surrounding wall was barely shoulder-high, not much of a barrier to a determined attack.

Having brought Strick's Bolg to mind, she wondered what was happening there. Had the plague reached it yet? While the manner of her leaving the village had been discouraging, still, she had nothing against Moralei, for instance.

She had a notion to ask Royin to save Strick's Bolg, but she had a feeling he'd have to turn her down because of the immediate danger, and he'd feel bad about it. No, she couldn't do that to him right now, not with armies descending on them.

A small group of armed men were advancing toward them from the town. This would be part of the local armed forces. Royin had told her, "We found it necessary to have an armed force in the Colony to keep down tribal raids. We don't usually keep many magicians at Nalagang Bay, and it isn't good use of resources to use magic to counter every little raid.

"We've hired a couple of hundred local tribesmen to do what fighting is necessary."

The leader of the troops was bareheaded, his helmet slung at his waist. As they came nearer, Alison could see the differences between him and the average Rosthanite. He had a snub nose, freckles, and deep red hair. Most of his followers wore helmets, but what she could see of them seemed much the same.

Like peoples coming up against "civilized" people everywhere, the local tribes were probably glad to work for the people in the Colony, especially if the pay was, partly or wholly, in goods that the "City People" could supply.

Well, at least future generations wouldn't have a skin-colour barrier to come up against. *'Be real, girl! If people want to be prejudiced, they'll find an excuse!'*

She shook her head. She had no authority, only a limited ability to convince Royin to pay attention to her, and there were some things he wouldn't try to command. Telling people how to treat strangers was almost certainly one of them.

Besides, she was basing her dire predictions on what she knew from her own world. Who said they had to go the same way here?'

The man in charge of the escort had a heavy accent, but his Rosthanite was comprehensible. "Welcome, Grand Master! I called Firchan Swifthunter, heading those who fight for the town. They command me to bring you safe into town."

"Thank you, Firchan. I understand troops are advancing on the Colony?"

"Oh, yes, they do be! We knocking them back on their rumps, though."

"How many troops does the Colony have?"

"Two hundreds and a half-hundred. But we having magic on our side, is it not?"

"We have, indeed. But magic can only do so much."

Firchan was not to be dismayed. "Ah, then. The rest my fighters doing!"

Royin decided not to try to make the man see how dire the situation was. It might demoralize him, but Royin doubted anything could demoralize this flame-haired force of nature.

He nodded, then, and said, "Fine. You have a plan for the defence of the Colony?"

"Ah, yes, for certain, plan having! Maybe best, though, we get back to town. Where is what you call it? The land-picture?"

"The map?"

"Yes, yes, the map! Fine thing that being! Picture showing every hill, valley, creek, and wood. Only better would be showing where right now the beasts are for hunting!" a wide grin spreading across Firchan's face.

They had set small blocks of wood on the map to show the advancing troops.

"I don't suppose we could be lucky enough to have these fellows come down with plague before they get here," Ormant muttered.

"Perhaps they will," Royin said, "But we can't count on it. Firchan, is there any place where you and your men might slow them down?"

"Ah." The freckled forehead wrinkled in thought. "Here is wood, and here, and here. My men might hra---hasr---. What is word? Pester?"

"Harass?"

"Yes, yes, we harassing them right good!"

"Fine. I can leave you to work out just how and when?"

"You want starting now?"

"As soon as the meeting's done."

"Good, good!"

"Fine. Now, Wizards, has anyone done any thinking about what spells we can use to defend the Colony?"

It turned out only a few had, and most of those few had come up with notions which needed more power than they could afford. Growing an impenetrable wood around the soldiers, for instance, would not have been a straightforward task even at the height of their powers, back in Gagapeng. *'Curse Tangral!'* Besides, to make it work properly, they'd have to wait until the three bands of soldiers had converged before the town, which left too much to chance and to the assumption that they would converge.

Thick hedges of thorns to block some of the approaches were a little more possible, and it was only a little more trouble to make it poison thorns. Sufficiently poisonous to kill was unnecessary, just enough to put a man out of combat for a day or two.

"I've been thinking about the Poison Smoke we used in the last fight," Royin said. "Holding a large bank of it together is too wasteful of resources. I'd suggest we send out small puffs of smoke at a time, enough to take down one or two at a time, make the rest think again about coming at us."

He put on a firm expression and looked around at the gathered wizards. "You'll notice that I've brought Melungtal in. I know that some of you don't like him much, if at all, but he's one of the most capable wizards here, and the soldiers will put a spear through him as fast as through any other, so he's working with us.

Anyone here who absolutely cannot work with him, see me, and I'll put you in a different section.

"Before you come see me, though, ask yourself if your personal feelings are that important, and ask yourself whether or not you want to be called to my attention."

He swept his gaze around them, and said, "Think about that for a moment, then come see me if you wish."

The troops came on. Firchan and his warriors raided them, causing little actual damage, but slowing them down, and lowering their morale for all that.

Melungtal could provide help beyond anything they'd looked for. He produced several bags of seed, which he brought to Royin. "If you get that flying thing, and scatter these along the approach of the soldiers, they'll grow overnight into fields of blue flowers.

"The flowers put out a delightful smell, but anyone walking through them, or even too close to them, will fall into a sleep that'll last as long as the flowers bloom. That will be only one more night, but it should be useful."

"Useful? It'll have them looking at every strange-seeming tree, bush, or flower along the way and worrying! Which gives me another idea. Loniswal, get hold of the juniors and have them make plans to put illusions on various trees and bushes. Nothing too powerful, just things that look different, and perhaps for those that can manage it, a touch of Panic along with the illusion."

"Yes, Grand Master." '

The troops came on. They took losses, but they came on. The fields of flowers shook them, and some even died, from the effects of the narcotic the flowers produced.

The junior wizards competed to see who could put the most subtle spell on a bush, tree, or shrub, and still cause the soldiers to shy away.

"They're deserting, Grand Master," reported a wizard who manned the Detection Spell. "Not in great numbers, but in ones and twos."

"Every little bit helps," Royin answered. *'But will it help enough?'*

"They must have some way of co-ordinating their advance," Ormant said. "They're moving just fast enough that they'll all be able to gather and attack us at once."

"Wizards," Royin answered. "We tend to forget that, just because the centre of everything used to be Gagapeng, that there are no competent wizards in other places. Practically anyone can send writing through fire."

"They don't seem to be able to do much about the blue flowers or the thorns."

Royin shrugged. "Maybe they're just not that strong. Or maybe they're saving their power for when they get closer."

❀

The soldiers went through the thorn-hedges, with predictable results. After having taken many losses, they brought up fire and burned a path through, taking more losses doing that. "Never thought of it that way," Royin said, "but it isn't surprising that the smoke from the burning thorns is poisonous itself. Enough to put down anyone who breathes it for too long."

"Not enough, though." Faral was looking worried.

"Oh, we're a long way from being finished yet."

Bushes in the path of the soldiers' advance sprang into flower, trees shifted shape and colour, even grass occasionally seemed threatening.

One of the bush-illusions whiffed away, leaving a mere bush behind. "Aha, that wizard, or one of them, has a bit of learning!"

"You're not cheering for them, are you?"

"No, Ormant, just making an observation. Will you see if you can pinpoint the wizards, or any one of them? If we can get rid of them, that will help us a lot."

"Right." He went to work and shortly said, "Got one!"

Royin produced a small puff of poisonous smoke which he sent drifting at the enemy wizard. They watched the Detection Spell as the man fell and did not rise.

"Can't find the others."

"If they had any kind of hiding-spell they hadn't used before, they may have done so now. I wonder if one of the reasons they weren't using so much magic was that they have some spell up to tell when any of them were attacked."

The last stage of the fight saw the three bands of troops, not quite so numerous now, converging on the town.

Royin had all the adult male population standing by, most with only makeshift weapons. He hoped to stand the troops off with magic, but there were no guarantees. If they continued to be as stubborn as they seemed, there was going to be hand-to-hand fighting at the wall of Nalagang Bay, and Pangwa Household was going to take some losses.

Royin gathered all his personal resources and sent a small cloud of poison smoke whipping along the front rank of the soldiers. He felt someone, someone unfamiliar, add their power to his, and most of the ragged front rank was down. His power exhausted, he could only watch as the man helping *'Melungtal?'* sent the smoke halfway back down the second rank before his strength failed him.

The remaining troops came up against the wall and the determined but untried defenders of Nalagang Bay, and people were beginning to fall. There was nothing Royin could do but watch.

The balloon swept by, dropping its noisemakers into and behind the soldiers. In his foggy mind, Royin understood they were not using the light-flashes for fear of blinding the defenders. However, even the noise was likely to distract some, perhaps fatally.

Nor was that all which was coming from the balloon; someone, actually more than one person, it seemed, was shooting arrows into the soldiers from the balloon's basket. He observed with detached approval that among the first to be hit was the commander, and then they seemed to concentrate their arrows on the underofficers.

He also noted the bowmanship was not excellent, but one shouldn't criticize Sannat's gifts.

Even with that, it would likely have ended with the destruction of Nalagang Bay, but for a sudden attack into the rear of the no longer carefully ranked soldiers.

The attack was no neat soldierly formation, but a mob of armed men, Firchan and some of his men charging out of the brush.

The king's soldiers had fought their way through so much, come on despite the sight of comrades dying or fleeing, but this was more than they could take. As soon as they realized they were under attack from the rear, not by any illusion, but by men wielding metal weapons, they began to scatter.

Royin's legs were buckling. Some hazy part of his mind said this was not the time for the Grand Master to fall on his face. He looked around. "You, Solitang, come here!"

Solitang, concern on his face as to what he might have done wrong, came rushing over.

"Yes, Grand Master?"

"I need to stay upright a bit longer. Lend me a shoulder."

"Uh---? Yes, Grand Master."

So, leaning on the shoulder of a junior wizard, the Grand Master of Pangwa Household watched the destruction of his enemies.

Chapter Thirteen

The tribesman seemed to fill the wood-panelled room that the Colony Administrator had insisted that Royin take over. Firchan was manifestly proud of himself. "Well, Grand Master, we finish your foes for you! This make big song, I think!"

Royin smiled. He had got some rest, enough so he could trust himself to talk sensibly and not fall asleep where he stood. "You have our gratitude, Firchan."

"Gratitude fine thing, Grand Master. For gratitude, you willing to allow my men to take away weapons and armour from the slain?"

"Iron is a valuable commodity. I will allow one part in four to your men."

Firchan had clearly not expected to have his first offer taken up, for he showed no anger, just an increased intensity. "One part in four? I spit on your one part in four! Three parts in four!"

"Perhaps as much as half."

"Half? For the blood we shed, half? Two parts in three!"

"All right, then, two parts in three is agreeable." Neither of them mentioned the notion of adding in whatever the tribesmen had picked up on their harassing raids, nor was Royin going to bring it up. He'd have nothing but their word on what they might have picked up, and putting one over on the Grand Master because of an oversight was better than putting one over on the Grand Master by sharp dealing.

Besides, they'd need good relations between themselves and Firchan's men for the future.

"Seventeen men dead, twenty-five with wounds, five of those serious," Ormant reported. "One of our wizards, Kalthan Rodda's-child, overstressed himself, and I don't think he'll recover."

"We can't afford anything like that again."

"We won't have to. The plague will take care of it for us. The Sannat-blasted thing is spreading fast."

"I don't like the idea of being saved because a plague devastated the land."

"What do you plan to do, Royin? Try to save them so they can send more soldiers against us?"

"No." Royin frowned at him. "First of all, by the time they can get another army together, it's likely to be three years or more along the road before they can start bothering about us. Then they'll have a lot of civil disorder to handle before they can get round to Nalagang Bay, out on the border.

"Third thing is by that time we'll be further along in the mastery of Magic, and we'll be that much harder to beat."

He paused. "We're going to start, soon as we can, putting the antidote on every village around us. We'll also have to work with Melungtal to try to find out possible changes the plague will go through, so we can fight them, too."

"You expect the villages to be grateful for that? They've gotten it into their heads that we're the Plague-Bearing Wizards; they still won't like or trust us."

"Not right away, but it'll come. We need them on our side. If we let the plague take them away, they can't hurt us, but neither can they help us. If we save them from the plague, by the time another army comes from Gagapeng, at least some of them will be willing to lend us a hand." '

❀

Royin had needed a lot of convincing, but Alison had finally worn him down with facts and arguments. Solitang was more than willing to come along and help, but they also needed a wizard of higher rank to do the Plague Detection Spell.

In theory, the procedure she had planned should work and if it did, well, she'd have done something useful besides the business of boiling water.

It was a good thing, she mused, this culture had built up this business of baths, even communal ones. She grimaced. It made personal hygiene so much easier. Now if she could just invent an anti-bacterial soap....

The balloon landed.

The village had been hit hard by the plague before Royin could put the anti-plague antidote on them. This culture had maps, but not every little village or hamlet was on them. They'd spelled this village as the plague was running wild, but the survivors had deserted the place. Having no way of knowing they were immune, and likely unwilling to trust any messenger from Nalagang Bay who said so, no one had attempted to dissuade them. The village could be re-occupied somewhere in the future.

"All right," she said, "let's get to work."

The village was not a pleasant sight. Several houses had been burned, probably a first attempt to stop the plague. As the plague had continued to spread, however, there would have been fewer people to do even that, and fewer people, Alison suspected, who were willing to go near a plague-stricken house.

Some people had fallen in the act of fleeing the village, and some had fallen in the act of getting water or working the fields.

The smell was bad, though not so bad, Alison supposed, as it would be in an enclosed space. *'I hope I can get what I need without going into any of the houses.'*

She took a hesitant scraping from a dead hand, smeared it on a slide, and told Solitang "All right, hit it."

He did, projecting the image onto a sheet set up on a wooden frame for the purpose. "A little bigger. That's it."

"Now, Fangan, cast the Plague Detection Spell, just on the slide."

It needed not simply power, but finesse to do something like that, another reason why they needed an experienced wizard.

She watched the slide and the projection in turn.

"Nothing. Is---." She stopped herself from asking Fangan if the spell was really working. He was really quite even-tempered, but she didn't need to upset him. The best of wizards seemed to have a trace of prima donna in their makeup.

He'd caught it, though, despite her shutting her mouth on the question itself, and smiled gently.

"Most times, if the magic doesn't work, there's a reason. This time it's because there's nothing to detect." There was only a hint of sarcasm there, more like a warning shot across her bow.

"Apologies, Fangan. I can't use magic myself, nobody on my world could, so I have a bit of a hard time wrapping my head round it."

She looked around. The communal well was nearby, a round stone casing with a bucket, along with a rope to let it down the well to haul water up.

"I think we should check the water. Not in the well itself, but let's check the houses."

She was happy to see Fangan's prima donna attitude did not extend so far as refusing to do non-magical work. In fact, she had more trouble convincing herself to enter a house.

The smell from the doorway was horrific.

It was not just rotting flesh, either, but rotting excrement as well, along with various other food-items which had spoiled. She recognized the sort of earthenware crocks which the people of Strick's Bolg had used for storing water. She removed the lid and saw at the bottom a couple of tablespoonfuls of water.

She hauled the crock out into the comparatively fresh, clean air in the street. Fangan was coming out of another house with a crock, and Solitang was coming out empty-handed. "Crock's empty. Should I try another one?"

Alison shook her head. "No. Let's see what we have here first. Fangan, this time before I prepare the slide, could you cast the Detection Spell, just on the water that's in it? Could save us all a little time and trouble."

"Certainly. First, I should replenish my available power. Solitang, light a small fire."

Alison felt a touch of annoyance at his assumption of the right of command, but said nothing. That was the way of it in a Household; a senior member could give orders to a junior member, and the junior obeyed. There were restrictions on this right, but they were all traditional, learned as one grew up, but not written down anywhere for handy in some manual for strangers from Foreign Worlds.

The fire was soon burning. Not a large one, just big enough to burn up the few grains of cereal Fangan tossed into it.

He then spoke the words of the spell. Alison nearly cracked up as Solitang muttered "Alakazam!" in her ear.

The water in the crock glowed. "Aha! How long will it stay glowing, Fangan?"

"A difficult question, Alison. Not longer than half an hour, I suspect."

"Should be plenty."

She went to work as quickly as was consistent with careful work, dabbing a little touch of water on one of several slides.

"Try this one, Solitang."

The first attempt showed scattered blotches of red on the slide. "Crank up the magnification."

Solitang spoke, and the blotches showed up as little rod-shaped things with a touch of red round the edge. "There! Gentlemen, behold your plague!"

Solitang was already pinning a piece of paper to the sheet. "It's moving! I can't trace it accurately if it moves."

Alison looked at the older wizard. "Fangan, is there anything you can do?"

"Yes, just a moment. I don't think I can make the bateriya itself hold still, but I can make the image on the paper hold still, long enough for someone to trace round it."

He paused for a moment, then said, "Ah, yes, this is the one." He spoke a phrase, and the image on the paper stayed still. Solitang went to work.

"So, Alison, have we got what we came for?"

"We have a very minimum of what we came for. I'd like to check various things, see whether the bacteria can hold on to cloth, fleece, and the like. I hate to sound macabre, but I could have wished for some samples of liver and kidneys to see if it lived there, too."

"Cutting up dead bodies?"

She suddenly realized she'd never thought to ask anyone about taboos involved with death or dead bodies. She shook her head. "Wouldn't be worth it, not in the condition these are in. That's something to be left for another time, if ever."

She tossed the in last two words in an effort to assuage any bad feelings Fangan might have about the matter. She'd try to put it off entirely until she had a chance to ask Royin about what she might be getting into.

"To test the other things, do you really need to see the bakeertia themselves? Is it not enough to use the Detection Spell on each item?"

"You're right, of course. I've been thinking too narrowly again."

While Solitang finished up the tracing, Fangan went round putting the Detection spell on things Alison indicated, and she wrote the results on a tablet. She wrote in English, sometimes putting in the Rosthanite name after, if she was sure of it. On the trip back, she'd have to put the notes into Rosthanite so anyone could read them.

When Solitang had finished, and when they'd completed a fairly full catalogue of just what things the plague-bacteria could be found on, Fangan asked, "So. Are we done, then?"

"Close to. I'd like to do magnifications of some things, fabric, hide and the like, just to be absolutely sure." She caught the look on his face and said, "Just for my peace of mind, Fangan. I'm the non-magical foreign woman, and I need to be sure. We need as much evidence as we can pile up to convince the doubters back in Nalagang Bay."

After a brief moment, he smiled in return. "As you say, Lady."

She didn't miss the familiarity. *'God! I'm going to have to get Royin to do me a list of dos and don'ts, including how not to sound like I'm challenging the competency of a wizard!'*

❋

"Now, gentlemen, watch what happens when Fangan casts the spell to kill all this sort of bacteria. Fangan?"

The wizard obligingly cast the spell, and the red glow in the jug of water faded and disappeared.

She looked around. There were still doubting faces out there, but a few more of them looked thoughtful.

She considered pressing the matter, having one of the doubters come up and clean the plague out of another cup of water, but decided not to. They'd already set this up with several dozen—or so it seemed—spells to detect spells, so everyone would know there was no jiggery-pokery going round with extra spells, particularly illusion-spells, to make it look as though something was happening, when in fact nothing was.

She'd even taken the precaution of having one of the doubters cast the Plague Detection Spell.

A young wizard—not a junior—in the second row spoke up and said, "You say these bacteria come in all shapes and sizes?"

"Back where I come from, they come in five main shapes. I haven't seen enough bacteria here to say for certain, nor even guess, though I haven't seen any that don't fit the five main shapes. As for sizes, there are limits to that, but unfortunately I can't tell you what they are.

"The only thing I can say for sure is that only one of them, that we know of, can be seen by the naked eye."

"So, then," the young wizard continued. "We could cast a spell to kill anything in the body shaped like this?"

"God, no!" This was further than she'd wanted to take the bacteria business. "There are many beneficial bacteria. In fact, a good deal of digestion is handled by bacteria. Kill every bacteria in the body, and you'd probably make a person very sick, if it didn't eventually kill him."

At this point, there was pandemonium, with several wizards demanding to be heard at once. Royin stepped in to call for order, then recognized Kalangas. "Kalangas, you wish to speak?"

"Yes, I do! This is all confusing! First, we are told that these little things cause all sickness, including the plague. Then we are told that sometimes they are beneficial, so we dare not kill them all. And yet we are also assured that this knowledge will help us fight the plague, not only the one Melungtal and his Saljashinite friends loosed on us, but others as well.

"So if we kill these plague bacteria, how do we know we have not unwittingly killed ourselves?"

Alison refrained from pointing out this was as fine a job of selective listening as she'd ever encountered, and strove to keep her voice calm as she said, "I believe you have misunderstood me. *'Purposely, you twit!'* We are just beginning to identify bacteria here, starting with the plague, as is vital to us at the moment. I have said that killing all bacteria is not a good thing, because some of them are beneficial. Some, but not all. This bacteria," she pointed to Solitang's drawing, "is one of the ones that is definitely not. Killing it wherever we find it will be definitely beneficial, because it will stop the spread of the plague.

"It must be a spell that effects this specific bacteria, though, since we cannot safely kill all the bacteria of a similar shape.

"I am not sure yet at what distance this plague-killing spell can be used, nor even how great an area it can cover; that is for the wizards, who have abilities I will never have. *'See how humble I am? Twits!'*

"There is a long road ahead for those who choose to follow the paths of bacteriological wizardry. We will have to learn how to identify harmful bacteria, develop spells to kill them, and maintain lists of what we discover.

"We will also have to work out lists of beneficial bacteria, making sure that these are not destroyed along with the rest.

"I will not ask every one of you to help, though that would be useful. On the other hand, I will ask that those of you who cannot bring yourselves to help wholeheartedly should not actively work against us."

There were more questions, often as not covering the same ground which had already been covered, and Alison maintained her patience, answering each one as though no other magical twit had asked that same one in different words.

Finally, Royin spoke up. "It's clear that we're going over the same ground, again and again. I am going to ask Alison to dictate a paper to Solitang, giving as much detail as possible, and have this copied so that each of us can read it for ourselves.

"I will also ask, no, command, that those of you who find they cannot accept this thesis do not hinder those of us who do.

"I have one thing more to say, which makes all this the more important. Long range use of the Detection Spell has shown areas of plague which seem to have developed out of one of those sent by Saljashin. This means we are facing a new threat before we have properly dealt with the old one.

"Further, today's demonstration has been against only one of the plagues. We still have to discover what bacteria cause the other two, as well as dealing with the blight.

"At present, the blight is a serious problem only around Gagapeng, but it will spread, and therefore it must be dealt with.

"Now, we all have much to do. To work, everyone."'

❇

Melungtal was weary. Not merely weary in body, he realized, but weary in mind and spirit as well. Trying to work from this end, calculating possible changes in the plague, was near to futile. There were too many possibilities.

They had managed to narrow down the Detection Spell so it would find and hold on the new plague. Could they be so lucky as to have only one of the plagues change? Or was that mere wish too much temptation to the gods who dispensed luck?

Worse still, what god had declared that the plague should change only once?

For all his work, he had nothing tangible to show, save for a Detection Spell for the new plague, important in its way, but not what the Grand Master needed.

He had attended Alison's lectures, and his longstanding work with diseases as noxious vapours had been no barrier to his saying to himself, "Yes, this model fits." The demonstration of the killing of the bacteria with the spell, that had been the clinching proof for him.

Royin had been using her theories. Having something specific, not a shapeless, formless, invisible, noxious vapour made fighting the plague a good deal easier. It still took some amount of power to kill the bacteria in any large area, but not so much power as casting the antidote spell.

It occurred to him the antidote, if tailored for that one bacterium, might be more useful and effective as well.

He'd have to suggest that to Royin or Alison. Privately. He wouldn't want to risk tainting the idea as having come from the Saljashinite Plague Maker.

He paused to make a note.

He looked out to seaward, to the far horizon a black line in the distance. How easy it had been, back in Saljashin, where black was black and white was white, and a Rosthanite was an evil life-twister bent on becoming another Blue-Blossom Wizard!

Sometimes he was sorely tempted to use that escape-spell of his to take him out to that far horizon, putting himself beyond regrets and guilt forever.'

"It's insanity, Alison! You'll kill yourself!"

"Not if I do it right. I'd dress up in a suit that covers me from head to foot, and when I'm done, I burn the suit. I'd wear a cloth mask over my mouth and nose, so I don't breath anything dangerous. When I get back, I have someone kill everything living on the balloon, and on the surface of any container I bring back.

"We have someone cast the Detection Spell on whatever I bring back, then I look for bacteria in it. Solitang can cast the Magnification spell from a safe distance. I trace out whatever bacteria shows up in the right colour. Afterward, we have someone cast a spell to kill that exact sort of bacteria in me, for safety's sake."

"You can't fly the balloon!"

She scowled. "So what do we do? Magic up a robot to go do the collecting?"

"A robot?"

She spent some time describing just what a robot was, and Royin shook his head. "People have tried, from time to time, to make some sort of magical servant, but it's never been possible, starting from a plant or plants.

"There are rumours about wizards doing this sort of thing starting with a human being, but it's something reputable wizards wouldn't stand for, and they'd probably band together to punish anyone who did.

"Even trying to do it, starting with animals, is a little dodgy."

"Hmm. You people say 'Do it with magic.' Back in my home it's 'Make a machine to do it.'"

"And your way is better, of course?"

"No, no, not better, just different. Besides, since you don't have the technology I know, I can only make vague suggestions. Magic doesn't work back home, so we had to approach everything differently."

He grinned. "And some of your suggestions make people think of new things to do with our magic. I suppose you could even get hold of some of our metalsmiths and make some of your technological devices."

"Starting with what we've got, and jumping to radio-controlled robots? I don't know enough to advise on how to make the tools to make the tools to start off. I'm a botanist, not an engineer.

"But we're getting away from the real question. How do we go about getting samples of the new plague?"

The balloon settled into the village. This village was smaller than the last one, and water was drawn from a stream that ran through it.

Alison looked at Royin. He had finally agreed this was necessary, but he was not willing to order any of his wizards to take the risk. She had to admit that there was danger, despite the fact that she'd minimized it.

"All right." He said. "Let's get this done."

Alison didn't bother to answer, but pulled out her equipment and set it up.

Royin cast the Plague Detection Spell. A pink glow settled over just about everything. She wished they could have come up with some colour other than that ugly pink, but on the other hand, the plague was ugly, particularly when it had been made by men, and turned loose on other men.

She wished she didn't feel so much satisfaction in knowing that the new plague was spreading into Saljashin itself.

Royin, without further instruction, was inspecting houses for water, or anything else that might hold plague bacteria.

Alison started at the other end of the village. In the first one, the water-jug was dry. The stench in here did not seem to be so ferocious as she'd remembered from the previous village. She looked around; which of the pink-glowing objects should she take?

Alison ripped a piece from the hem of a woman's garment and noticed that the pink glow spread to her fingertips. She ought to be wearing rubber gloves, but no one here knew about rubber. She imagined if she suggested it to Royin, he could produce some form of rubber tree, but she had no notion of what one did after collecting the sap. It would just be one of those tantalizing notions until they had someone or some ones to go to work on that complete process for a project.

'Concentrate on the job at hand, girl,' she muttered to herself.

Royin had brought out a pink-glowing cook-pot, his own hands glowing pink. *'I hope he doesn't have any open cuts on his hands!'*

Alison took a container, put her piece of cloth in it, and poured water over it. She took another larger container and put Royin's cook-pot in it, and sluiced water over it.

By that time, the water immediately around the piece of cloth was pink, so she squeezed the cloth and was rewarded with the sight of the pink glow increasing in the water.

"All right, Royin, kill whatever's clinging to me."

"We may have to handle more things."

"If we do, we do. I'd prefer to be safe."

"All right, then."

The spell Royin used caused a prickly feeling over Alison's bare hands, but the pink glow disappeared, both there and from her feet.

When the decontamination was done, she used a glass rod to put a droplet of water onto a slide. The droplet itself was pink, so she should be able to find what she was looking for.

"All right, Royin, crank up the Magnification Spell." She occasionally had to explain herself when she put an English colloquialism into Rosthanite, but often as not the meaning was clear from context. She'd noticed that some of the wizards, particularly the juniors, were using some of those phrases in their own conversation, often to the annoyance of their elders.

Royin used the same level of magnification which had shown the original plague bacteria. The pink one showed up clear and bright, with only some touches of resolution needed; it was similar, but not identical to the original.

Royin muttered a phrase, and the outline of the bacteria was burned into the sheet of paper on which it was projected. She looked at him, and could tell by his eyes, he was grinning under the cloth mask. "Faster than a pen."

"Ah, the Laser-printer spell."

He was still grinning. "Whatever 'leyzerprintr' is."

"More technology. Don't bother about it. Let's see what we can get from that cook-pot."

Using an uncontaminated glass rod, she prepared another slide of the pinkish water around the cooking pot. The droplet had only a very faint pink tinge, but she was able to find another bacteria on it.

Royin traced the outline of the bacteria again, while Alison took the contaminated water and put it into sealed containers to take back to Nalagang Bay for further investigation.

Royin decontaminated all surfaces when the containers were stored in the balloon, then decontaminated the two of them, including the soles of their feet.

When that was done, Alison noticed his frown of concentration.

"What's up?"

"Just trying to work out a 'Kill everything that looks like this' Spell in my head." He shook his head. "I think I'd better leave it for when I have time and writing materials."

Faral showed deep concern on his face. "More people coming in, refugees from some of the villages that aren't on the map. They're begging our mercy, asking us to lift our curse from them."

"You told them it wasn't us?"

Faral looked a little offended. "Of course! I told them we hadn't done it, that we had a spell to prevent it. I put the antidote spell on them and all. They asked me how long they must be our slaves in return."

"What did you tell them?"

"To go back home, that we don't need slaves."

"But they're still here, otherwise you wouldn't have brought this to me, right?"

"They say there's nothing left for them at home save death, that the fields haven't been planted, so they'll starve to death."

"And we're supposed to support them?" Ormant broke in.

Royin glanced at Ormant. "It'll mean more calls on our resources, but we can do it. But we don't keep slaves. We'll feed them, supply them with seed grain and implements, and they can take up lands just outside the borders of the colony. They can pay us back, a year at a time, out of what they grow."

"And where does this seed come from?" Ormant demanded. "We've hardly enough for our own needs."

"We'll assign one of our stronger wizards to accelerating some of our cereal fields. We can get a couple of harvests, maybe three. That should be enough to ease the grain shortage."

"Yes, and accelerating those fields means they have to have time to recover, or a lot of fertilizer."

"We'll do it. One thing we have here is an abundance of land, but not enough people to work it. We've already got some of the servants doing field work, but they were never trained for it, and a lot of it's not being done right. We need these people."

Royin paused, then something came to him. "Do any of them have wizard potential?"

"I never asked."

"Go ask. We won't take children under twelve, unless they're orphans with no one to look after them. Nobody too young to decide for themselves that they want to be wizards, but you're allowed to paint as golden a picture of life as a wizard as you can manage."

"I'd say we ask them to turn over everyone with wizard potential, everyone old enough to walk!"

"No, Ormant, I won't add the reputation of child-stealer to that of Plague-Wizard. Go on, Faral, take my word to the people at the gate.

"Ormant, I need to talk to you. I have a report that the spell to kill the new plague specifically has been tested, and appears to work perfectly. The only problem we have is that we still have to find an outbreak of plague before we can make use of it, and that means someone has died already. Melungtal says that an antidote spell is possible, but he has to work at it longer.

"What news do we have about the blight on the plants?"

Ormant tossed his head. "Pretty simply, really. It's sort of fungus; all we need to do is cast a 'Kill this' on the affected areas, and that's it. I don't know how they expected it to be a potent weapon."

"With everyone, including wizards, dying of plague, the blight could easily have gotten such a hold that it'd have taken excessive power to eradicate it."

"Yes, there is that, I suppose."

"One further thing," Royin said. "I want to approach Firchan, ask him to spread the word among the tribes, we'd be willing to train any of their local wizards, even if it's only to handle the plague."

"Tribesmen? You'll let tribesmen in on our secrets?"

"Ormant, you know as well as I that Tangral smashed up wizardry in Gagapeng pretty badly. We of Pangwa Household can't clear the plague from all of Rosthan yet. We don't need it springing up among the tribesmen too, and changing into something new again, and coming roaring back at us!

"We won't be losing out of this either; I'm sure we'll get a tribal wizard or two who decide to stay with us, and everyone builds us up a bit closer to what we were when Tangral caused his disaster."

He could tell that Ormant still didn't like the notion, but had no good arguments against it.

Solitang spoke a phrase, and the outline of the bacteria stood black on the paper. Alison looked up in surprise. "I didn't think you knew that one!"

He grinned. "I didn't. I went to the Grand Master and asked him to teach me. He figured it was a good idea, given my work with you, so he taught me. I need a couple of grains of cereal every time, though, so I don't know that I could do more than five a day, not if I want to be good for anything else as well."

She sat back on her heels. "Well, we're not working on the plague any more, not anything, life-threatening at all, I think. I wonder how many of these things we want to eliminate entirely. Seems to me I heard theories that if the human immune system doesn't have a chance to work on anything from time to time, it gets weakened. Might we end up with a bunch of people who get flattened every time a new disease comes from outside their borders?"

The immune system was no longer a strange subject to Solitang; Alison'd explained it to him some time back, even showed him on slides about how the immune system worked. He had, in turn, started thinking about theories on how to make it work 'harder.'

Since her field was botany, not biology, and since she knew only a bit about magic-theory, her ability to critique these theories was limited.

"I suppose I'd be too cold," he said, "if I wished for an outbreak of smallpox? That's one nobody would mind seeing eradicated."

Alison had found it interesting, first time it was mentioned, that the Rosthanite word translated directly to English 'smallpox'

"Yes," she said, "to both. It would be too cold, and nobody would mind seeing it eradicated. Now write the name on that picture, so we know what it is."

"Right."

Magical healing had usually been a hit-and-miss thing, aimed at symptoms. By the nature of magic, this often had a contagious effect on the actual disease, knocking it out as well. At other times, it removed the symptoms for up to a day, after which followed a relapse. Such relapses varied from mild to serious, depending on the person and the disease, but this relapse could be cured again with magic.

There were cases on record of up to twelve relapses in one patient, and depending on the disease, the patient ended up extremely debilitated, often dying from the next relapse. Sometimes, though, they survived.

Alison suspected that the effect had been like several vaccinations until the body had its immune system ready for the disease. *'Either that or the disease just got sick and tired of trying.'*

Knowledge of bacteria, along with a 'Kill this' spell, would revolutionize medicine, Alison thought. In theory, it ought to eliminate the relapses, since once every instance of a germ was killed, it shouldn't come back.

She thought that over. It would be best to get the whole family together and cast the 'Kill this' on the house and everything in it. That would give a new meaning to 'holistic medicine.' She grinned at the thought.

And make freaking sure they boiled their drinking water.

Chapter Fourteen

"You, Melungtal siTalrun, are declared Suspect of Misuse of Magic, in that you produced and released a deadly plague upon your own people." The grim Watcher made a gesture. "Remove him!"

Melungtal tried to protest that he hadn't done it, that he'd refused to agree to it, but all that seemed to come out were the words of the plague-killing spell.

The hands gripped him and pulled him away. He screamed.

And woke sitting up in his bed, screaming.

He rubbed the palms of his hands on his face. This was not the first time he'd had that dream recently, nor the first time he'd woken up screaming.

He still remembered the first time the Watchers declared he had magical potential. That was something he couldn't deny, in part because he was still a child and this grim-faced adult had made a declaration about him. He realized now that even if he'd had, as a child, the nerve to deny that declaration, such a denial would only have led to him being put on a list for careful Watching, with condemnation as Suspect not much further down the road.

Then he'd been selected for magical training. Saljashin needed wizards, if only to help track down rogue magicians. This time, there was no possibility of refusal. To turn this down would be to condemn himself as Suspect, obviously someone who had leanings toward becoming a rogue wizard.

Then he'd been chosen to work on the project. Once more, refusal would have been fatal. To tell the truth, he'd been sufficiently indoctrinated regarding the reign of the Blue Blossom Wizard, as well as the nature of wizardry in Rosthan. Rosthan, where any dealer in magic had some potential to be a new Blue Blossom Wizard.

Working against that possibility had been a laudable goal.

But Hadjalloni had taken the opportunity of Tangral's disaster to put the program into action, though he, Melungtal, had pointed out the dangers of that action. He'd been justified in the end, but justification had a sour taste when one realized those pink blotches on the map represented people dying.

Could he have been more insistent? Should he have tried something besides meekly accepting Hadjalloni's declaration, then running off to Rosthan to counter what he feared? He shook his head. All he would have been able to achieve was condemnation as a Suspect.

His flight to Rosthan had achieved less than he'd hoped. He hadn't been able to counter the plague. Or rather, plagues. All he could do was wrest free a moment here and there to cast the 'Kill this' spell on some of those coloured blotches on the map of Saljashin.

He couldn't ask Royin to set some of his wizards to helping Saljashin, which had produced this horror, not until Royin had made more progress in making all Rosthan safe. He couldn't ask to be relieved from other duties to save his country. All he could do was what he was doing, to save another little bit of it every day.

Worse still, the 'Kill this' only endured for a day, if that, and afterward the cleared space would turn pink at the edges again.

He might have as much success bailing the ocean out with a pitcher.

He sat for a long while, listening to the sea-birds as they circled in the air, smelling the scent of the sea which came from the tide-line. '

❁

A young messenger leaned in the doorway. "There's a fellow at the Gate, a Saljashinite, asking if Melungtal's here."

Royin looked up from the papers on his desk. "A Saljashinite, looking for Melungtal? Probably not a friend, but let's have Melungtal look at him before we make a decision."

They went to Melungtal's workroom; Melungtal looked up as they entered. "No progress as yet, Grand Master. Even knowing something of the nature of a change of one of the plagues is only of limited help in trying to make these sorts of predictions."

"Actually, we've come about something else entirely. There's a Saljashinite at the Gate, asking for you. I can't imagine anyone from there just wanting to look you up to natter about old times. Do you have any notion about who might have come looking for you?"

Melungtal stood staring for a moment.

'The man's worn to a stump,' Royin realized.

"No one. Perhaps one of the Watchers might have tracked me here, but I don't know. This is a bit far for them to come."

Royin nodded. "Right. I'll do a Watch-spell, and you see if you recognize him."

He poured water into a bowl, then said the spell. The face of the water rippled, then cleared, showing the man at the Gate. Melungtal stared at the picture wearily.

'I wonder if this fellow is in a state where he'd even recognize his own mother?'

Then Melungtal's head came up. "It's Slider. He's a rogue wizard from Saljashin. He helped me get away."

"Why would he be looking for you?"

Melungtal rubbed his face. "I've no idea, Grand Master."

"Well, I suppose we could go ask him. Are you willing?"

Melungtal paused. "Uh---. Yes, of course."

"I'll keep some protections up around us until we have a better idea what he wants."

They walked the path to the Gate. The path was rutted and rough. That was one of the things wizardry couldn't do much about; increased cart and wagon traffic which came with the increase in size of the Colony meant roads took a beating. With the other pressing problems, road conditions were way down on the list of priorities.

Slider's facial expression only changed to a slight smile when he saw Melungtal. "Peace to you, Melungtal. Can you vouch for me with these fellows?"

"Possibly so. I thought you had no intentions of leaving Saljashin?"

"I didn't and I wouldn't, except for the plague. I was hoping you fellows would have an antidote for it by now."

"Not quite. We do have a spell that kills it, though we can't always prevent it from coming back."

Melungtal stopped and glanced at Royin, suddenly aware he might have said too much.

Royin nodded. "It's all right, Melungtal. We've been trying to tell everyone, so it shouldn't hurt us if he knows."

He then addressed Slider. "You're a wizard yourself."

Slider nodded. "Good enough to have managed to slide away from the Watchers for years."

"Right. We're sort of top-class wizards. We'll teach you the plague-killing spell in return for your helping us with our work here."

Slider considered for only a moment. "I'll agree to that." '

❀

Royin was bent over a table studying pictures of bacteria with Alison when Ormant flung open the door and strode in.

"Another Saljashinite, Royin? And you accept him with open arms!"

Royin straightened. "It wasn't quite that casually done, Ormant. He'll help us out, but he'll have limited access to the library, at least until he proves himself."

"But another plague-making Saljashinite wizard!"

"He's not one of the ones that worked on the plagues. He's what they call over there a rogue wizard, one who practices in secret, and hides himself from the authorities for fear of execution."

"Even worse! He's an outlaw to his own people and you've welcomed him here! Can't you see the sort of risk you're running?"

"Ormant, our entire existence from the time Tangral cast his spell without shields has been running risks. We ran risks staying in Gagapeng as long as we did and ran risks in leaving. We've run risks getting here and staying, and in our work on the plagues. I've weighed each risk, every time, to the best of my abilities.

"I think the benefit of having another high-ranking wizard is worth the risk of whatever secrets he might steal."

All this time, Ormant was pacing up and down. By the time Royin had finished speaking, he seemed a little mollified, but only a little. He said nothing, but Royin was sure he was thinking deeply.

With no hint of warning, Ormant stepped behind Alison, his left arm around her neck, holding her chin up, while the point of his small knife was pricking the skin over her jugular vein.

"All right, you've taken the decisions that brought us here. I happen to think that many of those decisions were mistaken. While I can't undo most of them, I can see that you don't make any more decisions.

"What you'll do is start walking. Once I think you've gone far enough away to be no more harm to us, I'll let her go join you. You try to come back. We've got enough magic to stop you. After all, you're just barely above me in rank."

Royin considered. Alison was standing stiff, apparently paralyzed with fright. Ormant might have a slightly exaggerated notion of his ability compared to Royin's, but there was no doubt he knew how to open a vein on an animal or human. Nor was there any doubt he could press the knife home before the Grand Master could do more than start a spell.

"All right, let her be. She has nothing to do with it. If you want to be Grand Master, go ahead."

"No! She has everything to do with it! Tangral brought her over with that spell that killed all our magicians. The lack of magicians gave Melungtal and his Saljashinite friends the opportunity to send the plague against us.

"Worse, she's been coming up with these notions, upsetting everything we know, and leading you around by the nose. Or by the---."

Alison moved. With his attention on Royin, Ormant's reaction was just a little slow. Her left hand caught his right, just below where the knife protruded, and twisted.

Before Royin himself could start to move, she kicked back with her right foot to catch Ormant in the knee. She straightened his arm, continuing to twist until the knife dropped. By now she was facing him, and her knee drove up into his groin. The bottom of her fist slammed against the back of his head as he bent over, and when he fell, she stamped her foot on the back of his neck for good measure.

She wheeled toward Royin, her hands coming up into what appeared to him to be a ready stance.

He held his hands spread out from his sides, trying to look as non-threatening as possible. "It's all right, Alison. You're safe now. Easy, now."

He continued to speak in a calm, reassuring voice, just quiet words to put her at ease.

After what seemed like a long time, she slowly lowered her hands. "Royin. Ormant was.... Did I...?"

"He's on the floor behind you. He had a knife at your throat, but he was concentrating on me. You moved. I've never seen anything like it."

She spoke, almost as if in a dream. "It was like that other night. That man had a knife, too. I didn't know what to do."

"It's all right, Alison. You're safe, now. It's all over."

She turned and looked down at the body, then bent and felt for a pulse at the throat. She straightened. "I think he's dead. Will his family want me killed in return?"

"His family?" Royin asked, blankly, then suddenly remembered the situation from which he'd taken her at Strick's Bolg.

"No. His family is Pangwa Household, and I'm the Head of the Household. They'll take my decision. None of us have any close blood relations left, not after Tangral's disaster."

He looked around. "Well, I'd better call someone to take care of the body."

"How'll you explain that?"

"Explain? I'll tell exactly what happened. He tried to use you as a hostage to make me leave, and you killed him."

She wrapped her arms around herself as if she were cold. "It's not as though I enjoy killing people. I don't. I just don't want anyone to be able to..." Her voice trailed off.

He longed to take her in his arms and comfort her, but he sensed that would be no help. He rang a bell, and a servant came in shortly. The servant took in the scene, and his eyes went wide.

"Don't stand there staring, man. Master Ormant tried to use Alison as a hostage to take over the Grand Mastership. She killed him. First thing I want is for you to get some woman servant to take care of her; it's been a hard thing for her. Then get some people to remove the body and have it prepared for burial."

"Yes, Grand Master."

As the man went out, Royin realized he'd been very brusque with him; he'd have to make it up later.

He'd have to get the wizards together very soon and announce what had happened. There were going to be a half-dozen rumours flying around by the time the servant returned.

He looked at Alison. No, he couldn't offer her much comfort, but he could make sure she wasn't alone. He waited.

"Generally speaking, Slider, they don't think much of Saljashinites here," Melungtal said. "You may find it a bit different personally, having been a rogue wizard and not connected to the people who made the plague, but I'm afraid a lot of people will still see Saljashinite and think 'Plague-maker.'"

"But you're still here."

A shrug. "Where would I go? And besides, I was actually one of the ones who produced the plagues. It seems only right that I should be one of the ones to fight them."

He stared off across the sea. "Sometimes though...." He pointed. "See that insignificant speck on the horizon? That's an island. Not much there, from what I can find out. Sometimes I want to use my Escape spell and go there."

Slider looked at the horizon, then back at Melungtal. "That distance, it'd kill you.

Unless you've done a lot of work on it since you gave it to me."

"No, I haven't done any more work on it. As for it killing me, does that matter? I'd hoped to be able to save Saljashin from the results of a mistaken decision, but all I can do is a bit here and a bit there. Not enough to do much good.

"I can't ask Royin to help save Saljashin either, not when he's stretched to the limit saving his own people."

"You think too much and too deeply, Melungtal. Be a little easier on yourself. You sound as though you're taking personal responsibility for the plague and everything that came from it. As I understand it, it was Hadjalloni's decision, taken against your advice."

"I've told myself that. Still, I was one of the ones who helped to develop the plagues to the point where they were when Hadjalloni made his decision. Worse yet, I did it willingly because I was preventing the rise of another Blue Blossom Wizard.

"It wasn't until I got to Rosthan and the plague actually came that I realized what a horror I'd created. To prevent some hypothetical Blue blossom Wizard from coming forth, I was willing to kill hundreds of thousands of people whose only crime was to live in Rosthan.

"Worse, I was right about the plagues changing. One of them already has, and it's moving into Saljashin at a terrible rate. So now people are dying whose only crime was living under a government that would use plague as a weapon. Not that the people would have been able to stop it; the project was being kept secret, and some poor fellow in Orsiya, for instance, had to pay for what I did in his name."

"You're sounding as though the whole thing were an invention of Melungtal siTalrun. There were a lot of other people involved."

"But am I not responsible, because I took such a willing part in it? I can't assign blame to other people, not when I know what I did myself.

"No, I think it's time to go."

He muttered a phrase and was gone.

Slider stood for a moment, staring off at the island, though there would be nothing he could see at this distance. Then he cursed and ran back to the town. '

"Grand Master! Melungtal's gone! He may have killed himself!"

Royin whirled on the messenger. They'd just about gotten Alison calmed down, and they didn't need someone coming in shouting.

He gestured brusquely toward the door and the messenger, a young servant, backed out, fear and confusion on his face. Royin followed him. "Now, quietly, what is it?"

"The Wizard Slider, Grand Master. He reports that he and Melungtal were walking and talking on the beach. Melungtal was--- uh, unhappy about his role in producing the plague, disturbed at what he had done to his homeland. In the midst of the conversation, he used a certain Escape Spell he'd developed to take him to an island offshore. From what the wizard Slider says, using this particular spell to go such a distance would result in death."

Royin looked back at the door behind him, then at the messenger. "Wait here."

He opened the door and stepped in. Alison was asleep on the bed with a woman servant sitting in a chair beside her. The servant looked up.

"Another emergency. I'll be back shortly."

"Yes, Grand Master." The servant's manner suggested that the two women would be much better off without a man looming around in the background.'

Slider was extremely calm, but Royin supposed a lifetime spent on the run from Saljashinite authorities would give a man a clear appreciation of the relative state of danger.

Slider explained quietly and clearly. "We were talking, talking about the plagues, and his part in producing them, and how he was generally upset about things. He couldn't do enough to save his people, and even the fact that he was right about it being too soon to send out the plagues was no consolation when Saljashin was dying.

"Then he started talking about this Escape Spell he'd developed, to get himself out of Saljashin, that he had a great urge to send himself off to that island on the horizon. I tried to make him see that the guilt wasn't all his own, but he'd finally made the decision. The spell only took a moment to work, then he was gone."

It occurred to Royin the rogue wizard might have had more to do with Melungtal's death than the passive role he described, but he himself knew how hard Melungtal had been driving himself, and had some sense of the man's state of mind. No, it was most likely the situation had gone just as Slider had said.

"He's dead, then?"

"Unless he's refined that spell greatly, then plotted out some complex method of escape, yes. And I don't think he intended to escape. Not alive, at any rate."

"Sannat's toes! He was too good a wizard to lose like this!"

"He was too good a man for this world. If he hadn't gone today, it wouldn't have been much longer."

Royin agreed. "Yes. I'm thinking of things from the perspective of the Grand Master of Pangwa Household. Everything is a resource to be used, and to be used carefully so as to get all possible benefits out of it. Melungtal's death is a tragedy, and the least I can do for him is to think of him as a person."

Slider nodded. "I understand, better than you might think. All my life has been lived with the goal of keeping ahead of the authorities. I did a few things for people, but everything I did still had that notion in mind, to avoid the Watchers.

"There are a lot of decisions I might've made differently if that hadn't been on my mind all the time."

Chapter Fifteen

The balloon settled down next to the battered plinth.

Alison stepped out of the basket and looked around. It was a ghost city, a warning of what single-minded fear can bring about. The others had spread out to do their own searches.

She looked at the weathered floral frescoes on the front of the building across from the plinth. From the description, that was it. Ten years was a long time, but they could still hope that some of the records were there.

She walked to the door, and Royin was beside her. He'd said that any wizard worth working for put protective spells on his or her records, and usually some sort of anti-vermin spells as well.

The records were important, though perhaps not vital. They could give hints as to where the Saljashinite wizards had started, the processes they'd gone through, any of which might just be a help in fighting the new plagues that kept coming roaring out of Saljashin every year.

Every year they went through the process of isolating the disease, and using a "Kill this" spell wherever it showed itself. "Kill this" did not grant immunity, though. In some cases, it did, but no one could work out just how or why. They were still working on the "traditional" method of treating the symptoms, every time anyone fell ill, all the time trying to isolate what bacteria might be the actual cause. They were still doing that in Nalagang Bay, trying to send teams out whenever another plague broke loose, to isolate the bacteria and kill it all across the land. Sometimes they did so before it got too far, other times they didn't. Over the last five years, Rosthan had ceased to be a primary source for new versions of the plague, but that was not the case for Saljashin.

It would have been nice to be developing vaccines, but Alison's knowledge didn't extend that far, didn't even extend far enough to guess where to start.

She and Royin had discussed the necessity of clearing the plague out of Saljashin, if only to cut back on the yearly plagues. He agreed, but there were a lot of vengeful old men back at Nalagang Bay who would get all fired up about doing anything for Saljashin, even if the end result was to do something good for Rosthan.

The door to the building was gone, possibly a bad sign. Royin went in and started up the stairs.

Another problem they had, in the use of resources, was that the new king in Rosthan was making noises about the people of Nalagang Bay owing him allegiance and tribute, and how it didn't look right for them to be so independent of the crown.

This could mean another war, though Royin doubted that. The 'Plague-Wizards' reputation hadn't completely gone away. They were the people who developed the means of fighting the yearly plagues that came out of Saljashin, and to some minds, they might be able to cause plagues if they wished.

There were only a few hotheads back at Nalagang Bay who actually considered turning the plague loose on Rosthan. Everyone knew entirely too well what the original plagues had done to Rosthan, despite the best efforts of Pangwa Household.

Royin pushed rubble out of the way, continuing to move upstairs. Ah, here was the door. Unlocked, too. A good sign, or bad? Theoretically, one could spell one's records against malicious damage, but the necessary power made it not worthwhile.

The walls were lined with cabinets, none of which seemed to have been opened.

Royin opened one of the cabinets at random and pulled out a scroll. Taking it out of its case, he opened it carefully. It was written in tiny Saljashin-style letters, too small to make out in the available light. He rolled up the scroll and put it away, then turned to Alison.

"All right, I think we've found what we came for. Let's call in the others to start loading up."

Royin and Alison went about gathering the others for their return to Nalagang Bay, where they would then spend the next while going over their findings and hopefully find an end to the plagues for good.

Solitang left the doorway of one of the ruined buildings and approached them.

He was now a somewhat serious young wizard, well on his way to becoming one of the best of the post-Tengral crop.

Then he grinned, and the serious young wizard was replaced by the laughing young man. "Any more words you need help with before we go?"

She grinned back at him. "Not right now, thanks."

He turned to Royin, serious once more. "We'll be on our way, then, Grand Master?"

Royin nodded with a grin on his face. At this, Solitang turned and walked toward the balloon,

Firchan Swifthunter cleared his throat behind them. "I think that this journey warrants a song, about danger undertaken by a few for many. It would among my people."

His command of the language, Alison noticed, had improved greatly since he had first met them coming to Nalagang Bay. A lot of tribespeople, even some who were not on completely friendly terms with his tribe, had come to the Colony to lend their abilities, to farm some of the free land, and make themselves useful. A fair number of tribal wizards were in training here, too, and she knew that there were hopes to recruit some of them to the Household.

"It deserves something," she said.

The rest of the group reached the balloon, entered the basket, and disappeared. A moment later the balloon began to fill, tugging at the mooring lines. Crews cast the mooring lines away, and the balloon began to rise, rapidly. As it rose, it turned and headed off, back toward Nalagang Bay.

* * *

Thank you for reading this story, please consider leaving a review.

Also by JP Wagner:

The Avantir Chronicles:

The Guardian of the Sword

The Crystal Crown

Talisman Series:

Stonecaller

Talisman of the Winds

Standalone:

The Search for the Unicorns

Railroad Rising: The Black Powder Rebellion

Maid of the Westermoor

Watch for more at J P Wagner's site.